MW00646908

On Thin Ice

A full-length romantic comedy

Avery Kane

KissingShark Publications

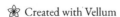

PROLOGUE

TEN YEARS AGO

January Jackson might've been a college student, but that didn't mean she could drink like one. Two cocktails was her limit. She was floating and feeling happy, buzzed to bliss. Right up until the moment Jacob Jeffries—or Jake, to his friends, which she was not—plopped down next to her in front of the roaring fire at Sylvan Slopes Ski Resort & Lodge.

"Oh, it's *you*," January complained.

"It's me," he agreed with a charming grin, his dimple coming out to play and setting off his dark hair and eyes. January hated that dimple with a fiery passion. He only whipped it out when he was trying to charm someone. It was never for her benefit, although she'd seen her fair share of it because they went to high school together. For some reason, the teachers at Bellaire High School thought alphabetized seating charts were the height of sophistication, so they were always seated in the same row. Her in front of him, so when she turned ... he was always there. Smiling that stupid smile.

"What are you doing here?" January knew she sounded rude, but she didn't care. It was Christmas break. Her first

Christmas as a college student. She knew when returning home to Bellaire, Michigan that she would see people from high school. She'd hoped that Jake wouldn't be one of those people.

"My dad owns the resort," Jake reminded her. He was the picture of comfort as he draped one arm over the back of the couch and regarded her with unreadable brown eyes. "What are you doing here?"

"I'm skiing," January replied primly.

"You're not wearing skis."

"I was skiing earlier. I'm done now because it's cold."

"So why are you still here?"

January squirmed under his scrutiny. She'd never felt comfortable around Jake since elementary school when he'd punched her in the arm and declared her a cooties magnet. She'd been furious ... and a little afraid. When she told her mother about the incident, however, her response was to laugh.

"Oh, that just means he likes you, January."

Confused, she'd ruthlessly questioned her mother on how that could possibly be true. Her mother had gone on and on about boys not being able to express their feelings correctly. Because she'd been nine at the time, the story made sense to January. So she approached Jake the next day and blurted out that she liked him too.

That was the beginning of years—more than a decade, really—of strife between the two. Jake's response, of course, had been to declare girls "grosser than gross" and mime gagging. Apparently, he couldn't mime gagging without actually doing it, so he'd also thrown up on her shoes. Embarrassed and horrified, January had responded the only way she could and kicked him in the knee.

They'd both been called into the principal's office over that incident. After that, they needled each other incessantly.

Jake razzed January when she got an A in school. She always got As, so that meant a lot of razzing.

January mocked Jake when he was suspended from the football team because he was on academic probation.

Jake had found out that January was moonlighting as the school mascot one month—she was filling in for a friend who had developed an unfortunate allergy to the costume head—and had proceeded to squawk like a chicken and torture her whenever he saw her. The mascot was an eagle, not a chicken, and January wanted to saw off Jake's beak to shut him up.

Then there was the time Jake brought a date to the winter formal. She was a pretty girl from Traverse City who also happened to be dating a guy from Mancelona. January knew because she'd seen them in the township library together, and she let everybody at the dance know that Jake was getting two-timed.

That resulted in Jake convincing one of his friends to ask January to the junior prom ... and then standing her up.

There were more instances—*so many more*—but the highlight reel in January's head didn't paint a pretty picture of either of them, so she ruthlessly shoved it to the side.

"What were we talking about again?" January asked when she realized Jake was watching her in expectant fashion. He was obviously waiting for an answer about something.

"I'm wondering why you're here," he replied. There was no edge to his voice, only curiosity. "We've established why I'm here."

"Yes, you're entitled, and your father lets you run all over the resort without having any responsibilities," January confirmed.

Jake's lips twitched. "I guess that's true. I'm going to school, though, just like you."

"Yes, Northwestern Michigan College, right?" January kept her smile flat and polite. "Good for you."

"Oh, don't take that tone with me."

"I didn't take a tone." January was the picture of innocence. "I think it's great that you're going to college." She turned her head away from him. "A community college," she added under her breath.

"And there it is!" Jake jabbed a finger in her direction. "I knew we would get to the condescending portion of tonight's festivities at some point."

"I have no idea what you're talking about."

"You do so. You've always looked down on me. You know I was supposed to go to Western Michigan University but didn't get in even though my father went there. I should've been considered a legacy."

"Oh, I *did* hear something about that." January tapped her bottom lip, feigning contrition. "It's great that you're furthering your education. I recommend everybody do that."

"Says the girl going to Michigan State University on a full scholarship," Jake muttered.

"Hey!" January straightened. "I worked hard for that scholarship."

"Yes, I'm well aware." Jake's tone was withering. "I got to hear all about your scholarship for four straight months before we graduated. That's all you talked about."

"So?"

"So watch a movie or something. Not everybody wants to talk about school."

January didn't like his tone. He had an ability to talk down to people without actually saying anything derisive. It drove her insane. "I watch movies."

"What? *The Book Thief*?"

"That was a great movie."

"I wouldn't know. I need movies that don't put me to sleep."

"Oh, of course. You have *connoisseur* written all over you when it comes to cinema."

Jake's eye roll was so pronounced, January couldn't figure out how he didn't fall over. "Who even talks like that? You sound like some snooty blue blood when we all know you grew up in that dump on Monroe Street."

January stilled, her entire body going rigid. "I should probably go," she said out of nowhere, averting her gaze and grabbing the arm of the couch so she could stand. Her knees were shaking, although she couldn't focus on that when her eyes were blurring.

"Oh, god, I'm sorry." Jake moved with her. He looked horrified by his own words.

"It's fine."

"It's not," he countered. "I didn't mean to say that. I don't think that. I—"

January didn't wait for him to find the correct words. "I should head home. I was going to spend the night up here with the others—I heard they had use of one of the guest lodges tonight—but I think I'll just call my mom." What she didn't say was that her mom was working the night shift at the local diner, and there was no way she could drop everything and pick January up. That had been made very clear when her mother dropped her off.

"I know. I'm the one who got us the lodge. Wait." Jake grabbed her wrist to swing her around and then backed up when January brought her fist toward him, swung, and narrowly missed his face. "I'm sorry," he barked when her anger—and potential tears—became obvious. "That was a horrible thing to say."

"Then why did you say it?"

"Are you kidding me? You called me stupid."

"I did not." January was scandalized at the mere thought. "I said it was great you were going to college."

"Community college."

"Yes, well, education is education. As long as you're learning, that's the most important thing." January couldn't ignore the burning in her cheeks. It was guilt, but she refused to acknowledge it. There was no reason to let Jake know he'd gotten to her. "I didn't mean to insult you."

"Well, I didn't mean to insult you either."

"How else was I supposed to take the 'dump' comment?"

"Fair point. I didn't mean to actually hurt you though." Jake dragged a hand through his dark hair. "You just always push my buttons. I try to be the bigger person, but I can never manage it. You won't let me. You still bring up that time in sixth grade when I accidentally got gum in your hair."

"You put your gum on the edge of your desk and trapped my hair there at the same time. How was that an accident?"

"Well, I didn't mean to get your hair. I just wasn't paying attention."

"I had to have three inches cut off. I'd been growing it forever."

"It was an accident!"

"Whatever." January folded her arms across her chest. She didn't know what to say, and yet knew she had to come up with something. She couldn't call her mother. She had to stay at the lodge tonight or find a couch somewhere in the resort and hope security didn't roust her. "Did you really arrange for us to have a lodge?" she asked finally.

"Yup." Jake managed a smile. "It will sleep twenty people. I think everybody is already over there."

"I know. I just ... wanted a bit of oxygen before I headed over."

"It's a lot of people," he confirmed. His tone was softer now. "I get it."

"I'm used to people now." January had no idea why she

felt the need to keep talking. "There are a lot of people on campus. I just ... occasionally need a few minutes to myself."

"No, I get that." Jake managed a rueful smile. "You can walk around outside if you need air at the lodge. It has a big patio with a hot tub."

"I didn't bring a bathing suit."

"I'm pretty sure nobody is going to be wearing them tonight."

January's mouth dropped open. "What now?"

Jake's laugh kindled the anger she'd thought abated. "It's not a big deal. A little naked soaking never hurt anyone. It's not like you can see anything with the bubbles churning. I bet you could wear your bra and underwear if you want."

Since her bra and underwear were cotton —and from Walmart—January couldn't see that happening. "I think I'll just enjoy the view from the patio."

"Okay, but you're missing out." Jake held out his arm at an odd angle.

"What are you doing?" January asked when she realized he appeared to be waiting for something.

"I'm going to walk you over." Jake wiggled his elbow.

"You want me to hook my arm through there?" January was naturally suspicious. "Why would I do that?"

"Um, because I'm being polite."

"You've never been polite to me."

"I would be if you weren't such a pain."

"I'm not holding your arm." January lifted her nose. "I will, however, walk across the parking lot with you. I mean, if you want me to."

"I don't even care what you do at this point."

"I've had two drinks," January admitted. "I really came over here to walk off the drinks. I don't hold my liquor very well."

"I'm shocked," Jake drawled.

"If we walk together, I won't have to worry about slipping."

"Very pragmatic."

"I can't hold your arm though. That's weird."

"Consider the arm dropped."

They eyed each other again, a weird *sizzle* passing between them. It was something January had never felt before, and she wasn't certain she ever wanted to feel it again. Well, probably not. Most likely not. Maybe though.

"Let's go," Jake said when January didn't respond for a really long time. "I think I could use one of those drinks you're trying to walk off."

"You should be careful about binge drinking," January warned as they started for the glass doors. "It's a killer for college students."

"Even community college students?"

"Oh, geez." January wrinkled her nose. "Will you let it go?"

"Probably not until my third drink."

"Well, I can't wait until we get you that third drink. Does it count if we get them for you all at once?"

"Now, see, that's the most interesting thing you've said all night. I think that's a fabulous idea."

"Of course you do. That's so ... *you*."

"And that response was so you."

"Maybe I'm okay with that."

"Maybe I am too."

She slipped as she was walking out onto the stone stairs that led to the parking lot. Jake caught her before she could fall, her arm wrapping around his.

"I knew you wouldn't be able to resist this arm over the long haul," he said smugly.

It took her a moment to catch her breath, and when she

did, her glare was at the ready. "You think a lot of yourself, don't you?"

"Yup. Even though I go to community college."

"Oh, let it go."

"I'll let you know if I'm willing to do that in an hour."

"I can't wait for the update."

ONE
PRESENT DAY

"Y ou guys have the maps ready, right?"

January Jackson was the picture of efficiency as she ticked items off her to-do list. First up was the front desk at Sylvan Slopes Ski Resort & Lodge. She was the activities director and event coordinator at the Northern Lower Michigan resort that offered skiing in the winter and golf in the summer, and she took her duties seriously.

Misty Dobbins, while a good worker, was less efficient. She ran the front desk at the resort on weekdays and was supposed to be organized. Unfortunately, expectations and reality rarely synced up when January had to work with Misty.

"The maps?" Misty's forehead creased. She was forty, on the right side of a bad divorce, and scatterbrained to the nth degree.

January forced herself to remain calm. "The resort maps," she confirmed. "We had special ones made up to give out to the guests so they wouldn't get lost. We have the Winter Extreme Games coming to the resort in days—not *weeks* but *days*—and we need those maps. I know they were delivered because I checked the delivery for accuracy myself."

"Oh, right." Misty tapped her bottom lip. "I know they were in a box."

January wasn't the type of person to yell for no reason. In fact, she didn't like to yell at all. The Winter Extreme Games were a big deal for Sylvan Slopes, however, so she needed things to run smoothly. Misty was making her job harder, and there was nothing she hated more than somebody making her job harder. "Have you checked the office?" January pointed toward the door behind the desk. It led into what could loosely be described as a break room. Most of the workers avoided it because it had become something of a catchall over the last few years and it was cluttered. If January had to guess, however, that's exactly where Misty would've shoved the box.

"Oh." Misty's eyes flashed bright. "I bet that's where they are. Hold on." She darted toward the office, leaving January to tap her fingers on the desk and survey the huge lobby.

Sylvan Slopes—although a name change would be coming soon because the owner, Jacob Jeffries, thought the golf course was being overlooked—had been a huge part of her childhood. Skiing had been one of the few extracurricular activities she was allowed and only because her mother had stumbled across a pair of used skis at a garage sale one summer while feeling generous. January, always determined, had taught herself how to ski by saving up money for all-day lift passes at the resort, starting when she was thirteen. Then, miracle of miracles, she'd actually won a lifelong ski pass to Sylvan Slopes when she'd entered a raffle at school, which meant she finally had an escape. She could get away and not be the girl who lived on the poor side of town. Skiing had offered her freedom, and she'd embraced it. Then her scholarship to Michigan State University had awarded her a different sort of freedom.

It had been a fluke, really. January worked five nights a week at a local diner to save up money while in high school, essentially pulling off a part-time job and going to school at the same time. She didn't get to socialize a lot because of it, but she did get to attend some dances and parties. The job allowed her to apply to several schools—something her mother wasn't going to pay for because it was extra money they didn't have to squander—and not only did she manage to get accepted to Michigan State University, but she qualified for one of their all-inclusive scholarships. It had been a dream come true.

Sure, she had to work on the campus for extra money, but she was used to that. She got a business degree with an emphasis on hospitality and applied to Sylvan Slopes right away upon graduating. Her first job had been in the public relations department, but she'd moved her way up quickly. Within six years, she was one of the top five managers on site. It was everything she could've hoped for, even when people like Misty weren't completely dedicated to their jobs.

January worked overtime to keep her face impassive when Misty exited the office.

"They're in there." Misty jerked her thumb at the office.

"Great." January unleashed her patented "I'm a great boss" smile. "I need you to unbox them and set up a table over there in front of the windows so the guests can have easy access to them."

"Today?" Misty looked horrified at the thought. "I'm only here another hour. I don't have time to get a table and set that up before I have to go."

Patience, January internally chided herself. *Not everybody has the same work ethic as you.*

Actually, that lesson had been a hard one. It wasn't until college that January recognized exactly how rigid she was. A school counselor pointed it out when she melted down because the other people working with her on a group project weren't pulling their weight ... at least in her estimation. She melted down in fantastic—and public—fashion and earned herself a trip to one of the school counselors. That single trip turned into two years of therapy, where Heather Gordon helped January develop coping skills and realize that she couldn't control everything. January hated to admit it—and would deny it if pressed—but she didn't think she would be where she was today if not for that counselor. Yes, she still liked her lists, but she'd learned patience.

Well, at least mostly.

"Not today," January replied. "It doesn't even have to be done tomorrow. It *does* have to be done before the games start and the guests begin arriving."

"So ... next week?"

January allowed her annoyance a window to climb through. "Hand me your phone, please." Her tone was crisp.

Misty handed over her phone without asking why.

January took it and pulled up the woman's calendar. She set a reminder for the maps and handed it back. "When that reminder goes off, set up the table."

Rather than be offended, Misty actually looked relieved. "Cool. Thanks."

"Don't mention it." January mentally ticked an item off her to-do list as she hit the stairs that led to the main suite of offices. It was closed to the public, which meant she didn't have to fake smile once she was beyond the barrier. She headed straight for Jacob Jeffries's office rather than stop by her own. She had several updates to give him.

The door was open when she arrived, so she didn't knock, but she could hear his voice when she poked her head inside. He sounded angry. That was unlike Jacob. He never sounded anything other than calm and collected.

Concerned, she cocked her head and watched her boss pace in front of the huge windows that looked out on the ski slopes. It was a beautiful view, especially after a fresh snow.

Jacob's wife, Enid, sat in one of the chairs across from her husband's desk, and the look she shot January was indecipherable.

"Should I come back?" January asked automatically. Sure, she wanted to tick another item off her list, but she knew better than to interrupt.

"Actually, I think you should stay." Enid flashed a smile that didn't touch her eyes. January didn't know the woman all that well—Enid opted not to spend a lot of time at the resort because she wasn't a sports enthusiast—but she liked the woman.

"Did something happen?" January asked as she lowered herself into the chair next to Enid and clasped her hands on her lap. "Oh, please tell me the Winter Extreme Games haven't been canceled."

"It's not that," Enid reassured her quickly. "As far as I know, everything is on track for the games."

That's good, January told herself. *The games are fine.* Whatever else they were facing would simply be a minor detail. She could handle minor details.

"I'm done!" Jacob roared into the phone at that moment, causing January's shoulders to jolt. He held up his hand in apology when he realized he'd frightened the event coordinator. Then he adjusted his tone. "Actually, Jake, I should rephrase that. *You're done.*"

January managed to keep her face impassive, but it took work. Jake. Of course it was Jake. He was still out there being a boil on the butt of humanity. Unlike everybody else in their graduating class, he'd never bothered to mature. He was still stuck in high school mode. Well, at least that was what she heard through the snippets of gossip that filtered her way when at work. It wasn't as if she bothered to check on Jake or anything. No sirree. She had no reason for that. None at all.

"No, Jake, I'm not ordering a hit on you," Jacob snapped. "I am, however, cutting you off financially."

Enid stirred in her chair as if she was going to say something, but Jacob pinned her with a "Don't even try it" look.

"That sounds horrible, Jake," Jacob drawled after several seconds of silence. January could only imagine the whining Jake was doing on the other end of the call. "I'm truly sad you won't be able to afford a penthouse at the Bellagio." Another pause. "Yes, that was sarcasm."

January felt uncomfortable being present for this conversation. It was a family matter, and she didn't want to get involved in family matters. Heck, she could barely handle her own family, and all she had to deal with was a warring mother and grandmother who refused to talk to one another. Other people's family problems were way too much for her.

"I'm being serious, Jake." Jacob's tone was flat now, as if he were turning into an immovable boulder that Jake wouldn't be able to dislodge no matter how hard he tried. "The gravy train is over. You're not getting another dime of my money, and that includes paying for your penthouse. I already called and canceled your credit cards."

January slammed her mouth shut and stared at the desk as she tried to keep a peal of laughter from escaping. Oh, sure, it was wrong to laugh at other people's misfortune, but Jake deserved it. He was a playboy who flitted from thing to thing. He romanced women for one night, maybe more, and then took off for his next destination, all the while squandering his father's money. He was thirty now, for crying out loud. He should be a responsible adult at this point.

"I don't know how you're going to get home, Jake," Jacob replied. "It's quite the conundrum. I'm sure you'll figure something out. You are an adult after all."

January slid her eyes to a visibly blanching Enid. She wanted to have sympathy for the woman—she'd never been anything but nice to January—but she was too busy reveling in Jake's misfortune.

That was another thing she would never admit out loud.

Her attitude regarding Jake had been set in stone at a young age. They'd made a career out of irritating each other. There'd only been one night when they'd broken their pattern. One night when things had shifted.

January briefly pressed her eyes shut as images of them kissing—and doing other stuff—flooded her mind. She shoved them right back out as quickly as she could. She would not dwell on that night. As far as she was concerned, it was an aberration. She'd drank too much, even though she'd only had the two cocktails, and that caused her to make the dumbest decision ever. It was not something to think about—or try to rationalize. It was part of her past, and it wouldn't be part of her future.

"That's also not my problem, Jake." Jacob was firm. "You're on your own for paying your bill and getting home. You lost me more than seven figures with a snowmobile deal that not only fell through but was never real to begin with. They were grifters, something I believe I warned you about."

January's forehead creased at the new information. *Seven figures?* Did that mean Jake had somehow squandered a million dollars of his father's money? That sounded both preposterous and likely.

"Jacob, you can't just strand him in Vegas," Enid insisted in a worried voice. "That's not fair."

Jacob lowered the phone from his ear. "How is it not fair?" Jacob shot back at his wife. "He's an adult."

"Yes, but he'll get thrown in jail or something. And he's too pretty for jail."

"I'm not paying for his indulgences one second longer!" Jacob's face flushed red. He was clearly angry, something January rarely saw.

"Then I'll pay for it." Enid picked at invisible lint on her skirt. "I'll pay for it, and he'll pay me back."

"Where are you going to get the money to bring him back?" Jacob demanded. "Are you talking about using my money to do it?"

Enid shot her husband a quelling look. "You're not going to want to go there." Her tone was icy. "We're married. You're not my king."

January shrank in her chair. This conversation was getting even more personal than she'd anticipated. She wanted nothing more than to escape to her office and let the Jeffries family deal with their own crap. She was not part of it.

"You're right." Jacob held up his hands in surrender. "That was wrong. I don't believe it's just my money. At all."

Enid appeared appeased. "Thank you."

"It's not his money," Jacob shot back. "I'm sick of him doing absolutely nothing to contribute. It was bad enough when he was just traveling on my dime and bedding every woman he came into contact with, VD be damned. He's now actively losing me money though."

"I know." Enid shifted on her chair. "You still can't leave him in Vegas. I agreed to the rest of your plan. Abandonment is not allowed, however. He's my only son."

Jacob blinked twice and then nodded, lifting his phone again. "Are you still there, Jake? It seems your mother refuses to abandon you. She's much softer than I am. That means we are going to bring you home. I'll pay for the hotel and plane ticket. Your accounts are frozen though."

January could only imagine the meltdown happening on the other end of the call because Jacob was silent for a long time.

"Save your breath," Jacob said after several seconds. "It's done. There's nothing you can do to change my mind." Silence for another beat. "What will you do? Oh, I don't know. How about you get a job?"

January didn't realize she was smiling until Enid's forehead creased. The woman was focused on her. January quickly blanked her expression.

"Oh, don't worry, Jake," Jacob drawled. "I'm well aware that you don't know how to find a job for yourself. I have years and years of experience watching you do absolutely nothing. I'm arranging for you to have a job here."

January's heart skipped a beat. That wasn't what she wanted to hear. *It's karma,* her inner voice chided. *You laughed in the face of Jake's misery, and it's going to come back to bite you. He's going to be working at the resort, and you'll have no choice but to cross paths with him.*

"Shut up, Jake," Jacob snapped. "I'm done listening to you. Call your mother, and she'll arrange for you to pay your bill and get home. I don't care how it happens, but you will be here tomorrow to learn about your new job." He disconnected the call before Jake could start arguing again. "He's your son," he barked at Enid. "You get him back here and ready to work."

Enid looked beaten down more than irritated by his tone. "I'll talk to him," she promised as she stood. "You have my word that he'll get it together."

"Awesome." Jacob glared in his wife's wake long after she was gone.

"Maybe now isn't a good time for an update," January hedged when she realized Jacob wasn't going to ease the tension in the room. He was seemingly lost in his own little world.

"What?" Jacob jerked his eyes to her, emerging from his reverie. "No, it's fine." He waved his hand to brush away January's concern. "This was a long time coming. I'm sorry you had to witness it, but since it affects you, I felt it was only fair."

January went rigid in her chair. "Affects me? How?"

"Jacob is my son. Eventually, I'm going to want him to

take over this place. That obviously can't happen right now. He needs to learn responsibility."

"I'm still not sure how that affects me."

"You're the most responsible person I know, and you went to high school with him. You get him."

"Still not understanding." January was practically breathless at this point.

"I need you to help rein him in, show him the ropes. He's not going to do your job or anything, but he needs to start learning about the business. With the Winter Extreme Games coming here, I figured this was a good time to give him a bird's-eye view of what we do."

January was convinced she'd somehow wandered into a nightmare. "You want me to do what here?"

"Just show him the ropes. You're in charge, of course, but he needs to learn that this resort doesn't run itself. He needs to get it together because eventually I'm going to want to retire."

"Why me?" January didn't realize how petulant the question sounded until it was already out of her mouth.

"Because you're the best employee I have. I need Jake to learn from the best. I will, of course, be giving you a bonus for doing this. Consider it hardship pay for helping my son mature."

January had to bite back a sigh. Jacob knew exactly where to hit her. In her pride. "I can't wait to help," she said finally, the words painful as they escaped. "It's going to be a great event."

"It certainly is. I will accept nothing less."

Two

J ake had more swagger than was likely advisable when he made his way through the resort's lobby. People called out to him, and he waved, flashing that devastating smile that people had become familiar with, but inside he was frowning. How had he gotten himself into this situation? That was all he kept saying, over and over again, as he made his way to his father's office.

Leo Sandusky, the head of security, stopped him as he was heading up the steps that led to the executive offices.

"I heard you were back." Leo beamed at him. He was a gregarious man with charm oozing out of every pore. It was one of the reasons he was so effective at his job. People liked him so much, they didn't mind doing what he asked. He was both respected and adored, something Jake was desperately trying to achieve himself.

So far, it hadn't been going very well. He had no problem being adored. His mother had set that precedent when he was young, and the adoration had never stopped. There were times Jake was convinced she'd done him a disservice, made life too easy on him, but he liked being Bellaire's favorite son and let it slide. That was ultimately a mistake on his part, he realized. His need to be liked by everybody had left him hating himself. He was working on that. Or he was until he'd made a mistake on a snowmobile deal, and now he was really in the doghouse.

"I'm back." Jake's smile was a reflex, and it made an appearance. People assumed he was never upset because he covered well. "I'm excited about the Winter Extreme Games. I couldn't miss those."

"Uh-huh." Leo was the shrewd sort and merely stared at the younger man. "This place is a gossip mill. You know that, right?"

Jake swallowed hard and then sighed. "What have you heard?"

Leo smirked. "I've heard a little bit about a great many things. For example, Florence in the kitchen? She's supposedly banging Barry on the grounds crew."

Jake's lips curved down. "Aren't they both married to other people?"

"Yes." Leo bobbed his head. "And both those people work at the resort, so it's only a matter of time until that blows up."

"Huh." Jake didn't know what to say. He wasn't a fan of infidelity, something he was convinced his father had participated in on a regular basis when he was younger. Jake worried that it remained a commonplace occurrence in the present. "Well, that sucks."

"It does. I don't mean for you to focus on it though. I just want to remind you that everybody already knows your business, so pretending is going to get you absolutely nowhere."

Jake scowled. "Bunch of vultures."

Leo chuckled. "You're the golden boy. They can't help but be interested in your antics."

"I wasn't trying to entertain. I was actually trying to do something. I thought a snowmobile partnership would be beneficial to the resort."

"I get it." Leo utilized his most reasonable tone. "I know you have a good heart, kid. I also know you have good intentions. Your problem is that you don't look before you leap."

"That doesn't sound very flattering."

"I don't know that it is or isn't flattering. Sometimes, it's cute. Not all the time though. That's the part you've yet to learn."

In truth, Jake had always looked up to Leo as a father figure. He hadn't gotten along well with his own father growing up, and he'd glommed on to Leo at a young age. He was always at the resort anyway. Why pay for a babysitter when you had an entire staff to keep an eye on your mischievous only child? Jake had spent more time at the resort than he had at his own home. Even now, when he returned home to Bellaire, he stayed at one of the resort's lodges rather than his parents' house. It was simply easier because Jacob Jeffries sucked up all the oxygen in a room, and when he was around his father, Jake could never breathe.

"I'll take it under advisement." Jake forced a smile he didn't feel. "I wish I could talk more, but I've been summoned." He angled his head toward the spiral staircase that led to the part of the resort the guests were forbidden to visit. "I don't want to be late, on top of everything else."

"Definitely not." Leo let loose a wink, likely in an effort to relax Jake, but it didn't work. "It's going to be okay." The security chief adjusted his tone. "You're a good boy. You always have been. Your father sees that. He just wants you to add some direction into the mix."

"That's what I was trying to do."

"I know." Leo held his hands up in mock surrender, Jake's shrill tone seeming to jolt him. "Remember that I'm on your side. Your father is, too, when it comes to it."

"No, he's not." Jake shook his head. "My father is on my

father's side. My mother is on my side. That's what's important. She still has some sway over my father."

Leo hesitated, and for a moment Jake thought the older man was going to say something negative about his mother. Instead, he mustered another smile. "Just go up there and tell the truth. Take your lumps."

"What do you think he's going to do with me?" Jake was grim as he glanced up the stairs.

"I think he's going to make you go to work."

"I was working."

"Son, you're wasting your breath on me." Leo was firm now. "I know you have big dreams of proving yourself to your father, but I've yet to see you do it the correct way. *This* is the correct way."

"What's the correct way?" Jake was baffled.

"You'll see." Leo's smile was crooked as he motioned for Jake to head upstairs. "Don't leave him waiting. It will just make matters worse."

"Yeah." Jake made a growling sound in his throat. "I'm sure I'll see you around if he doesn't kill me."

The dramatic response was enough to make Leo laugh. "Somehow, I think you'll survive."

Jake trudged up the stairs, one at a time, and each step matched an unhappy beat of his heart. *This is going to suck.* That kept repeating in his head over and over again. By the time he reached his father's office, the one that was three times bigger than anybody else's, he was convinced he might pass out.

Instead, he raised his hand to rap on the open door. He could see his parents standing together behind his father's desk. They looked to be having a deep conversation. Jake had no doubt who was at the center of that conversation, so he knocked to interrupt them.

When Jacob turned in his son's direction, the set of his jaw was rigid. Enid, however, looked thrilled to see her son.

"Jake!" Enid raced from behind the desk and threw her arms around her only child's neck. "I'm so glad you're home."

"Thanks to you," Jacob muttered as he sat in his desk chair and eyed his son critically. "Have a seat, Jake. Make sure you thank your mother for rescuing you from Vegas first. Otherwise I'm guessing the mobsters that run that town would still have a firm grip on you, even as we speak."

"Oh, well, that's not dramatic." Jake rolled his eyes as he extricated himself from his mother. "Thank you for helping me." He was sincere as he stared into her tearful eyes. "I appreciate it. I *will* pay you back."

Jacob snorted. "How many times have we heard that song and dance?"

"Jacob." Enid's voice was low and full of warning. "Just ... don't."

Jacob regarded her for a moment, his eyes probing, and then he sighed. "Sit down, Jake. We have a lot to discuss."

Jake had no doubt his father wanted him to settle in for a long rant, so he sat in one of the wingback chairs across from his father's oversized desk and braced himself.

"Your days of traveling all over the world on our dime are over," Jacob announced, his tone no-nonsense. "Your mother and I have had a long talk, and while she is more—let's say sympathetic— to the fact that you have yet to find your place in this world, I am not. Since I don't believe you're capable of working for anybody else, you *will* be working for me."

"What does that mean?" Jake asked. He was already worried. "Are you going to make me start on the grounds crew and work my way up?" Honestly, he didn't mind the idea of the grounds crew. That sort of mindless work would be good for centering himself. His father would consider it a punishment.

"I thought about that." Jacob almost looked amused. "I decided against it, however. It's not like you're going to continue with the grounds crew forever. I want to put you in a position where you can actually benefit from learning something.

"One day this resort is going to be yours, Jake," his father continued. "You're going to inherit this place and be expected to run it. Yet, at thirty, you know nothing about how we work here. Don't you find that odd?"

Jake found the entire conversation odd but knew that wasn't what his father was getting at. "Just tell me what you expect me to do." He was resigned to his fate. After all, there was one thing his father wasn't wrong about. There was nobody else who would hire him. He had no job skills to speak of, unless partying was considered a skill.

"You're going to help with the Winter Extreme Games, to start."

Jake perked up. He hadn't been lying when he told Leo he was excited for the games. "Like ... I get to work with the athletes?"

"That will be part of it," Jacob confirmed. "You will also be liaising with Jim Maxwell, as he is our biggest sponsor for this event."

Jake furrowed his brow. "He's that car dealership guy, right?"

"Yes."

"He runs the really religious ads, doesn't he?"

"Yes." Jacob's expression didn't change, but his body language did. "I've already received several notes from him regarding the length of women's skirts in the resort. We're talking the guests, not the workers. He's going to be difficult."

"But he's the money man," Jake surmised. "That means we chase the money."

"That is exactly what it means."

Despite his wariness about working with Jim Maxwell, Jake found he was mildly excited. "I can't believe you're trusting me with this." It was more than he could've hoped for. "I appreciate it, and I won't let you down."

Amusement flitted across Jacob's features. "Do you seriously think I'm putting you in charge of this?"

Jake shrugged. "You just said—"

"I just said that I want you to learn," Jacob replied. "I'm not throwing you into the deep end of the pool and expecting you to swim on your own right out of the gate. You'll be working with my event coordinator."

"Oh." Jake deflated a bit. Still, this was better than he'd anticipated. "Okay. That makes sense."

"She's a smart cookie," Jacob said. "She's got a firm handle on what we're doing. She checks and double-checks everything. She has lists all over the place and goes over the lists a million times. You're going to be learning from her."

"That sounds ... great," Jake muttered, his stomach constricting. The last thing he needed was some Type A pain in the ass ordering him around. He had zero choice in the matter. "Who is it? Is it anybody I know?"

"It is." Jacob steepled his fingers on the desk, and a very bad feeling settled in the pit of Jake's stomach. "You remember January Jackson, I'm sure."

Jake felt as if he'd been kicked in the stomach, and by Godzilla at that. "You've got to be kidding." He looked to his mother for confirmation. Enid's tight smile told him everything he needed to know. "We can't work together."

"And why not?" Jacob feigned patience, but his son knew better.

"Because ... because ... you know." Frustration clawed through Jake's throat. "She spent every waking hour before the age of eighteen making my life a living hell." *And then there was that one other night. No, don't think about that night.*

Jake willed his heart to keep from beating out of his chest. "She hates me."

"January is a professional," Jacob countered. "She's very good at her job. She was in on the ground floor of this event and has made every effort to ensure its success. She knows all the players."

"I don't care about that." Jake recognized he was coming across as aggressive—and maybe a little whiny—but he couldn't stop himself. "She's mean to me. She always has been."

"That is true," Enid hedged, her eyes imploring as they searched Jacob's face. "I know she's a good worker now, but they don't have the best relationship. Maybe another department is better."

Jake brightened considerably. "Yes, another department."

"Absolutely not." There was no give in Jacob's features when he regarded his son. "January is a consummate professional. She's organized. She's wonderful with people. Those are the things I need you to learn from her."

"She's horrible," Jake complained. "I'm not partnering with her. Don't you remember the things she used to do to me?"

"I do. I also remember the things you used to do to her. I particularly enjoyed being called into the principal's office because you told everybody in the school that her parents were brother and sister and that she was born with a tail. I believe you were ten then, and you made that poor girl cry. The other kids wouldn't stop asking about her tail for months."

A smile rushed to Jake's lips, unbidden, and then he quickly blanked his features when he found his father frowning. "She told everyone in school that I was born with both boy and dog parts, and you guys waited until I was thirteen to let me choose what I wanted to be, and I wore animal pajamas when I was home at night so I could wag my tail. Oh, and those pajamas had *Teenage Mutant Ninja Turtles* on them. You know, just to make it uber weird."

Jacob snickered and then sobered. "You two went at each other hard. I haven't forgotten. You were children then. You're adults now. I think you should both be able to put the past behind you."

"Uh-huh." Jake wasn't convinced of that in the least. "And what did she say when you told her about this arrangement?"

"She was fine with it."

Enid made a small, distressed sound but didn't speak.

"She was fine with it?" That was a lie, and Jake knew it. "There's no way she was fine with it."

"The difference is that she's a team player, and she didn't argue with me," Jacob responded pointedly. "This is what's happening, Jake. It's done. If you don't like it, well, then you're free to find a job somewhere else. It will not be here, and you will not be getting another dime from your mother and me. This is it, kid. It's my line in the sand."

Jake wanted to throw something. Instead, he shook his head and held out his hands. His father had him over a barrel, and they both knew it. "Fine. We'll be partners." The words were difficult to get out.

"Oh, you misunderstand." Jacob made a tsking sound with his tongue. "You're not partners. She's your boss."

"And the hits just keep on coming," Jake muttered. "You mean I have to follow her orders?"

"Yes, and if you don't, I'll know, and you're going to be in big trouble."

"You'll know because she'll tattle?"

"I'll know." Jacob was firm. "Now, if that's all, I have some meetings to get to."

"I'm sure you do." Jake stood. "I can still stay at my normal lodge, right? You haven't yanked that away too, have you?"

"You can stay there," Jacob hedged. "It's just, well, we've loaned the lodge out for the next few weeks to one of the workers, so you'll have to share the space. Once the games are done, the place will be yours alone again."

"A roommate?" Jake was horrified. "Unbelievable."

"You could always come home with us," Enid offered.

To Jake, that possibility was worse than having a roommate. "No, I'll deal with the roommate." His expression was pinched and tight. "Who is it? Please tell me it's someone I know."

"Oh, you know her." Now Jacob looked diabolically amused. "January is already set up in the lodge. She knows you're coming and will point you to your room when you get there. I believe she's expecting you."

Jake had never wished for a hole to open up beneath him and swallow him whole as much as he did now. "That is just unbelievable. You cannot expect me to share a lodge with January Jackson. It's inhumane."

"It's two thousand square feet," Jacob countered. "You'll survive." With that, he turned to his computer, and Jake knew he'd essentially been dismissed.

"It will be fine," Enid assured her son as he moved to leave. "I bet you'll find that you and January can laugh about all that old stuff and be friends."

Jake didn't have the heart to tell her exactly how wrong she was.

Three

J anuary sat at the kitchen table in the lodge and tried to focus on her work. Her eyes kept drifting to the clock on the wall, however. She knew Jake would be arriving at any second, so it was like a countdown to Armageddon.

Tick.

Tick.

Tick.

She let loose a sigh and went back to looking at her laptop. She had to focus. The Winter Extreme Games were her baby. They were her stepping stone to bigger and better things. That meant everything had to be perfect. Well, as perfect as possible. Even she knew there would be hiccups. It was how she handled those hiccups that mattered.

The sound of the front door opening made her frown, and when she moved to the hallway to stare at the entryway, her back went rigid as she and Jake locked gazes. It had been eight years since they'd seen each other. Ten years since they'd... She'd rather not think about that. There was no reason to think about that.

The years had been good to him. He'd filled out a bit, and

in all the right places. His cheekbones were still high. His dimple was still present. His eyes were still piercing.

God, why did he have to be so hot?

"Hello," Jake said blandly.

"Hello." January had no idea what to do with her hands. Her pants didn't have pockets. They were formfitting L.L. Bean thermal wear, and she loved them. They made her ass, which she often thought was nonexistent, look like it actually had some definition. The trade-off was a lack of pockets.

"Long time no see," Jake said. He sounded as uneasy as January felt.

"Yes." She was tentative as she moved forward. "I take it your father informed you I was staying here."

"Yeah." There was no warmth in Jake's voice. "He informed me of several things."

January didn't like his tone. "So knowing that I was staying here, you didn't think you should knock?"

Jake's eyes flashed with annoyance. "Why would I knock? This is my lodge."

"No, this was your lodge. Then it was my lodge. I was supposed to have it for the entire games so I could be on site and put out any fires. Because you're you, it's now *our* lodge." Her smile bordered on a sneer. "So, thanks for that I guess."

Jake made a rumbling sound in his throat. "This is always my lodge when I'm here."

"Were you expected here this week?" January sounded prim. "I must've missed the parade and welcome home party. My mistake."

"Oh, don't take that tone with me." Jake hefted his large duffel bag over his shoulder and started down the hallway, heading to the room on his left without asking.

"Wait!" January moved to head him off, but he was quicker and disappeared in the room. He tried to shut the door in her face, but she stopped him, and she was a huffy mess when she landed beside him. "I've already set up in this room."

"So I see." Jake's eyes drifted around the room, ultimately landing on the bra resting on the end of the bed.

Embarrassed, January scooped up the bra and tried to shove it into her nonexistent pockets. "I've been here for days. I didn't realize that I would be sharing the space with you."

"It's fine." Jake sounded despondent. "This is just my normal room. It's fine though." He turned to leave, but she was standing in his way, and they bumped into one another, chest to chest. "Move," he ordered.

January couldn't remember the last time she was such a fluttery mess. She'd matured since leaving high school. She'd learned how to present herself and hopefully blunted some of the edges that people complained about when she was younger. She'd learned that being organized didn't mean she also had to be uptight. Unspooling her complicated emotions and reactions was still a work in progress.

"You could say please," she complained, her annoyance on full display. "I mean … that would be the polite thing to do."

"Oh, are we playing at being polite now?" Jake's eyebrows winged up. "I must've missed the memo. My bad. I thought we were still playing the game where you call me names and I try to pretend you don't exist."

"We never played that game."

"Um … sophomore year?" Jake's gaze was pointed. "You told everyone at the winter dance that I had a skin disease that was contagious, and none of the girls would go with me."

"Your hands were dry and flaky."

"Because I got frostbite! I had to go to the dance with Mindy Wellington. I mean … Mindy Wellington!"

"Mindy is a perfectly nice girl." January sounded prim. "She's married."

"I know she's married," Jake snapped. "I don't dislike

Mindy. It's just ... she's gay. She's married to a doctor. A female doctor! I knew then that she was gay. That meant I was her..." He didn't finish what he was going to say.

January did it for him. "Beard?"

"Knock it off." Jake's testy attitude eased some of the anxiety January had been feeling before his arrival. If he'd been nice to her, she would've freaked out. This was better.

"Whatever." January moved out of the way so he could go to the other bedroom, which was markedly smaller than the one she'd claimed for herself. She was amused as she moved behind him and watched as he tossed his duffel bag on the bed and went to his private bathroom to poke his head inside. "When you're done unpacking, I have some things to go over with you," she said.

Jake slid his eyes back to her. "Go over with me? Listen, if you're worried I'm going to try to share that bed with you, I have other things on my mind. There's no need to lay down ground rules or anything. There will not be a repeat of ... that night."

January managed to keep her face expressionless, but it took every ounce of strength she had. "I'm not sure what you're referring to, but I was talking about what you'll be working on during the games. I have a binder containing your duties. Your father asked me to put it together."

"Of course he did." Jake's shoulders drooped. "Just give me a few minutes, huh? I need to change my clothes."

"Sure." January was more than happy to get away from him ... and the bed. It wasn't that she was tempted, of course. It was more that it was another reminder of what had happened— and what she so desperately wanted to forget.

To give herself time to calm down, she grabbed a Diet Coke out of the refrigerator and popped the tab. Because she was a creature of habit, she poured the drink over ice, rinsed the can, and added the empty to the recycle bin before sitting back down at the table. Then she took one refreshing sip of the soda before sliding her eyes to Jake. He'd appeared in the kitchen without alerting her to his presence.

"What?" she demanded, annoyance playing across her features.

"You said you weren't sure what I was referring to," he prodded.

January kept her face impassive. "When?"

"When we were in the bedroom."

"Um ... okay?" It was January's lone goal to make him think she had no idea what he was talking about. If she embarrassed him, perhaps he wouldn't bring up their drunken night together years before. That was what she wanted more than anything.

"You said you didn't know what I was referring to," he insisted.

"You keep saying that. I'm not sure why though."

"Because I was referring to that night when we were in college." He said it as if she was supposed to respond with a knee-slapping laugh of acknowledgement.

"We didn't go to college together." January figured if she was going to feign ignorance, she should go all the way.

"I know we didn't go to college together." Jake sounded as if he was running out of patience. "I know that better than anyone. Trust me."

"I can't figure out what you're trying to say." January made a big show of choosing her words carefully, as if she was afraid to set him off. "I just don't know what you're referencing."

"I'm talking about that night when we were here," Jake exploded. "It wasn't this lodge. It was one of the bigger ones. We were on winter break from college, we were here for the same party, and we ... you know."

January merely blinked. *I should be an actress,* she thought as she patted herself on the back. "I have a vague recollection of being here for a party." She cocked her head. "Were you here for that?"

"Of course I was here. We ... you ... that is, you and me ... we..."

January almost felt sorry for him. Then she remembered the time he announced to everyone in seventh grade that she stuffed her bra and went so far as to throw tissues around the room, making her want to die. "We talked that night?" she prodded, feigning confusion.

"No, we had sex!" Jake barked out the words in frustration. "We had sex in one of the bedrooms after too many drinks."

"Yeah, I think I would remember that."

"You do remember it. You just don't want to admit you remember it."

"If you say so." January's neutral expression never shifted. "So, duties." She lifted the binder for him.

"We had sex!" Jake insisted. "In fact, we had it twice. We slept in the same bed all night. Then, the next morning, before we could even talk, you took off."

"I don't know what to tell you," January said. "That didn't happen. Are you sure you're not confusing me with somebody else? Lana Peterson, perhaps."

"It wasn't Lana Peterson." Jake looked horrified at the thought. "She kissed like a broken Slurpee machine."

"Jane Baker then, maybe."

"It wasn't Jane!" Jake gripped his hand into a fist and shook it. "It was you."

"If I say it was me, will you take this binder and start going over your duties?" January pretended she was doing him a huge favor.

"I don't want you to say it was you to shut me up. I want you to say it was you because it was you."

"But it wasn't me."

"It was so!" Jake's chest was heaving at this point. "Why are you trying to drive me insane?"

"I think that's just your natural state." January was matter of fact. "Either way, you can just assume whatever you want. I need to get back up to the resort. What I need from you is an acknowledgement that you understand that I'm bestowing this binder on you, and it contains your duties."

Jake's eyes slitted, but he reached over and took the binder from her. "I know what you're doing."

"Yes, I'm working."

"No, you're trying to make me think it didn't happen when it did."

"If you say so."

"I know so!"

January managed a soft smile as she skirted around him. It was a pitying smile, however, as if she was placating him. That only made matters worse. "We'll talk about your duties when you're not jet lagged and grumpy. How does that sound?"

Jake didn't respond. January could feel his eyes on her back as she moved toward the front door, however.

"Just take a nap or something," January said as she shrugged into her The North Face coat and tugged on her gloves. "I'll see you in a few hours."

"I know what you're doing!" Jake screeched at her back. "I'm not going to let you get away with it."

January didn't respond. She didn't have to. She was smiling when she shut the door and started out toward the resort. Perhaps this wouldn't be as terrible as she initially envisioned.

JAKE'S FOUL MOOD FOLLOWED HIM from the lodge to the resort bar. He took the binder with him, even though he wanted to toss it into the fireplace, and made a series of disgruntled noises as he sat on a stool and waited for one of his former classmates to get to him.

Luke Gordon was all smiles when he arrived in front of his old football buddy. "The prodigal son returns." He gave Jake a hearty slap on the shoulder. "What's up?"

Jake didn't even bother to smile. "I need a big drink. Like, huge. We're talking as big as you can make it, and keep them coming."

Luke's eyes went wide. "Um, okay. Whiskey?"

"Yup."

Luke set about making the drink, but Jake could feel the bartender's eyes on him as he leafed through the binder. "What's that?" Luke asked when he delivered the cocktail. "Is that all the women you've banged while you've been traveling all over the place? I'm not jealous or anything," he added. "I just want to live vicariously through you."

Jake snorted and shook his head. "No. These are my new duties." He lifted the binder so Luke could see how thick it was. "There's a full page in here on what is and is not considered appropriate clothing for the Winter Extreme Games."

Luke's lips curved. "Yeah, we all got that sheet. Let me guess, January Jackson?"

"She's the devil." Jake was still furious that she refused to acknowledge their night together. "Just the absolute worst."

"She's not so bad."

Jake froze. "Excuse me?" He was incredulous. "Since when do you like January?"

"Oh, I didn't say that I liked her." Luke rested his elbows on the bar. It was a slow night, so he and Jake could converse without risking anybody overhearing. "She's still wound a bit too tight, and she makes a face like a constipated squirrel when something happens that she doesn't like."

Jake laughed, as he was certain his friend intended.

"She's organized, though, and even though I wish she would lighten up, she's good when it comes to a crisis. Honestly, I'm much happier to see her when something goes wrong than your father, because she doesn't yell."

"No?" Jake found he was intrigued. "What does she do?"

"She makes the same noises my mother used to make and says 'I'm disappointed' before outlining ways we can all do better."

"And you don't find that infuriating?"

Luke shrugged. "Listen, do I want to hang out with her? No. She's uptight, and I swear my scrotum shrinks whenever I hear her voice. Things run smoothly around here when we have big events, though, and we couldn't say that with the previous team. Also, your father is the type of guy who likes to yell until he gets red in the face. She never does that."

Jake had to grudgingly admit, if only to himself, that dealing with January was better than listening to his father rant and rave. That wasn't saying much though. "She's staying in my lodge."

Confusion lit Luke's features. "I don't understand."

"The lodge I usually snag when I'm here. She's already in it, and because we're booked solid, there's not another one available. So I either have to stay there with her—and in the guest room because she already snagged the master—or stay with my parents."

"Your parents have a huge house on Torch Lake. They have a maid and butler too, right?"

"A house manager," Jake corrected.

"A house manager." Luke adopted a hoity-toity tone. "I would totally take a house manager over living with January."

"Yes, but my father sleeps there."

"That's true."

Jake was morose. "At least this way I can hang out here."

"And drink."

"And drink," Jake agreed.

"Because if you're staying with January, you're going to need to drink."

"Most definitely." Jake flipped another page in the binder. "Just out of curiosity, did she mention that she and I would be staying together?"

"Oh, she doesn't talk to me unless she has to. She's tight with a few of the other workers, although I don't know if she's ever invited out for girl's night or anything."

"Why wouldn't she be invited out?"

"You've met her. Besides, nobody wants to go out with the boss. Everybody remembers what she was like in high school and how she tortured you. Who do you think we're loyal to? That's right. You. And it's not just because you're the boss's son."

For some reason—and Jake would have to think on this later when he wasn't still so riled up—he didn't like what Luke was inferring. "You shouldn't hold high school against her. I mean I gave as good as I got."

"Yeah, but you were fun."

And the boss's son, Jake silently added. That had always been his lone insecurity. Did people only like him because he was Jacob Jeffries's only son and heir? For some people, he was certain that was true.

"Well, don't be mean to her on my account." Jake was firm. "I don't want that. Besides, we're only going to be sharing the lodge for a few weeks. Then she'll go home, and I will have the place to myself." He determinedly focused on the binder. "Keep the drinks coming. I have to get through this entire thing tonight. I will not give her the satisfaction of not finishing what I'm supposed to finish."

Luke winked at him. "You got it. I'm so glad you're here, man. It will be just like old times."

Jake couldn't decide if that was a good or bad thing.

Four

January's favorite thing now that she was staying at the lodge was to make her coffee first thing in the morning, put it in her thermal mug, bundle up, and sit on the back patio so she could watch the sun spread over the ski resort peaks in glorious fashion. She already had her coffee in her hand when she walked into the living room ... and almost tripped over Jake's prone form when she realized he was passed out on the floor.

Her mouth dropped open, and her first assumption was that he was dead. He'd somehow tripped when coming in and hit his head. That notion didn't last long, however, because there was an obvious pool of drool by his mouth. Oh, and he was snoring.

She did a quick inventory of the situation. The front door was closed, but she could tell by the position of the lock that he hadn't bothered to secure them inside the lodge and make sure they were safe. His boots were off but not on the mat where they were supposed to be. He looked to have been wrestling with his coat when he passed out. It was halfway on, and he was using the second arm as a pillow.

Annoyance flooded January as she glared at him. Instead of waking him softly and asking that he go to his room, she turned on her heel and stalked back to the kitchen. There she filled one of the pitchers in the cupboard with water and stalked back into the living room. She had only a split second of hesitation before she threw the water at Jake's face. Then she watched with grim satisfaction as he made a yelping sound and rocketed to a sitting position.

"What in the hell?" Jake was clearly dazed as he took in his surroundings. He had an indentation from the zipper on the coat embedded in his cheek. His hair stood up in a million different directions. There was also mayhem lurking in his eyes. "What did you do?" he demanded as he took in his surroundings.

January was calm as she regarded him. "I was just making sure you weren't dead." She made sure there was no apology in her features. "You look alive to me." Calmly, as if playing a part on a television show, she returned the pitcher to the kitchen. When she appeared in the living room, she had her coffee mug in her hand and a scowl on her face. "Your bedroom is down the hallway. You should try sleeping there this evening."

Jake narrowed his eyes. "You could've shaken me to wake me up."

"That's not my job. Now, if you'll excuse me." She grabbed her coat from the rack, slipped into it, and moved out toward the patio. "Clean up that mess. Don't leave water on the rug. It will mildew."

"I'm not responsible for this mess," Jake barked at her back.

January pretended she hadn't heard him as she got comfortable on her usual chair. It hadn't snowed the previous evening—or not enough to coat the chair—so she didn't have to worry about anything but watching the sunrise. She found the entire process soothing on a normal day. Unfortunately, today her attention kept floating back to the man sharing her roof. Why did he have to be so ... Jake? It was beyond frustrating. Still, January was nothing if not determined. That was how she'd managed to make it as far as she had at the resort before the age of thirty. She focused hard, her eyes glued to the sun. She was so focused, in fact, that she didn't hear the door open to allow Jake to join her.

"You look like you're about to crap your pants, you're concentrating so much," Jake announced.

January scowled. "Don't you have something better to do?" She refused to look at him.

"Apparently not. Once I'm awake, there's no going back to sleep." Jake plopped down in the chair next to her. "Give me some of that." He reached for her coffee.

January cradled the mug close to her chest and shot him a death glare. "You know how to work the coffee machine. Or at least I'm guessing you do. You never were a quick learner. I can schedule a tutorial later if you need a refresher course."

"Just give me some of your coffee," Jake complained. "I need to wake up."

"No." January's temper came out to play. "Make your own."

"Why are you being so difficult?" Jake sounded as if he was at the end of his rope. "I need the coffee to wake up."

"No." January's eyes flashed. "This is my coffee. Besides, I can only have one latte a day. I make it with almond milk and sugar-free syrup. It's thirty calories. I can only have the thirty calories."

Jake blinked several times and then made an exasperated sound. "Thirty calories is nothing."

"That's why I'm allowed one latte a day."

"But you're not fat."

January's glare was withering. "There's a reason. I stick to a 1,500-calorie-a-day diet. Also, don't say 'fat.' It's rude. I know you idle at rude, but it's still mean. You should learn to use your words."

Jake looked as if he was about to start throwing around insults. Instead, he merely shook his head. "I've known you your entire life, January. You've never been overweight. Your mother was, but you've always been thin." It was as if he realized what he'd said and finally looked at her with new eyes. "Oh, *that's* why. Your mother."

January glared at Jake. "My mother is a good person."

"I didn't say she wasn't."

"She raised me on her own."

"Okay."

"She worked two jobs the entire time I was growing up just to keep a roof over our heads." January recognized she was growing shrill, but she couldn't seem to stop herself.

"I'm not trying to insult your mother," Jake barked. He was clearly exasperated. "That came out wrong." He sucked in a breath and pinched the bridge of his nose. "Let's start over," he said when he had a better grasp on his emotions. "I wasn't saying there was something wrong with your mother. I was just saying there's nothing wrong with you. You've got a nice body. You don't need to limit yourself to thirty freaking calories a day for coffee."

January's cheeks heated despite the cold, and she averted her gaze.

"Aren't you going to say something?" Jake asked after several seconds of silence.

"I don't think so," January replied finally.

"Are you going to give me some of that coffee?"

"Definitely not." Even though she was determined to keep hating him, January couldn't fight off the small smile that appeared over the rim of her coffee mug. "I think sharing your spit once is my limit." She hadn't even realized what she'd said until it was already out of her mouth. By then it was too late to take it back. She risked a glance at Jake and found him glaring at her.

"I knew it!" he hissed, annoyance evident. "We did sleep together."

January couldn't decide which part of that statement bothered her more. "Why does it matter?"

"Because you denied it happened."

"Maybe I wish it never happened. Have you considered that?"

"You can't rewrite history just because you want a do-over," Jake snapped. "That's not how it works. Trust me. If I could right a wrong after the fact, I wouldn't be here."

January reacted as if she'd been smacked. "Right a wrong?"

"You know what I meant." Jake waved his hand. "Don't go reading something into my words that wasn't there. There's also no need to gaslight me."

"Gaslight you?" January's eyebrows practically flew off her forehead. "That's rich." Her mind involuntarily flew back to the morning after her ill-advised tryst with Jake. She'd woken up feeling like an idiot, hopeful that nobody would find out what had happened between them. At the very least, she was convinced they would have a new understanding of one another. Instead, she found herself alone, and when she snuck into the living room to find her boots, she'd overheard Jake boasting to his friends about helping pull the stick out of her ass finally. She'd been mortified and snuck out without saying a goodbye to anybody in the lodge. She hadn't seen anybody in the group since, and she wasn't sorry about it.

"You pretended we hadn't slept together," Jake snapped. "I knew we had. I was almost positive."

"You were *almost* positive?" January's tone was acrid enough to peel paint. "Wow. How many women do you have to sleep with to be 'almost positive' you had sex with someone?" She used the appropriate air quotes. "That's not insulting at all."

Jake narrowed his eyes. "What is your problem with me? You're acting like I killed your dog or something."

Worse. I'm acting like you broke my heart. That couldn't be further from the truth. *What is wrong with me?* With deliberate intent, January sucked in a breath to center herself. The therapist she'd started seeing in college had taught her some breathing exercises. She said January was wound way too tight and needed to take a breath whenever the world started closing in. That was easier said than done sometimes, but January was committed to the process. Otherwise, she feared she would lose everything she'd worked so hard far.

"It doesn't matter," she said finally. "The past is the past. I certainly don't need to dwell on it. It's not like the sex was memorable or anything. We should just forget it ever happened. It was a million years ago."

Jake's mouth dropped open. "Hey!"

For some reason, the look of insult on his face made her grin. "I was just saying," she supplied primly.

"You're unbelievable." Jake made a growling sound deep in his throat. He seemed to be chewing on something, if January had to guess, and after several seconds of contemplation, he held out his hands. "We need to put the past behind us."

"You once stranded me at the grocery store at ten o'clock at night because you thought it was funny to seduce my ride. Mickey Jordan followed me home and tried to get me into his truck the whole walk. I was terrified the entire time. Some of that stuff I can't just let go."

Jake's face drained of color. "I didn't know that."

"Why would you? You got what you wanted and left me there. I had twenty dollars for groceries for the entire week, and when I left with the milk and eggs, I had to practically run to get home before they went bad. Mickey chasing me was motivational, I guess."

Jake blinked several times and then rubbed his cheeks. "I never would've even thought about that being a problem." He stared at his stocking feet, which should've been cold given the weather. "January, I'm really sorry." Genuine contrition reflected back from his eyes when he looked at her. "I did not mean for that to happen. I just thought it would be funny if you came out and realized your ride was gone. It never occurred to me that I would be putting you in danger."

"That's the problem, Jake." January kept her tone flat and icy. "You never thought about any of it. You came from a family that didn't have to survive on one carton of eggs a week. You could afford to take multiple cartons out and egg houses when you were bored. Not all of us lived the same life as you."

"No." Jake kept rubbing his cheeks. It was as if he was trying to wake himself up from a bad dream. "I'm still sorry. That was wrong. I have no excuse."

It wasn't the response January was expecting. She thought he would play the victim or something. It was the exact opposite. "It's done," she said finally. *You don't feel sorry for him. You can never feel sorry for him.* "If I remember correctly, I told the cheerleaders from Kalkaska that you made your penis out of bologna and sewed it on so you wouldn't look awkward in the locker room, and that explained why you smelled all the time a week later."

Jake's lips quirked. "You're forgetting the part where you stole the bologna from the lunchroom and actually put it in my coat pocket. Even I couldn't stand the smell of me."

That earned a genuine smile from January. "That *was* one of my favorites."

"My dad was furious." Jake's smile slipped. "He said I stunk up the entire house and threatened to send my dog to a farm if I didn't get it together. I loved that dog, but he was always threatening to send it away."

January's smile disappeared in an instant. "That doesn't seem fair. You shouldn't always live in fear."

Jake's eyes were clear when they caught with hers. "You always lived in fear as a kid, didn't you?"

"I'm not a kid any longer. It doesn't matter."

Jake hesitated and then held out his hands. "I'm still sorry."

"For what?" January briefly wondered if he was going to apologize for all the pranks he'd played on her during their youth. She was quickly relieved of that notion.

"I'm sorry for the time you had to walk home with Mickey following you," he replied. "I think he was mostly harmless, but that still had to be scary. That wasn't fair. My only excuse is that I was an idiot and didn't think through any of the things I did to you."

She blinked twice, debating, and then nodded. "It's fine. I obviously survived."

"You not only survived, but you're thriving. My father can't stop talking about what a great worker you are."

"I like my job. I like that it's close to home. I like that people respect me now and don't just see me as the girl from the trailer park."

Jake snapped his eyes to her, and January instantly regretted the last part.

"This job is important to me, Jake," she said pointedly. "Very important. I get that you and your father are working stuff out, but I need you to get it together. Your job performance will reflect on me. Your father has made that very clear. I can't let you just float, which I'm assuming is exactly what you want to do."

"You know what they say when you assume something," Jake muttered. He looked tired as he dragged a hand through his hair. Maybe a little defeated too. "I won't go overboard again. I don't even know what happened last night. I ran into Luke at the bar, and the next thing I knew I was drunk and trying to keep myself on task when walking back to the lodge in an icy parking lot."

"You were with Luke?" January pursed her lips.

"He was in the main building bar. I was just looking for a drink."

"Well, I'm not your boss."

Jake managed a quirky smile. "Actually, you literally are my boss."

"That's true." January brightened considerably. "As your boss, I would suggest that drinking until two in the morning on a weeknight is a bad idea. I get that you had a troubling day yesterday though. Maybe going forward, you could save the partying for days when you don't have responsibilities to fulfill."

"Is that what you do?"

The question was like a knife twisting in January's ribs, but she brushed off the quick jab of pain. "People don't want to party with me. I'm not fun. That doesn't matter though. This event is important to the resort. We have to make sure it goes off reasonably well."

"I know how important it is," Jake said. "I don't want to screw this up for anybody, including my father. Things just got out of hand last night."

"Well, try to make sure that doesn't happen again, huh?" January's voice was light. "I need this to go well. My whole future is riding on it. I think yours might be, too, if your father is to be believed."

Jake scowled. "He's a blowhard."

"Maybe with you but not with me. I need this to go well, so you have to get it together. Otherwise, I'm screwed."

"I'll get it together," Jake promised out of nowhere. He looked so earnest January almost believed him.

"We'll see," she said, refusing to soften her stance. "We have a meeting with Jim Maxwell in one hour. He's the main sponsor for the Winter Extreme Games. That means we have to schmooze and delight him."

"I will be on my best behavior," Jake promised.

January studied his face. She almost believed he meant it. "Just try not to be late. He hates it when people are late." She leaned in to sniff Jake and made a face. "You also need to shower. He's not going to be impressed with the smell of stale beer and pot."

Jake's cheeks colored. "I'll get right on that, boss. You don't have to worry about me. I can schmooze with the best of them."

"I guess we'll see."

"No, I promise. I won't let you down at this meeting, January. I've got this. Trust me."

FIVE

J ake hydrated and showered before dressing in a pair of khakis and a polo shirt. He didn't have a lot of clothes with him that would be considered professional and made a mental note to stop at his parents' house to go through his old wardrobe. He might have to hit Traverse City to pick up a few things, but with an important meeting breathing down his neck, there was little he could do.

He gave himself a cursory glance in the mirror, hated what he saw, and then headed out anyway. His head was in a bad place.

It wasn't just his relationship with his father that was bugging him. The story January had told about having to walk home with the town pervert following her bothered him more than he was willing to admit. He hadn't even thought about how she would get home that night. The trailer park was a hike from the grocery store. He'd been laughing about screwing with her when he flirted with Becca and convinced her to leave with him. He hadn't even benefitted from that little maneuver because he didn't even really like Becca. He hadn't wanted to spend time with her. He'd just wanted to mess with January because she was always messing with him.

He didn't feel good about himself now that he had a clear picture of what had happened that night.

The other thing that bothered him was mention of the food. Everybody in school had known that January didn't have a lot of money. She never had a vehicle to drive and was always at the mercy of others in the cold months to get places. The mere thought of her having to worry about how she spent twenty dollars—money that made the difference between her eating that week or not—made him feel sick to his stomach. He didn't even want to unpack what she'd said about the thirty calories. He couldn't imagine being that rigid about the number of calories he ate in a day.

The whole thing left him feeling uneasy.

His mother was in the lobby when he arrived. Enid was talking to the restaurant hostess when he appeared, and she quickly waved off the other woman and headed toward him.

"You need better pants," Enid complained when she saw the khakis. "Don't you have any dress pants?"

"Not with me." Jake slapped at his mother's hands when she tried to smooth the pockets. "I'm going to run to Traverse City later and pick up some clothes." Something occurred to him as soon as he said it. "Although I don't have a credit card right now since Dad stopped paying mine."

Enid gave him a serious look. "I'll handle the pants. Just email me your sizes."

Jake was horrified at the thought. "I can pick out my own pants."

"Your father will melt down if I give you my credit card," Enid argued. "He's been very clear about how he expects this to go. I need to do the shopping."

Jake made a grumbling sound but nodded. He didn't have

time to argue with his mother about shopping, of all things. "Fine. I'll email my sizes. Don't get anything weird though."

"I know how to shop. Who do you think picks out your father's wardrobe?"

The question didn't make Jake feel any better. He refused to dwell on it. "I have a question," he said out of the blue.

Enid arched a perfectly manicured eyebrow.

"Dad pays January well, right? Like, he doesn't expect her to do the job she's doing for peanuts, does he?"

Enid looked taken aback at the question. "I believe she does quite well."

That wasn't the answer Jake was looking for. "But she can afford to live somewhere decent, right?" Why he was so bothered by the prospect of January living in a potential shack was beyond him, but he couldn't get it out of his head. "It just seems like she deserves to be making good money for the amount of work she's doing."

"Your father is quite fond of her. You don't have to worry." Enid, who was still smoothing Jake's shirt, studied his face. "How are you and January getting along now that you're staying under the same roof?"

"Well, she woke me up by throwing a pitcher of water at my head this morning and refused to share her coffee. She also made me feel bad about the time I stole her ride home and she had to walk three miles with eggs and milk and Mickey Jordan sexually harassing her the whole way. Other than that, it's great." Jake shot his mother a sarcastic thumbs-up.

Her eyebrow remained arched. "I'm not sure I understand," she said finally.

"It's nothing." Jake waved off her concern. "I'm just starting to wonder if I was even more of a douche than I realized when I was growing up."

"I don't like that word." Enid was stern. "I happen to think you were perfect. Why do you think I only had one child? When you hit perfection the first time, you don't mess with it."

Jake adored his mother, but the statement grated. "I was never perfect." He glanced around the lobby, which was buzzing with energy. "I have a meeting I have to get to. I'll email you my sizes for the clothes. I don't want to be late though."

"I know about the meeting," Enid supplied. "It's with Jim Maxwell. He's the main sponsor of the Winter Extreme Games, and he's a bit of a ... pill." She looked uncomfortable talking badly about the man, but there was a fierceness to her eyes. "That's why I'm here. I want to make sure that you don't put your foot in your mouth."

Jake wanted to be insulted by the statement, but he knew better. "What's the deal with him again?"

"He's very set in his ways." Enid lowered her voice. "Their family is very religious. Like *very* religious. They don't believe in premarital sex or drugs, and I'm not sure how they feel about drinking." She leaned in and sniffed her son. "You smell okay. No mimosas this morning, right?"

Jake managed a hoarse chuckle. "Mimosas are your thing, Mom. I haven't been drinking. I'm not surprised about the religion thing either. I seem to remember that from when we were younger. Their kids went to school down in the Detroit area, right?"

Enid nodded. "Yes. They went to a very prestigious private school."

"But they were up here for summers. I remember the girls being rigid—like they were no fun at all—and the boys were kind of wild."

"I don't think any of them are wild," Enid countered. "I've met some of those kids, and they're following in their father's footsteps. They're all married, and they're not fun. You need to be careful. They like an orderly individual."

"Which is probably why Dad has January handling them," Jake mused.

"Yes. Just follow her lead. She's dealt with Jim before."

"Trust me. I have no interest in stealing her thunder. I'm going to let her do her thing and be quiet for a change."

"That's smart." Enid seemed hesitant to let him go, and it made Jake suspicious.

"What aren't you telling me?" he demanded.

"Your father is sitting in on the meeting this morning, which is something he doesn't normally do," Enid volunteered. "I think he might be a little worried about your presence. I just wanted to prepare you."

Jake's heart sank. If things weren't bad enough now, his father was going to be there, on top of everything else. "I'll be good," he said automatically. He knew that was what his mother wanted to hear. "You don't have to worry."

"That would be a nice change of pace, huh?"

JAKE KNEW HOW TO SCHMOOZE PEOPLE. He hadn't been exaggerating when he told January that on the patio. That was why he walked into the meeting room with a bright smile on his face. Thankfully, only a handful of people were present, and all of them seemed focused on a piece of paper that had been spread out over a conference room table.

"Jake." Jacob eyed his son with an impenetrable stare. "Thank you for joining us."

Jake recognized the tone. His father was already agitated. He flicked his eyes to the clock on the wall, found he was three minutes early, and flashed a smile for his father's benefit. "Of course. I wouldn't miss this meeting for the world."

Jacob didn't roll his eyes or sneer, but it was impossible for Jake to miss the momentary flash of annoyance in his father's eyes. "Yes, well..." He cleared his throat. "Jim, this is my son."

"Ah, Jacob Jeffries Jr." Jim Maxwell tore his gaze from what looked like a map and beamed at Jake. "I've heard a lot about you. It's great that you're joining the Winter Extreme Games team for the next few weeks. I hear you've been wheeling and dealing in other states. I'm so glad you could make it back." He extended his hand in greeting.

Jake shook it without hesitation. If he'd picked up one thing from his father, it was a firm handshake. "I'm thrilled to be part of the games," he assured the sales entrepreneur. "I wouldn't miss these games for anything. They're going to be a great boon for the area."

"They are," Jim readily agreed. "That's why I agreed to sponsor them."

"Jim will be one of the primary faces of the games," Jacob offered, drawing his son's gaze to him. "January will be one of the other faces." There seemed to be a warning there, and yet Jake couldn't quite suss out what it was.

"Well, if anybody has a face made for attention, it's January," Jake replied easily. He didn't mention that he couldn't quite seem to keep his attention off of her. She'd filled out since he'd last seen her—in all the right places—and he couldn't decide where he wanted his gaze to rest. His eyes wanted to dance all over her.

January narrowed her eyes as she regarded Jake with overt suspicion. Given they had an audience, however, there was nothing Jake could do to set her mind at ease. That would have to wait until later.

"What are we looking at?" Jake asked as he moved closer to the map. It wasn't hard to ascertain what the map represented when he grew closer. "This is the resort?"

"All three resorts," Jacob replied. "We'll have so many guests that the hotels at all three of the resorts—not just the main one here—will be full to the brim. We needed a map that indicated where the shuttles would be located. We don't want the guests getting lost if this isn't their primary resort."

"That makes sense." Jake smiled at the map. "It looks pretty good. Did you have an illustrator do it?"

"Actually, January did it," Jim replied. "She has a program, and she did it on her computer." He said it in such a way that Jake couldn't help picturing the older man giving January a condescending pat on the head. It was almost as if he thought she was a shiny new toy and seemed delighted that she'd surpassed expectations.

"Nice job." Jake smiled at January, but she didn't return the expression. "I didn't realize you did all of this."

"It's amazing what you can get done when you don't sleep on the floor," January replied pointedly.

"Sleep on the floor?" Jim let loose a wild laugh. "Who was sleeping on the floor? Am I missing something?"

One look at January told Jake that she realized too late that she said out loud what she should've only thought. Because he still felt bad about the night she had to walk home—likely terrified the whole time—Jake was determined to fix the conversation.

"It's just a private joke," he volunteered quickly. "January almost tripped over me this morning when she was going out to the patio to drink her coffee, and we've been needling each other ever since. We like to verbally spar to get the juices going in the morning." He'd meant it as an offhand comment, but the way his father was waving his hands in a "Stop right now" manner behind Jim's back had him pausing.

"You're staying together?" Jim's tone changed slightly as he glanced between Jake and January. "I didn't realize you were married. I must've missed the announcement."

If Jake had been drinking coffee at that moment, he would've spit it all over the other man's face. Instead, his eyebrows nearly made a run for the Canadian border off his forehead, and he opened his mouth to dissuade the man of that notion right away. Unfortunately for him or maybe fortunately—it was too soon to say—his father inserted himself in the conversation.

"They were married a couple months ago," Jacob lied smoothly. "Neither of them wanted a big wedding—they're both shy that way—but my wife has been working on them, and we expect to at least have a big party to celebrate their nuptials this summer."

Jake's mouth fell open. Next to him, January's body went rigid. Jake had never known his father to lie that way, especially when doing business, but there had been no hesitation before Jacob threw it out there. The only way to correct the situation was to call Jacob a liar in front of a huge sponsor. Jake wasn't an expert on business, but he knew that would go over poorly.

"Is that a fact?" Jim looked absolutely delighted. "You two are married?" His eyes immediately went to January's naked ring finger, his lips curving down.

"January's ring had to be sent in to be resized," Jacob explained, doubling down on the lie. "She'd been wearing it even though it was too big because she couldn't bear being separated from it, but since fingers shrink in the cold, I put my foot down. It's too expensive to lose, even if it is insured."

"Oh, that's very wise." Jim bobbed his head sagely. "It's too bad. I love a beautiful wedding ring. There's nothing better than seeing the proof of true love." His eyes sparkled when they landed on Jake.

Because he was suddenly uncomfortable—and also didn't want to explain a missing second ring—Jake shoved his hands in his pockets to keep them away from Jim's prying eyes. "Yes, well, hopefully the ring will be done soon. There are only a few jewelers in the area who can handle precision work, and we wanted the best one for January's ring."

"Yes, it shouldn't be long," Jacob readily agreed. "Back to the map though." He drew Jim to the map, leaving his son and January to stand in their wake, both of them blinking back horrified disbelief.

"This is unbelievable," Jake muttered under his breath, his eyes moving to January's shocked pallor. "Did you know he was going to do this?"

She shook her head, seemingly unable to form words.

"I can't believe he just threw us under the bus like that." Jake felt himself gearing up for a rant. "I just ... cannot believe it."

January's expression suggested she was feeling the same thing. Unlike Jake, however, she kept her mouth shut.

"We can't just let this guy think we're married," Jake insisted, fighting to keep his voice low. "That will come back to bite us. We need to explain to him that it was a misunderstanding or something before this gets out of hand." All he could picture was having to pretend January was his wife for the better part of a month. The notion terrified him.

The suggestion was enough to snap January out of her mute reverie. "Don't say a word," she hissed. "Not one single word. If you out your father as a liar, Jim will pull out as a sponsor."

Jake was taken aback. "Why would he do that?"

"Because that's who he is." January pinned him with a serious look. "If you don't want to ruin the entire games, keep your mouth shut for a change. Do you think you can manage that?"

Jake didn't like her tone or what she was insinuating. He didn't want to make the wrong step though. He'd been back a grand total of twenty-four hours. If he screwed up, there would be no making it better. That was the one thing he realized above all else.

"Fine, but we're fixing this as soon as the meeting is over," he said. "We can't let people think we're married. Nobody who knows us will ever believe that."

January looked as if she was on the same page, and then she darted her eyes to Jim and her resolve solidified. "Just sit there and look pretty," she whispered. "Don't do anything we can't take back. We're in this now. Let's just hear what your father has to say before melting down."

That was easier said than done, Jake internally mused. He'd never been so agitated with his father in his entire life. Unfortunately, he didn't know how they could fix this. It seemed like a lost cause.

If there was one thing Jake hated, it was a lost cause. That was why he hated himself on a regular basis.

Six

January had no idea what to do. She followed Jake and Jacob to the latter's office, as if she was a robot going through the motions, but she couldn't fathom how this had happened.

She was married to Jake? Sure, it was a fake marriage, but even pretending they were in a relationship was too much for her. And for Jacob to be the one to force her into this position? That was not the man she knew. He was always so professional. How could he think this was a good idea?

Jake walked in front of her, and the square of his shoulders, along with his gait, told January that he was spoiling for a fight. She decided to let him do the talking when they slid into Jacob's office. He would be able to talk his father out of this decision. She was certain of it.

"What were you thinking?" Jake exploded as soon as the door was shut. His face was a mottled shade of red.

"I was thinking that Jim Maxwell was going to pull out as a sponsor if he decided you two were living in sin," Jacob replied evenly as he sat at his desk. He looked tired, January mused. She couldn't remember the last time she'd seen him looking so tired.

"Why should he care?" Jake demanded. "I mean, seriously, why should he give one fig what we're doing?"

"I happen to agree with you on this one," Jacob replied evenly. "I don't think it's any of his business. That doesn't change the fact that *he* thinks it's his business. The entire family is religious."

"So what?" Jake was not backing down.

As for January, she was still absorbing her shock over Jacob's actions, so for lack of anything better to do, she lowered herself into one of the wingback chairs and stared at nothing in particular. She kept her ears open, however, in case Jake could somehow manage to extricate them from this situation.

"We need the sponsorship, Jake!" Jacob's eyes flashed with warning as he regarded his only son. "The Winter Extreme Games are going to bring a lot of money to the area. I mean *a lot* of money. They're going to give some much-needed exposure to the resort, and Bellaire as a town is going to thrive. Heck, some of the other towns are going to see an influx of money too. This is good for everybody."

"That still doesn't explain why I have to pretend to be married to January," Jake gritted out.

For the first time since Jacob had dropped the bomb on them, January managed a genuine reaction. She glared at Jake's profile. He made it sound like she was the problem in this scenario.

"Jim Maxwell is old school," Jacob fired back. "He has a boatload of kids. Like, I don't even know how many. It's at least seven or eight. He's a stickler regarding certain morality judgements. I had to actually sit for a question-and-answer session regarding my marriage when he first showed interest in being a sponsor."

January jerked up her head. "I didn't know that."

Jacob shot her an apologetic look. "It wasn't a big deal. Listen, I'm sorry you have to be part of this, but you know how he is. If he thinks you two are living together but aren't married, then he's going to kick up a fuss."

"I like how you're sorry that she has to be part of this but not me," Jake complained.

If looks could kill, Jake would be dead. The glare Jacob settled on him promised mayhem. "You've been through way worse situations and come out fine," Jacob shot back. "Your reputation won't be the one taking a hit if this goes badly. January is the woman, which means people will judge her while giving you a pass."

Jake looked incredulous. "Do you know how many questions I'm going to have to answer if people from high school think I'm married to January?"

January's stomach constricted, but she managed to keep her face placid. Just barely.

"Oh, please." Jacob waved off the argument. "You should be so lucky to marry January. She would have your life whipped into shape in four weeks flat. You're just upset because this means you can't do what you normally do and bed-hop through the cleaning staff."

Jake's mouth fell open. "Is that what you really think of me?"

"Last time you were home, we had to find a new maid, gardener, and three new employees up here at the resort because you slept with them all before, um, what's that term?" he asked January. "What did they say he did again?"

"He ghosted them," January replied calmly. "It means he had sex with them and then refused to call or interact with them after the fact."

"Right." Jacob's eyes narrowed when Jake opened his

mouth to argue. "Don't bother denying it. Your mother may make excuses for you, but I won't. I'm sick of you being you."

Jacob worked his jaw but didn't lose his cool.

"It's a few weeks," Jacob continued in a conciliatory tone. "You don't have to actually be married. You're sharing the same roof. Just wear rings in public, and don't be obnoxious to each other. How hard is that?"

"She told the temporary guidance counselor at high school that I dreamed I was having sex with my mother, wanted to wear a diaper in public, and sucked my thumb for sexual gratification," Jake growled.

"That was only after you told the counselor I wished my ovaries were testicles and was trying to figure out a way to fondle them," January shot back.

Jacob let out a growly sigh as he rubbed his forehead. "You two have history. I get that. Most of that history is bad. Jim Maxwell is our main sponsor, however. He might be a kook— and from everything I've heard, that's a mild word to be using for him—but he's who we're stuck with. We don't have time to get another sponsor. This is what's happening."

January had been trying to work out a way for them to escape their predicament since sitting down. She hadn't come up with anything. The more she thought about it, the more she realized Jacob was likely right.

That didn't mean she was going to go quietly.

"I'm not kissing him," she warned in a low voice. "It's not going to happen."

"Oh, like I would want to kiss you," Jake shot back. "I would rather ghost the entire resort than kiss you."

Jacob wagged a warning finger at his son. "If you're seen with one of the women up here, you're going to be fired, and there's not a thing your mother will be able to do to protect you," he rasped. "You'll be cut off. There will be no lodge to sleep in. No travel money. No nothing. Good luck finding a job without a single reference."

Mutiny sparked in Jake's eyes, but he held it together through tremendous force of will. "What do you expect us to do?" he gritted out.

"Very little," Jacob replied. "Don't have sex with any of the other workers. Don't flirt with them. Don't have screaming matches in public. Just go to events together when necessary, wear wedding rings, and keep your mouths shut."

It didn't sound undoable, January mused. Jake wouldn't make things easy though. She needed to give him more of a road map, she realized. Otherwise, Jake would make a mistake. That was who he was.

"There will be sponsorship dinners and evening mixers for the athletes and bigwigs," she volunteered dully. "We're going to have to stand together during those events and make nice. The good news is that Mr. Maxwell is so religious, he actually believes that nothing good happens after eight o'clock, so the whole family goes to bed early. With the events finishing up around five o'clock in the afternoon, at most we're going to have to keep up with the charade a few hours a week."

Jake blinked several times, as if absorbing the news. January was convinced he was going to pull out and ruin everything. Instead, he ultimately nodded. There was no warmth to his gaze when it landed on his father. "I'll do it, but I don't want any crap from you about it. You might think I'm a screwup—and in your eyes I can see why you think that—but I don't want any verbal abuse from you. That has to be part of the deal."

"Believe it or not, Jake, expressing disappointment with your life choices is not verbal abuse," Jacob shot back. "That's neither here nor there. I don't want to talk to you any more than I absolutely have to. I'm still annoyed with you.

"This is your shot to prove you're more than just an empty

head with a pretty face," he continued. "Pull this off, and we'll all be sitting pretty."

Jake looked as if he wanted to push back, but he simply raised his chin. "Whatever. Where are you going to get these rings you want us to wear?"

"I'll handle that," Jacob replied. "There's a jewelry store over in the shopping village. I'm positive we can get the rings there. I'll put money down as a deposit, and you'll return the rings when the games are over in several weeks."

"Right." Jake's shoulders sank with exhaustion, and he pressed the heel of his hand to his forehead. "You do realize how messed up this is, right? The odds of us pulling this off are slim."

"You'll manage." Jacob's smile was bright. "Or, rather, January will manage. She always comes through. Just follow her lead, and you'll be fine."

January didn't miss the momentary look of angst that crossed Jake's features at the words, but she didn't comment. Instead, she followed him out of the office when he gestured for her to leave with him.

"If we're going to do this, we have to get the basics out of the way," he said grimly. "I think that means we need to get to know one another."

January nodded. It made sense. "Just superficial stuff, right?"

Jake rolled his eyes. "Trust me, January. I don't want to know your deep, dark secrets."

"That's good because I don't want to know yours either."

Jake's exhale reminded January of a deflating pool inflatable. "Let's get something to drink and meet by the main fireplace. We need to get to know each other if we're going to pull this off."

"Sure." January was more interested in her shirt than his probing gaze. "Ten minutes?"

"That sounds like a plan."

JAKE GOT A BOURBON AND COKE to drink before throwing himself on the couch in front of the fireplace. He was sullen, annoyed, and unbelievably disappointed in his father. Since when did Jacob Jeffries care what other people thought?

He frowned when January joined him. She, of course, had a mug of hot chocolate.

"If now isn't the time to drink, when is?" he demanded, glaring at the offending hot chocolate.

"It's early in the day," she replied dully. "I have hours of work to get through. If I start drinking now, I'll be ready for bed at three o'clock."

"So?"

She pinned him with a frustrated glare. "So some of us need to work to pay our bills."

"Oh, whatever." Jake sipped his whiskey, although he couldn't completely ignore the pang of guilt coursing through him. This felt like his fault, although he had no idea why. "Let's just get this over with. What's your favorite color?"

January's eyebrows hopped. "That's the first question you want to ask?"

"We need to get through the basics," he reminded her. "What's your favorite color?"

"Purple, and sometimes blue. What's yours?"

"Black."

"Black is not actually a color."

"Don't make this more difficult than is necessary. What's your favorite season?"

"Fall," she replied without hesitation. "I absolutely love when the leaves change. There's something magical about it. I like to head over to Dead Man's Hill and hike in the afternoons when October rolls around."

Jake couldn't hide his surprise. "Fall is my favorite too. I used to hike out there all the time."

"Well, look, we actually have something in common." Her smile was grim.

"What's your favorite movie?"

"*Pride & Prejudice*." Her answer was fast, telling Jake that was the truth. "I like the miniseries with Colin Firth, but I absolutely love the Kiera Knightley movie."

"I don't even know what that is," Jake muttered. "My favorite movie is *Avengers: Endgame*."

"Of course it is." January scowled into her hot chocolate. "God forbid you actually like something with substance."

"That movie has substance. Iron Man dies and everything."

"If you say so." January shook her head. "How did we hook up?"

Jake managed a sly smile. "I believe it started right on this couch."

January's exaggerated expression had Jake hiding a laugh. She was like a cartoon character sometimes, although that was one of his favorite things about her. Not that he had favorite things about her. All his childhood memories involving her were horrible.

"I mean what story are we going to tell Mr. Maxwell?" January snapped, clearly ascertaining where his head went. "Also, you can't say that we had sex before we got married in front of him. That's a no-no."

"I don't get why he's such a prude," Jake lamented. "Who doesn't try out the merchandise before slapping a ring on it and pledging forever?"

"I don't actually disagree," January said. "He's very prim and proper though. He said he could never sponsor summer games because the outfits were too revealing. You should've heard him go off about the women's beach volleyball outfits at our initial pitch meeting."

"You were there?" Jake's eyebrows hiked. "I didn't realize that."

"I was there, although I don't believe I spoke. Your father did all the talking. He's good at schmoozing people."

"My father is great at schmoozing people," Jake readily agreed. "It's when it comes to being authentic that he has problems."

The way January's lips twitched told Jake that she had questions. She didn't ask them, however. "Let's just say we knew each other in high school, didn't spend a lot of time together, then met again here at the resort as adults, and that's how it happened. We'll keep it vague."

Jake nodded. "That's probably best. We still need to know a few details about each other. Like are you allergic to anything? I don't want to be at one of these dinners we're going to have to attend and get caught shoving a crab leg in front of you if it will make you die or something."

That earned a genuine laugh from January, and Jake found himself grinning in return. "The only thing I'm allergic to is codeine. I found out when I had dental surgery about two years ago. I don't think that's going to come up."

"Probably not." Jake filed the information away. "I'm allergic to laundry detergent. It makes me break out in hives. It's not a big deal, though, so we don't have to mention it."

"All laundry detergent?" January asked.

"No, just one specific brand. My mother made sure that we didn't use that brand here, so I doubt it will come up."

"Okay." January tightened her grip on her mug. "What's your favorite sport? That will probably come up. You're a skier, right?"

"Yeah. You ski, too, correct?"

"Yeah, but not as much as I would like. Thankfully, your father arranged it so I can rent skis for free here. I'm getting better, but I'm never going to look coordinated out there."

"We can go out," Jake offered. "I can help you." He didn't even realize he was going to say it until it was already out of his mouth. "I mean, if you want."

"Maybe." January was noncommittal. "What do we do when they ask about kids?"

"You'll have to be more specific."

"The Maxwells have a bunch of kids and grandkids. It's going to come up."

"Oh." Realization dawned on Jake, and he looked momentarily thoughtful. "I want kids one day."

"You do?" January's surprise had Jake frowning.

"Don't you?"

"I don't know." January held out her hands. "My mother always said her life would've been easier if she didn't have to take care of me."

The statement, delivered with simple honesty, was like a punch in the heart for Jake. "She told you that?"

"She was just being honest."

Jake couldn't remember ever meeting January's mother. Well, other than a few instances in the principal's office when they were both in trouble. The woman had acted agitated every time, going on and on about missing work. She'd never been a presence at the school otherwise.

"Where is your mother now?" he asked.

"She's still around." January averted her gaze. "We don't need to bring her up in front of the Maxwells. It's been almost two years since I saw her, and she won't be coming here."

Jake's mouth fell open. "You haven't seen your mother in two years?"

January was clearly uncomfortable, given the way she shifted. "It's not a big deal. Not all families are built to last."

Jake had questions—so many questions—but her discomfort was enough to hold them at bay. "We'll just say your mother is doing her own thing, if people ask. As for kids, I'd like one or two. Not now or anything, but eventually. We can say we're still trying to figure that out."

"I don't think Jim Maxwell is the sort of guy who planned out his kids," January admitted. "He's more of a 'They're gifts from God' type guy."

"Well, we don't have to live our lives to make him happy," Jake reminded her. "He can mind his own business."

"Yeah." January sipped her cocoa again. "What about food? What's your favorite food?"

"I happen to love a good taco."

January laughed. "Me too. They have Mexican night weekly in the main dining room. You'll love it."

"Oh, see, that's something to look forward to."

"Definitely. I think we're going to need stuff to look forward to if we're going to get through this."

Jake merely shrugged. "It won't be so bad. I'm still furious at my father—don't get me wrong—but the other stuff won't be so bad. We'll keep it on the down-low, and nobody will find out."

The laugh January let loose was harsh. "Oh, you act as if we're going to have a choice in the matter. The gossip is going to spread. That's the one thing this resort does perfectly every single time."

"It will be fine. Have a little faith, huh?"

"If you say so."

"I do say so. Don't get worked up about something that's not going to happen. That's always been your problem."

"Yeah, we'll see if you're still singing the same song in a few days."

"It's going to be fine. Trust me."

SEVEN

For three days, January and Jake asked each other questions over coffee in the morning and then largely ignored one another for the rest of the day. Living under the same roof wasn't easy, and Jake found he had to take regular breaks just so he could breathe.

He would never say it to her face—well, at least not while sober—but January sucked up all the oxygen in the room. She was intense, to the point of no return, and it made him itchy.

Sure, he knew that his father wanted him to learn from January, and that was why he'd come up with this little arrangement. Jake wasn't entirely certain that Jacob hadn't purposely put January in his lodge as a way to teach him how to get along with others. He was frustrated though.

As for January, Jake wasn't a mind reader. It wasn't difficult to pick up on her moods, however. She was as frustrated with him as he was with her.

"We have to talk," she drawled as she appeared in the kitchen with what looked like a pair of his boxer shorts in her hand.

Jake, his hair still mussed from sleep, stood in front of the counter mainlining coffee as he looked up. He was shirtless, something January didn't appear to notice, which was irritating, and wore nothing other than a pair of gym shorts.

"If you want to talk about my boxer shorts, you should probably shave your legs," Jake replied without thinking. It wasn't that he wanted to flirt with her—that would never happen—but knocking her off that perfect pedestal wasn't out of the question. Why his father preferred her when she was so rigid was beyond him. Jake knew he had charm oozing from every orifice. January had none of that. She was just efficient. That was nowhere near as valuable as what he had to offer.

"What?" January's face twisted in confusion.

"Nothing," Jake replied as he snagged the boxer shorts. "Why do you have these?"

"You left them on the porch by the hot tub."

"Oh, right." Jake grinned at the memory. He'd had a few beers in the hot tub the previous evening and hadn't wanted to get his boxer shorts wet in the process. Since January was out with her friends—who was she even friends with?—he'd opted for a naked dip. "Thanks. I guess. I'm out of underwear. This saves me from having to do laundry until tomorrow."

January looked horrified.

"Or I could just run over to one of the stores in the shopping village," Jake mused. "I saw they have some flannel boxers over there. That will save me a few more days."

January narrowed her eyes until they were nothing more than judgmental slits. "I don't really care about your hygiene habits." She seemed to think better of the statement almost immediately. "Just FYI, though, there are things called snow fleas, and they'll totally crawl into your underwear if you leave them out. That's your decision though. I didn't come here to talk about your underwear in anything other than housekeeping terms."

Jake blinked and sipped his coffee, waiting.

"I would appreciate it if you didn't leave your underwear around the lodge willy-nilly," she complained. "We're sharing this space. I don't leave my underwear around for you to trip over."

"Uh-huh." Jake sipped his coffee again.

"I'm just asking that we both pick up our stuff. There's no reason for one of us to suffer because the other is a pig."

"I think you're calling me a pig in that scenario."

"If you expect me to deny that, I have no interest." She threw the boxers at Jake's chest, and he had to move quickly to catch them. "You need to get cleaned up."

Jake made a grunting noise as he looked at the clock on the wall. "It's not seven o'clock yet," he complained. "The sun isn't even out. Let me guess. You have one of those evil to-do lists you want me to get through. Well, I don't technically start until nine. You can wait to give me your list until then."

January's expression didn't change. "My to-do lists are helpful."

"If you say so."

"They are." January was firm. "We would never get everything done that needs to be done without my lists."

"Of course not," Jake drawled in sarcastic fashion. "Nothing in history has ever been accomplished without a to-do list."

January's eyebrows wiggled like caterpillars, and Jake knew she was about to unload on him. Good. He wanted her to start yelling. This sterile approach she was embracing at present drove him crazy.

"As I said, I'm here for a reason." She sounded prim and proper, and Jake was back to being irritated. "Your father has set up a breakfast date for us."

Those were the last words Jake was expecting to come out of her mouth. "What now?"

January scowled, finally making an expression that he

could relate to. "Apparently, Jim Maxwell is involving his children in his sponsorship. That means he's sending his daughter Abby and her husband, Cooper, over to have breakfast with us in the resort. We're expected up there in an hour."

That was so not the answer Jake was expecting. "Well ... crap."

"That was my reaction." January held her hands palms out. "They think they're having breakfast with a happily married couple. For that to be true, you can't be leaving your boxer shorts out by the hot tub. It's not allowed."

A slow smile spread across Jake's face as he sipped his coffee again. "Says who?"

"Says anybody with common sense."

"Uh-huh." Jake scratched at his morning stubble. "I think you're making that up."

"And I think I don't care." January turned on her heel. "We leave to walk up there in fifty-two minutes. Be ready. And don't forget your wedding ring."

Jake could hear the growl in her voice on the last two words. "How come fifty-two minutes?" he called to her back. "That's an awfully specific time frame."

"Because it takes eight minutes to walk across the parking lot if it's icy. I haven't been out since last night, but I'm betting it's icy after last night's freezing rain."

Jake worked his jaw. "Are snow fleas a real thing?" he asked before she was out of earshot.

She glanced over her shoulder, and the amusement glinting in her eyes made him swallow hard. "What do you think?"

"I think you're making it up."

"Then I guess that's your answer."

. . .

AN HOUR LATER, DRESSED IN COMFORTABLE
khakis and a polo shirt, Jake and January sat at the same table
in the resort restaurant and proceeded to elbow one another as
they tried to get comfortable.

"You're too close," January complained in a low voice. "I
need elbow room to eat."

"It's a round four top," Jake shot back. "We have to sit
next to each other. We're supposed to be married." He
squirmed on his chair when he felt a flutter below the waist.
He didn't believe in snow fleas. He knew she was just trying to
drive him nuts. That was why he'd googled snow fleas to see if
they were really a thing. Turns out they were, and now all he
could think about was fleas crawling through his boxer shorts.
"I need to go shopping for underwear after breakfast," he
muttered.

The triumphant look in January's eyes told Jake she knew
she'd won. It frustrated him to no end. Before they could start
arguing again, however, a couple showed up at the edge of
their table, and one look told Jake exactly who he was dealing
with.

"Abby and Cooper?" he asked automatically, straightening
in his seat. He caught January's left arm, which had been
flailing into his territory, without missing a beat.

Next to him, January went rigid. "Hello," she said automatically, a beatific smile appearing on her face. "It's so nice to
meet you."

Jake had to marvel at her transformation. Instantly, she
was the picture of perfection. In that moment, he could
understand why his father valued her so much. She could
handle any situation, it seemed, and even though she was irritated with him, by all outward appearances, she'd never been
happier.

That didn't mean he had to like her, despite the fact that
he was suddenly wowed by her ability to turn on a dime.

"Jake and January, right?" Abby's eyes sparkled like the diamond on her ring finger as she beamed at January. "My father has done nothing but gush about you," she said as she shook January's hand in greeting. "He thinks you're just the bee's knees."

Jake had to press his lips together to keep from laughing. Who said things like that? January seemed to take the comment in stride, however, and for the second time in as many minutes, Jake was impressed with her professional demeanor.

"I'm very fond of him too." January turned to Cooper and shook his hand. "Please sit. We were just discussing if we wanted to have the buffet or not."

Jake stood and shook Cooper's hand before giving a deferential nod to Abby. His manners were ingrained in him, thanks to the countless business meetings his father made him sit through when he was a child. "It's nice to meet you," he said.

"You too." Cooper seemed amiable enough. He pulled out Abby's chair for her and waited until she was settled to claim his own chair. Jake made a note of it in case that was how all the Maxwell family men acted.

"How long have you been married?" January asked smoothly. "I think your father told me it's been two years, correct?"

Abby beamed at her. "You have a good memory."

"Oh, well, it was one of those details that stuck." January waved off the comment quickly.

"Yeah, I don't think so." Abby let loose a nervous laugh. "My father likes to heap numbers on people to see if they'll remember. It's something of a test. I'm betting he told you how long all of us have been married in an attempt to confuse you. He'll be impressed when I tell him you remembered."

For some reason, the statement struck Jake as odd. Was

Jim Maxwell testing them? That didn't bode well for when he was spending more time at the resort during the games.

"Your father seems like a great man," January enthused. "I think it's wonderful that he's so proud of his family."

"Oh, family is everything to him," Abby agreed. "He wants us all close. My sister Becky wanted to move south to go to college when she was eighteen, but Dad lost his mind and refused to pay for it. She's at NMC now, though, and doing great."

Jake managed to keep from frowning, but it was a test of wills. Jim Maxwell didn't sound like a great father as much as a control freak. Since Jake had experience with parental control freaks, he recognized the signs.

"That's good," January replied without a beat. "I loved my college years. I'm sure she doesn't care where she ended up, as long as she learns."

Abby snorted so loudly she drew several sets of eyes from neighboring tables. "Oh, sorry." She looked legitimately contrite when she pressed her hand to her chest. "I didn't mean to react that way."

For the first time since sitting down, January's work persona slipped, and she darted a look toward Jake. She looked genuinely confused.

Because he didn't know how to convey that he felt the same way, Jake rested his hand on hers and gave it a reassuring little squeeze. That seemed to be enough to prompt a topic change from Abby.

"So, you guys are married, right?" she asked on an eye twinkle, her gaze falling on their stacked hands. "How did you meet?"

This was something they were prepared for. Or, well, at least Jake thought they were. "School," he replied, not missing a beat. "January and I grew up together."

"Aw." Abby made heart eyes as she looked at January. "Were you guys childhood sweethearts?"

It was Jake's turn to snort. He managed to catch himself, but it was already too late. Thankfully, January had snorted in tandem with him, so he didn't look like a complete and utter fool. Jake slid in smoothly to fix the situation when Abby frowned.

"We were actually enemies in school," he said, forcing out a warm chuckle. "Yes, the word 'enemies' has a negative connotation, but we actually hated each other in our younger years."

"Really?" The way Abby shifted on her chair told Jake he was going to have to do some damage control. "That is ... unfortunate."

"I think it was destiny," Jake replied. He recognized what sort of audience he was dealing with and knew exactly how to fix the problem. "I think we liked each other but we were too immature to realize it. I mean, we did meet at the same time I was telling my parents girls were icky and I just wanted to play *G.I. Joe* my whole life."

That earned an appreciative laugh from Cooper. "Oh, those were the days, right?" He held out his fist for Jake to bump.

Jake did it, but he was internally sneering the entire time. "Yes. I was a boy's boy, and I totally believed girls were the worst thing that had ever happened to the world. January was a girl's girl, and she hated me too. We fought all through school."

"But then how did you fall in love?" Abby asked.

Jake lifted one shoulder in a shrug. "It happened when we were in college. Well, at least for me. She went to a school down state, and I attended locally. She was up here for Christmas break our freshman year, and we sat in front of that fireplace right over there." He pointed toward the couch they'd sat on when asking each other questions days before.

"Oh, really?" Abby's expression brightened considerably. "I think I like where this conversation is going."

Jake winked at her, all that charm he kept in reserve making an appearance at the exact right moment. "We hadn't seen each other in, what, six months or so, January?" he asked, purposely including her in the conversation.

"That sounds about right," January confirmed. She looked uncomfortable with where the conversation was going, but Jake ignored her.

"We talked in front of the fire for a long time," Jake explained. "I don't even know how long. It felt like minutes though. I'm pretty sure it was hours, but it flew by. Then we went and hung out with some high school friends. I couldn't stop thinking about her all night. It was driving me insane."

"And then you asked her out the next morning, right?" Abby asked as she rubbed her hands together.

"No." Jake's expression dimmed momentarily. "And then the next morning she went back to college, and I stayed here. It wasn't until she got a job for my father that we crossed paths again." He was purposely keeping it vague, just like they'd agreed. They didn't want to get tripped up on the details. "I thought about her all the time after we talked in front of the fireplace though. I think that was the start of our true relationship, although I wouldn't have admitted it at the time. I was still mad from when she'd pulled my hair in second grade."

Abby giggled in delighted fashion.

When Jake glanced at January, he found her watching him with unreadable eyes. What did she think of the story? None of it was an outright lie. Sure, they weren't married, but they had connected in front of that fire. And their current relationship had started after she'd gotten a job with his father. Those were details they could both remember.

"He used to tie his coat around his neck in elementary school," January volunteered out of nowhere. "Even in the dead of winter. He pretended to be Superman. It drove me crazy because I was convinced he was going to get frostbite."

Abby's giggle doubled in intensity. "That's amazing. You guys have four Js for names, right? January Jackson and Jake Jeffries. That means you're going to have to name any kids you have with Js."

Jake involuntarily cringed at the thought. "Or we could break *that* cycle," he replied automatically.

"We haven't really talked about kids yet," January hedged.

"You want them though, right?" Abby persisted.

One look at her face told Jake all he needed to know about her. She couldn't fathom a world where adults didn't want to procreate. "Of course we do," he replied automatically. "We're just not ready yet. We're still enjoying the newness of being married."

"Oh." Realization dawned on Abby's face, and she nodded sagely. "Don't worry about that. Eventually, you'll get used to the S-E-X." She leaned forward to engage in a conspiratorial whisper. "Just remember, it's okay because you'll get a baby out of it eventually."

January blinked several times and then nodded as Jake gripped her hand in warning. "Thanks for the tip," she said. "I'm glad it will be worth it. Eventually."

EIGHT

"Looks like a great course." Jake, bundled up and on his skis, rested at the top of the steepest incline at the resort and looked down at the mogul flags. "I can't wait to run it."

"We've been waiting for you," Eric Simpson said. He was bundled up like his friend and gripping his ski poles. "Once we heard you were back, we knew we had to do it as a group. Isn't that right, Silas?"

Silas Hawthorne, another Bellaire High School graduate, nodded. His hair was longer than that of his friends—it touched his shoulders—and he'd garnered sidelong looks from at least three women since they'd taken up position on top of the hill.

"What is it with you and the chicks?" Jake asked when a trio of giggling teenagers slid past the group. Their attention was purely on Silas.

"He's handling skiing classes now," Eric explained. "He moved on to the advanced courses—he used to do the introductory classes—and now the older kids are noticing him. The teenage girls have started a rumor that he's hot, even though I don't see it." Eric winked at his friend. "I think it might be the hair. It fools people into believing he's hot."

"Oh, stuff it," Silas muttered. His cheeks had gone red, and it wasn't purely because of the cold. "He's exaggerating."

Jake wasn't so sure. When another group of young women got off the lift to their left, their eyes bounced between faces before landing on Silas. "Yeah, I'm pretty sure I've never felt more invisible in my entire life."

"It's humbling," Eric agreed. His eyes were keen as he looked over Jake. "Although ... I hear you have your own cheering section these days. A party of one, if I'm not mistaken."

Jake froze at the words and then did his best to brush them off. "We should run the course," he suggested.

Eric pretended he hadn't spoken. "January Jackson? I don't even understand how that happened."

"It's not a big deal," Jake replied. "It's also not what you're thinking."

"That's good, because there's a rumor you two are married."

Jake was grateful he'd taken off his ring. Even though it was fake, it felt heavy when he was wearing it. Because he couldn't be certain who he would run into while wandering the resort, he'd put it in a small drawstring bag and zipped it inside his snow pants. He wanted it to remain there for the foreseeable future.

Apparently, having the ring out of sight did not mean that he could push January out of mind, however.

"You know what they say about rumors," Jake replied dryly. He was curious despite himself. "What are people saying?"

"They're saying that you're living together," Silas replied. "We told them that was ridiculous."

"And yet we saw you guys crossing the parking lot at the same time two nights ago," Eric added. "You looked to be heading to the same place."

"Well, that part is true, although it's also not what you guys are thinking," Jake supplied. "My father is teaching me a lesson."

"By forcing you to marry January?"

"By giving her my usual lodge," Jake replied. "She needs to stay close because she's coordinating all the logistics for the games, and they need her on site in case there's a problem. All the other lodges are taken. I had a choice. I could either stay with my parents or crash in the guest room of January's lodge."

"I would've chosen to stay with your parents," Eric replied, not missing a beat. "I mean, it's January Jackson. Don't you remember how horrible she was to you back in the day?"

Jake grimaced. He'd been trying hard to push memories of his past with January out of his head. It wasn't as easy as he'd been hoping. "She's ... not so bad," he said finally.

Eric arched an eyebrow and darted a meaningful look at Silas, silent smiles passing between them.

"Oh, don't do that." Jake was aggrieved. "There's nothing going on. She's in one room, and I'm in the other. She's also technically my boss, which is its own brand of horror."

Eric barked out a laugh. "Oh, I can't even imagine. She's so unbelievably rigid. She was that way in high school, but she's worse as an adult. I heard Amy in purchasing say that January actually has to-do lists for her to-do lists. It's unbelievable."

"She does like her lists," Jake agreed.

"I bet she's still a virgin," Eric continued, barely taking a breath. "I mean, who would sleep with her? Nobody I know, that's for sure. I bet she'd be the most high-maintenance complainer in the world if you finally got her into bed."

Jake had to force his breathing to remain even. He'd only ever told one person about his night with January, and Silas had promised to never bring it up. Jake darted a look at Silas in an effort to gauge his friend's response to what Eric had said, but Silas's expression was hard to read.

"I don't think she's that bad," Silas said. "I know I don't have to work with her often, but she's really organized. You wouldn't believe how obnoxious the parents are when it comes to the lessons. They're the ones who forget, or screw it up, and January is the one who has to smooth things over. She takes the brunt of the disappointment on her shoulders and always manages to come up with a solution for everybody involved."

Jake was taken aback. Silas was one of the few people he'd heard stand up for January since he'd returned.

"Oh, maybe you're the one who has a crush on her," Eric teased. "I would be lying if I said she wasn't hot. All that hotness is burned away because she's a frigid bitch though. She reprimanded me—on the record—last week. She caught me in the storage room smoking and sent me to Human Resources."

"Why were you smoking in the storage room?" Jake demanded.

Eric shrugged. "It was cold out, man."

"That doesn't matter." Where Jake's newfound sense of responsibility had come from, it was impossible to say. He continued harping on his friend without a second thought, however. "You could've started a fire. There's a reason you can't smoke in the storage rooms."

Eric blinked twice and then started. "Good grief. Were you channeling your father or January with that little diatribe?"

Jake turned sheepish. "Probably my father. He's in my head right now, and I'm in a bad place."

"Which explains why you're living with January," Eric said. "There was a rumor he wanted to strand you in Vegas and force you to find your own way home with no working credit cards. Is that true?"

Jake's lower lip came out to play. "It's good to know that the gossip mill here is alive and kicking," he complained.

"That's the one thing you can always count on," Silas agreed. "It's like death and taxes. There's no getting away from either of them, and there's no escaping resort gossip either."

"My mother is trying to talk to him," Jake explained, suddenly realizing how lame that sounded. "It's not that I expect my father to fund my lifestyle. I really was trying to find a niche when it happened. I just made a bad choice and trusted the wrong people."

"Well, you learned from it," Silas replied diplomatically. "That should count as forward momentum."

"Yeah, my father doesn't really work that way." Jake's expression darkened. "He's nowhere near done punishing me."

"Hence why you've been saddled with January," Eric surmised. "I have to hand it to your father. He's a master at punishment. He must've realized nothing would hurt you quite so much as being forced to spend time with her."

Jake hesitated, an overwhelming urge to stand up for January washing over him. He had to battle it back. "It's not the end of the world. She's always busy with work. Most of the time, she's at the kitchen table planning stuff when I go to bed, and she's back up before me planning stuff again when I wake up. I don't see her all that often."

"You know, you could help her plan the stuff," Silas suggested. "I think that's what your dad had in mind when he paired you two together."

Jake involuntarily shuddered. "I'm not a big fan of lists."

"Or January," Eric added. "She's insufferable. She'll probably write him up before it's all said and done."

Silas's gaze was knowing when it landed on Jake. "Some people like a woman who is organized and together. They might not be willing to admit it, but that doesn't make it any less true."

Jake's heart beat faster. "We should really head down," he said. "There's a storm coming in, and I promised my dad we would get three runs in with feedback by the end of the workday."

Silas, understanding, clapped his friend's shoulder. "Let's not leave Mr. Jeffries waiting, huh?"

Eric nodded. "Let's do this."

JANUARY STOOD STARING AT THE WHITEBOARD in the conference room that had been designated for her use throughout the games and tried not to think how daunting the list looked.

"There she is," a friendly voice said from somewhere behind her, and when January turned, she found her friends Stella and Cady moving in behind her.

"Here I am," January agreed ruefully. "I feel like I live in here now."

"Except you live with Jake Jeffries," Cady teased, her eyes lit with overt amusement. "I have to think that's a lot more fun than living with ... *this*." Her smile slipped as she gestured toward the board. "Yeah, this is so much less fun than Jake."

January was a master at controlling her emotions. She'd been given coping mechanisms by her counselor, and she put them to good use on a regular basis. Her childhood had been out of control, thanks to her mother. Her adulthood would not suffer the same fate. "Let's not talk about Jake Jeffries," she said on a grimace.

"Oh, there's no way we're going to let this opportunity pass," Stella argued. She had dark hair that she let fall around her shoulders most days. She wasn't a fan of pulling it back. To January, it always looked out of control and effortlessly sexy, something she admired when looking at Stella and feared when it came to herself. "We want to know all the details."

"Yes." Cady rubbed her hands together. "Are you guys really living together? Don't leave a single thing out. We want every detail. You're not leaving this room until you tell us absolutely everything."

This was what January had been afraid of when she first heard Jacob's plan. She liked the man, respected him, but he had an unrealistic outlook on the resort's gossip mill. Just because he didn't hear the gossip—the workers were afraid of him, so they would never share—that didn't mean everybody else wasn't current on her living situation.

It made her unbelievably uneasy.

"Jake is being punished by his father," January replied. "Jacob believes Jake needs a firm hand. Right now, Jacob is busy breaking Jake down. Part of that is forcing him to live with me even though we hate one another. It's going to take weeks before Jake is in a place where he can be built back up. I'm just a means to an end here."

Cady's forehead puckered. "Did Jacob actually say that to you?"

"Pretty much," January confirmed. "He mentioned that my past with Jake meant I could elicit a reaction that other people couldn't, and he wanted me to essentially put the screws to Jake. He wants Jake to feel uncomfortable enough that he strives for control. Jacob thinks he's passive, and he can't very well hand the resort over to a guy who isn't comfortable making decisions."

"Ah." Realization dawned on Stella's face. "That sucks for

you. I don't suppose it ever occurred to Mr. Jeffries that you should have a say on the subject."

January's chuckle was light. "No, I don't think it crossed his mind for a second." Reading her friends' expressions, January felt the need to swoop in and smooth things over. "It's not a big deal," she insisted. "I want to help Mr. Jeffries. He's been very good to me."

"Yeah, but your past with Jake is the stuff of legends," Cady argued. "I remember when we were in middle school and Jake was caught sneaking into the girls' locker room. You were the only one in there, and he saw you changing your clothes. You slammed the locker into his face and that broke his nose. Then you tried to beat him to death with one of those pumps that you use to blow up basketballs. Mr. Jeffries can't possibly think it's a good idea to risk another basketball pump situation."

January scowled at the memory. She still remembered it like it was yesterday. She'd been mortified when she looked up and found Jake standing in the opening, his mouth hanging open as he stared at her. Thankfully, she'd had her jeans and bra on. She wasn't completely dressed though. Nothing had ever been as cathartic in her life as hitting him with that basketball pump.

"Yeah, that sucked," January complained. "I don't think Mr. Jeffries remembers all that stuff though. I know he was called up to the office with my mom a few times, but Mrs. Jeffries was normally the one who had to deal with our fights. She was prone to letting Jake off the hook more often than not."

"Yes, she's always been an indulgent parent," Stella agreed, making a face. "If you ask me, she was too indulgent. She's the reason Jake can't hold down a job. It's not as if he's stupid or anything. He's just lazy. She made him lazy."

January couldn't stop herself from thinking back to one of

the earlier conversations she and Jake participated in when they realized they were going to be stuck under the same roof for weeks. He said he'd been working on something, that he had a plan. He looked so crushed when saying it she'd felt bad for him. Sure, it was a fleeting emotion given their past, but her feelings had been genuine.

"It's fine." January waved off their concern. "It's only a few weeks. Once the games actually start, I bet I barely see him. I'll be just that busy."

"Well, you might think it's fine, but you should probably know that there's gossip flying around about you guys," Cady said.

"And it's only been a few days," Stella added.

January's throat went dry. "What sort of gossip?"

"Well, Linda in housekeeping says that you're pregnant by Mr. Jeffries and because he doesn't want his wife to know, he's forcing you to marry his son," Cady volunteered. "We told Linda that was ridiculous, but she says you asked for a virgin Bloody Mary the other morning, and I have to admit, that sounds suspicious to me. Why would you want to order a virgin anything?"

January was stunned by the story. "Are you being serious right now?" she asked when she could finally speak without tripping over her own tongue.

"Unfortunately, yes." Cady was rueful. "I told people it wasn't true, but now I'm afraid it might be true. She's right about the virgin Bloody Mary. Nobody drinks it without alcohol. There's no point."

"First off, I happen to love tomato juice," January fired back, her temper getting the better of her. "I don't even like regular Bloody Marys. I'm guessing what they saw was me drinking tomato juice."

"That's even grosser than a virgin Bloody Mary," Cady complained.

January ignored her. "Secondly, why would I sleep with Mr. Jeffries? He's old enough to be my father."

"He is, but he's rich," Stella argued. "Being rich makes up for being old. Plus, nobody ever sees him with Mrs. Jeffries. It only makes sense he's getting something on the side because ... well ... that's what happens when you're rich."

January was disgusted with the entire assumption. "I would never sleep with someone just because they were rich. I would most definitely never sleep with my boss. On top of that, Mr. Jeffries is devoted to his wife. Sure, they fight, but most of those fights are about Jake. Their marriage seems entirely healthy."

"Oh." Cady's disappointment was obvious. "I was kind of hoping it was true."

"Why would you hope that?"

"Because then you would get to marry Jake," she replied, not missing a beat. "Who wouldn't want to marry Jake? He's hot."

"So, basically, you're saying you're excited at the idea of me being pregnant by our boss and marrying his son to cover it up. That's what you're saying, right?"

"Well, when you put it like that..." Cady made a face. "I know it's gross, but you should hear the other stuff people are saying."

January swallowed hard. "Like what?"

"Well, for one thing, people are saying you're married to Jake, but he's embarrassed to acknowledge it, so you have to keep it secret."

"You would be shocked at the number of stories that are out there," Stella said. "I've heard a different one from every person I've talked to."

Resigned, January lowered herself into one of the chairs. "Tell me."

"You want to hear the stories?" Cady was incredulous.

January nodded. If she didn't know what stories were spreading, she couldn't combat them. If she didn't nip the gossip train in the bud soon, it would be out of control. There would be no reining it in. She couldn't risk it.

"Tell me all of it," January instructed. "Don't leave anything out."

NINE

J ake glared at his reflection in the mirror as he attempted to center his tie. He'd fallen into a routine at the resort—January providing him with a daily list of duties on the kitchen table before she left in the morning—and he was settling into daily life back in Michigan. There was something comforting about knowing exactly what he was going to do on any given day, and even though she could've run him ragged, Jake was surprised to find that January never gave him more than he could comfortably get done in an eight-hour shift.

He was both grateful and annoyed. Grateful because he didn't want to struggle to get through a workday. Annoyed because it felt to him as if she was refusing to offer up a challenge. *Because she doesn't believe I can level up at the resort?* He didn't want to think about it too hard, but there was a nasty seed of doubt starting to grow in the back of his mind. He ruthlessly shoved it aside when he heard heels on the ceramic tile.

"What is this stupid dinner about anyway?" he asked as he turned. His eyes went wide at the sight of her, and he felt as if the oxygen had been punched out of his lungs. Rocky Balboa was coming after him in that moment, swinging hard, and he forgot what he was going to say.

"What?" January asked.

He focused on her red dress. It wasn't ornate or even over-the-top festive, given the fact that Christmas was right around the corner. It boasted simple lines, an off-the-shoulder bodice, and a modest amount of cleavage that teased rather than taunted.

Or maybe it was the other way around.

"What?" Jake blurted. He had no idea what he'd been asking before he'd seen her.

January cocked an eyebrow. "You asked me a question."

"Yes, well... I don't remember what it was."

"You haven't been drinking already, have you?" January chided. "Your father will be mad if you show up tipsy."

"My father is going to be mad with me regardless," Jake replied, his hands returning to his tie when he caught sight of his reflection. Then he remembered the question. "I know this is a dinner—we've taken over the entire dining room, right?—but what are we supposed to do at it?"

Perhaps sensing his unease, January moved in front of him and lightly nudged his hands away from his tie so she could fix it. Her fingers were deft as she maneuvered them. "It's the entire Maxwell family and several of their workers," she replied. She was focused on the tie, not him, and Jake had to swallow hard at her proximity.

What is happening here? He'd never reacted this way to January. Not even the night they'd lost their heads and ... yeah, he couldn't think about that.

January smoothed his tie when she was finished and then smiled. "You look nice," she said.

Jake's heart skipped a beat. That smile... He didn't even know she could smile like that. She'd never smiled as a kid. Well, at least not at him.

"You look nice too," he offered honestly. "I've never seen you in a dress before."

The statement was enough to elicit a scowl from January. "I've worn dresses before."

"Maybe, but I've never seen you wear one. Especially not one like this." He lightly caught her wrist before she could pull away and ran his fingers over the delicate lines there. "You look really beautiful."

January's cheeks flamed hot and red to match her dress. "Thank you." She turned away from him—so he couldn't see her embarrassment?—and then headed toward the front closet. "It's going to be a harrowing walk across the parking lot in these shoes."

Jake arched an eyebrow as he glanced down. The shoes had ice-pick heels, and they made her legs, which were only visible from the knee down, pop. "I can carry you," he offered without thinking.

January's eyes went wide when she turned back to him. "What?"

He laughed at her response and then relaxed a bit. Just because she'd dressed in an alarm-red dress that seemed completely opposite of her personality didn't mean she wasn't still January. "Or you could hold my arm for the walk, and I'll be sure to keep you upright."

January hesitated and then nodded. "Thank you for that. This dinner is supposed to be low-key—a way for the sponsors to get to know the workers—but it feels like an audition of sorts."

"I thought you got along well with Jim Maxwell." Jake absently took her coat from her and helped her into it without thinking.

"I do," January reassured him. "Or at least I think I do. He's a little weird."

"Because of the marriage thing?"

"That, and he has a very rigid mindset when it comes to women," she replied. "Did you know that none of his daughters work in the dealership with him once they become pregnant? They're allowed to work with the rest of the family until they have a child, and then they're expected to stay home and take care of the kids. It's like a rule or something."

Jake frowned as he grabbed his own coat. "Maybe that's what they want."

"Maybe." January didn't look convinced. "I'm all for women doing what they want. If they want to stay home and raise kids, that's great. That's the hardest job in the world. If they want to work, though, it feels misogynistic for Jim to assume they can't raise children *and* hold down a job at the same time."

"I guess I didn't think about that part." Jake walked out to the front porch first and tested the wood with his boots to see how slippery it was. Once he was relatively certain January would be okay, he held out his hand to her.

She took it, gripping him tightly as she tested the porch herself. She was rueful when she glanced up. "Maybe I should change my shoes for the walk over and carry these."

Jake studied her for an extended beat, grinned, and repeated his offer. "Or I could carry you."

January balked. "I'm not a child."

"I didn't say you were a child. I know what a stickler you are for being on time, however. I could easily carry you to the main building in three minutes flat."

"That feels a lot like being saved," she hedged.

Jake's eyebrows slid up his forehead. "Is that a bad thing?"

"Yes." January's answer was automatic. "I have to be able to take care of myself. I'll lose everything if I'm not careful."

Jake frowned. "Why do you think that?"

"Because it's the truth." January was matter of fact. "I can walk." She was determined as she set out.

Jake watched her for a beat, confused, and when she slipped at the end of the sidewalk, he hurried forward and caught her before she could hit the ground. "I'm going to sweat through my shirt if I have to watch you walk across the parking lot," he complained, swinging her up in his arms with minimal effort and cradling her against his chest.

January sucked in a breath.

"I'm not saving you," he said as he started across the parking lot. His heart skipped several beats at the way she felt when pressed against him. Why did this feel so right? Why did she have to smell so good? Was that cookies? Who smelled like baking cookies? "Saving is different than helping, just for the record. Even if I was saving you in this instance, though, it doesn't mean you're not a badass."

January chewed on her bottom lip, conflict lining her pretty features. In the muted Christmas lights that were spread across the resort grounds, she looked breathtaking. It was another blow to his chest. Rocky was clearly feeling vindictive this evening.

"I just need to be able to take care of myself," January said. "It has to be that way."

Jake wanted to ask her why, but he knew now wasn't the time. Instead, he merely nodded. When they reached the front of the resort, he put her down behind the valet hut and watched as she smoothed her dress.

"Do I look okay?" she asked nervously. "My dress isn't wrinkled or anything, is it?"

"You look beautiful," Jake replied. The words easily slipped out because they were true. "Hold tight to me for the walk up the stairs, huh?" He inclined his head toward the expansive staircase that led to the lobby. "I'll keep you on your feet. You can trust me. Your badass rep will remain intact."

January let loose a breath and nodded. "Thank you for

your help, Jake. You didn't need to go out of your way like this."

He shot her a confused look as they started up the stairs. "I didn't go out of my way. It was nothing. You don't owe me your firstborn or anything. It was a three-minute walk."

She puffed out a laugh. "Thank you anyway."

He shook his head as they reached the top of the stairs and held open the door. "It was my pleasure, January."

"WE'RE HOPING FOR TEN."

January held her gin and tonic—she'd been nursing the same one since she arrived—and regarded Margie Lansing, one of Jim Maxwell's daughters, with a dumbfounded look. "You're hoping for ten what?"

"Children," Margie replied, not missing a beat. "The good Lord willing, I want two basketball teams so they can scrimmage against one another."

"Huh." January had no idea what to make of that. "I guess once you're used to the birthing drugs, it's not a big deal," she said finally. Given how wide Margie's eyes went, January realized in a split second that she'd made a mistake. "Or ... something else."

"Drugs are bad for the baby," Margie insisted. The look she shot January was suspicious. "Babies are born stoned when drugs are involved. Do you want a stoned baby? Because, let me tell you, stoned babies grow up to be stoned adults."

January pressed her lips together in horror. She was good with lists and getting things done, but when it came to people, she was less sure of herself. Before she could think what to say to smooth over the conversation, an arm slid around her waist and Jake's now-familiar presence appeared at her side.

"Did I just hear something about being stoned?" he asked in his charming way.

January laughed because she didn't know what else to do. Margie didn't so much as crack a smile.

"I hope you're not thinking of using drugs when your baby is born," she said pointedly.

Jake was unflappable in most social settings—something January had always marveled at—and that was on full display today. "Are we having a baby?" he asked January lightly. "I think I should probably be kept in the loop for that."

January choked on a harsh laugh and then managed to catch herself. Margie was not her father after all. The woman didn't have to like her. January just had to keep from offending her ... at least too much. "Would that upset you?" she asked teasingly.

"Nope." Jake shook his head, not missing a beat. "I want a little girl. We'll get her a label maker for her third birthday and be her favorite parents ever."

January's mouth dropped open. *How does he know about the label maker?* She shook herself out of her reverie and immediately went back to looking at Margie. "Margie here wants ten kids and doesn't believe in using drugs when giving birth."

Jake mock shuddered. "What a Viking you are. Wow."

Margie preened under the compliment, although January recognized the statement as a distraction more than anything else.

"How many do you have already?" Jake asked. "Of the ten, I mean."

"Oh, I haven't been blessed with a baby yet," Margie replied, her smile slipping. "I hope it's soon. I really hate working at the dealership."

"Oh, does your father insist you work at the dealership until you start having kids?" Jake asked.

Margie looked scandalized. "Of course not. It's just what my other sisters have done over the years. I can't not do what they do, can I?"

January studied Jake's profile as he considered the question. He seemed thrown by how he should answer.

"You should do what you want," Jake replied finally, tightening his grip on January. "If you'll excuse me, I would like to spend a bit of time with my wife. You understand, right? I mean ... there's mistletoe in every archway."

Margie's expression was so blank, Jake had to switch tactics.

"Or maybe you don't understand," Jake said. "There's just a few work things we need to discuss."

"Of course." Margie gripped her hands together in front of her. "I'm sure it will be a relief when you don't have to work again too. For now though..." She waved them off.

January was sputtering when Jake dragged her away from the restaurant and toward the bar on the other side of the central help desk. "There's something wrong with them," she hissed as Jake took her to the empty bar and nodded at Luke, who was serving drinks. "They're pod people or something."

"I think they've just been indoctrinated a bit too much," Jake replied. "They remind me of that family that got their own television show. They had a bunch of kids and counting. The girls were expected to raise the new babies and popping out babies was considered an Olympic sport."

"They're a cult," January countered, sliding her ignored cocktail onto the bar. "They make me distinctly uncomfortable."

"It wouldn't be so bad if they believed that everybody could live their own lives however they wanted," Jake acknowledged. "It's the part where they tell others what they should do that's an issue. And ten babies without drugs? Who cares if the babies come out stoned as long as the mother doesn't feel as if she's been run through some sort of medieval torture device?"

"Totally." January offered up her fist to bump, which she realized was out of the ordinary for her. Jake laughed and bumped fists with her.

When Luke slid over to take their orders, his gaze was on their bumping fists, and suddenly January felt distinctly uncomfortable.

"Do you need drinks?" Luke asked.

Jake nodded. "Give me a bourbon and coke please." He glanced at January. "What do you want?"

"Oh, I'm okay," she said automatically.

Jake made a face and reached for the cup she'd discarded so he could smell the contents. "Is this gin and tonic?" he asked on a nose wrinkle.

January immediately balked. "It's a dignified drink."

"It's a boring drink," he countered, resting his elbows on the counter as he studied the specials menu. "Have you ever had a cranberry martini?"

January shook her head. It wasn't hard to figure out where he was going with his line of questioning.

"She'll have the cranberry martini," Jake said to Luke. "Make sure you do all the fixings, including the sugar rim and the garnish. The drink will match her dress."

Luke blinked several times and then nodded. He looked baffled by what he was seeing, but he didn't offer up a word of complaint. Once he was gone, Jake turned so his back was to the bar and looked January over closely.

"They're a weird family," he said finally. His hand absently moved to January's exposed arm, and he brushed his fingers over it. January froze in place. It was a personal touch—something they didn't do—but she couldn't exactly make a scene given where they were and the fraud they were perpetuating on the Maxwell family.

"I wish they weren't our sponsor," January agreed, goose pimples appearing on her arm as Jake continued to sweep his finger up and down her skin. His touch was so light she could barely feel it. His presence, however, was like an anvil barreling toward her heart. Well, at least if they had been trapped in a cartoon. She couldn't think of a comparable real-world feeling.

"I'm guessing Dad didn't realize what a mess it was going to be," Jake said. "We're too close though. We're only a week and a half from the start of the games. We can't get another sponsor, so we have to make it work with this sponsor."

"I just can't help feeling that he's looking through me sometimes," January admitted. "I hate that feeling."

Jake's eyes sharpened. "You mean he makes you feel invisible. I get that. My father has a way of doing the same thing to me."

January's chuckle was uneven. "No offense, Jake, but I really don't think you do understand. I spent my entire childhood living on the wrong side of town. That meant I was almost never invited to parties, and my clothes weren't good enough for nice restaurants. My skis were secondhand and never the newest thing, so I couldn't come here at night because I only could use the lift tickets I got for free, and those were daytime tickets. There's a lot more to being invisible than facing your father's disappointment."

For the third time in as many hours, Jake felt as if he was being punched. He didn't like the forlorn look on her face. Thankfully, Luke picked that moment to appear with their drinks.

"Here you go."

January looked delighted when she accepted hers. "Wow." Her eyes sparkled as she lifted the beautiful drink. The colored sugar on the rim was dim compared to her smile, but Jake couldn't stop himself from grinning at the way she reacted to the drink.

He took his glass from Luke and waited for January to sample her cocktail. The way her eyes lit up at the taste told him he'd done the right thing suggesting the fancy martini.

"Come on," he said, prodding her away from the bar. "I'll wait until you're buzzed on your second cocktail and then force you to dance with me."

January's eyes were sharp when they landed on him. "You want to dance with me?"

He shrugged, noncommittal. "That's what married couples do, right?" He laughed at his own joke. "Besides, you're about the only person here who I can stand. I might as well make the most of it."

January looked caught off guard, but she ultimately nodded. "Okay, but I'm not a very good dancer. I think I'm a vacuum for rhythm."

Jake laughed, as he was certain she'd intended. "We have that in common."

"Then we can suck together."

"There are worse things," he agreed.

TEN

The storm they'd all been dreading for days hit Friday afternoon, as expected. January went to the summit hill area to check how things were going for the shutdown—even though it was fun to ski on fresh powder, the resort couldn't allow people to be out on the slopes during the storm in case someone got lost—and her chest tightened when she saw the way the snow was pelting the hills.

"It's going to be a doozy," Leo said as he appeared next to her.

January smiled. She was fond of the security chief. He had a penchant for stating the obvious though. "Is everybody off the hills?"

"Not yet." Leo's lips turned down. "Apparently, they haven't been able to get in touch with Jimmy down at the bottom of the lift. He's still sending people up, and they're not corralling everybody at the top of the hill like they should. The guests are excited by the snow. They don't understand it's a liability for us."

"Well, we have to get ahead of that." January rested her hands on her hips, glanced around, and made up her mind on the spot. "I'm going to grab a set of skis. I know ski patrol is out there, but somebody needs to take charge. I'll order the lift operator at the top of the hill to direct people inside and then head down to tell Jimmy the same. I should be the last one up the lift if all goes as planned."

Leo hesitated. "Are you sure you want to be the one who does that? It's not part of your job description."

January tried not to bristle. "It's fine," she assured him. "I know the hills as well as anybody else. I can handle it."

"I'm not saying you can't. It's not your job though."

"We all pitch in to help here." January was firm. "The ski patrol is going to be over on the Raptor. That's the more dangerous run. The bulk of the skiers are going to be on the first hill though. As long as people keep seeing others going down, they're going to keep going down. We have to nip this in the bud. It's going to get worse in the next hour. We need everybody inside, and the locals who aren't staying here need to get home."

"Okay." Leo flashed a smile that didn't touch his eyes. "I'll be here when you get back. I'll buy you some hot chocolate."

"Now that sounds like a great way to watch a storm."

JAKE HUMMED TO HIMSELF AS HE HELPED the ski rental clerks check returned inventory. That was one of the ways they counted heads. The storm was picking up—and, honestly, there was nothing he would've liked better than to take a run or two down the slopes himself—but he understood that the skiing was getting treacherous.

The most important thing was to make sure everybody—workers, ski patrol, and skiers—were off the hills. He was pitching in wherever he could to make sure the numbers added up.

"That's everything loaned out now accounted for, except

for the pair January took," Edgar Banes said as he checked his list. "I think we're good."

Confused, Jake drew his eyes to Edgar. "What do you mean? What skis did January take?"

"She took a pair of Nordicas about an hour ago," Edgar replied. "She was helping out on the mountain to make sure that all the skiers made it inside. Apparently, there was a problem with Jimmy at the bottom of the lift. They couldn't get a message down to him. She was going to take one down personally."

Edgar leaned closer, as if he was going to impart some great wisdom to Jake. "According to Leo, she felt someone needed to be in charge out there and decided she was the one who should do it. Isn't that just like a woman?"

Jake didn't like his tone. What he disliked more, however, was the pang of worry that shot through him when he thought about January being out in the blizzard. "Are we certain she's not back?"

"I mean... I can't be absolutely certain," Edgar hedged. "She's usually pretty prompt when returning gear. I mean ... she is the most responsible one on top of the mountain. That's what she always tells us anyway."

Jake battled back an irrational bout of fury. "I'll check on her. You can shut down. We'll lock up her skis in the front office if we have to. We'll get them back to you either way."

"I'm not worried." Edgar winked.

Jake hurried out of the rental shop and practically ran over Leo, who was walking down the hallway. Before he even realized what he was doing, Jake grabbed the front of the security chief's suit jacket and fixed him with a determined look. "Is January back?"

Instead of nodding, Leo looked grave. "I was just about to find someone from ski patrol. She hasn't come back. I've been up at the summit doors waiting for her. She said she would be thirty minutes at the most. It's been twice that."

Jake licked his lips, debating, and then made up his mind on the spot. "I'll head down."

Leo balked. "You can't go down there. It's too dangerous. The snow is coming down fast now. They say we're going to get up to two inches an hour for the next six hours, and it's blowing."

Jake didn't care about that. "We have people out there somewhere. That means I'm going down. Have they got the snowmobiles out?" He was hopeful.

"They have two of them over on the Raptor," Leo replied calmly. "Apparently, the skiers there are putting up a fight. I can redirect one of them to the main hill if you want."

"Tell them to shut the Raptor down," Jake barked. "If somebody decides to take shelter in the woods over there because they think they're being funny, we'll never find them. This storm is going to be going for hours. The cleanup after that is going to be a pain. We don't have time for nonsense." He turned on his heel and strode back toward the rental place.

"Are you going down on skis?" Leo asked, dumbstruck.

"It's the fastest way I know to get down there and check on them."

"January knows what she's doing," Leo argued. "She's a good girl."

"Even good girls need help."

Leo worked his jaw and searched Jake's face, seemingly looking for clues on what his response should be. Ultimately, he nodded. "I'll wrangle ski patrol. Don't dawdle at the bottom of that hill."

"I won't. I'm bringing her up."

"Then do it. Let's get this place buttoned up—and fast."

. . .

THE LIGHTS WERE ON AS JAKE MADE HIS descent. Hotel security was corralling every skier that came off the lift and forcing them into the building. They told him before he started down that nobody had been able to make contact with Jimmy. On top of that, even though they'd seen January go down the hill, nobody had seen her come back up.

Jake cursed to himself the entire way down. Thankfully, the main hill wasn't some twisty monstrosity like the Raptor. He ignored the moguls and headed straight down, tucking his poles under his arms and making the descent as quickly as possible. It still took him several minutes to reach the bottom, and when he did, he found January arguing with Jimmy Bolton outside the lift house.

"What are you doing?" he demanded as he executed a hockey stop directly next to her, spraying snow on her in the process. "Get up that hill!"

January's eyes went wide when she saw him. "Excuse me? I don't think I like your tone."

Jake thought he might blow a gasket. "You don't like my tone? Good grief, January, there's a freaking blizzard descending on us. Do you know what I don't like? Finding out that you're out in it."

"I'm fine." January drew up her normally small frame—she was padded in outerwear—and glared at him. "Jimmy is being difficult. He won't walk up the hill."

"There's no way I'm going out in a blizzard," Jimmy complained. He was halfway in the lift building, which was basically a small shed. "I'll get lost. I've seen movies. People get lost in blizzards."

Temper reared up and grabbed Jake by the throat. "You're walking up a hill, Jimmy," he snapped. "You're not wandering miles in the wilderness. The freaking lights are on."

Jimmy's jaw was stubbornly square. "I'm not risking it. I'll just stay here until it's over."

"It's not going to be over until tomorrow." Jake was determined. "You know what? Get on the lift. It will be quicker."

Jimmy's eyes went wide. "No way. I'm scared of heights."

"You're barely above the ground."

"It's not happening." Jimmy was adamant. "No way. No how. Nothing doing."

"Unbelievable!" Jake lifted his eyes to the sky, as if to lambast a deity for his lot in life. "Jimmy, you're walking up that hill if I have to drag you myself. As for you—he swung on January—you're going to give me a heart attack if you're not careful. Get your ass on that lift. You shouldn't be out in this."

January wasn't the type to take orders, Jake knew. She gave them and was happy to do it. "Maybe you should get your ass on the lift," she shot back.

"I will, just as soon as Jimmy starts up that hill and your ass is on the lift."

"I think I'll wait until Jimmy is heading up the hill and your ass is on the lift," she countered. "You are my subordinate, if I'm not mistaken. That means I'm responsible for you."

Jake was convinced he was about to turn into a cartoon character and blow his stack. Like, he literally thought it was possible for the back of his head to blow off so the steam could escape. "Are you trying to kill me?"

"Are you trying to kill me?" January shot back. "I'm the boss. That means you need to go up before me."

"Unreal." Jake let a string of curse words fly, and then the unthinkable happened. The lights on the hill blinked off. "Son of a bitch!" The bellow was lost in the howling wind.

January's shoulders jolted, something Jake could barely make out in the limited light. Because of the snow, it was brighter than it would've been on a nonsnowy night. That didn't mean they could see anything of substance.

"Well, that does it for me." Jimmy moved to lock himself inside the lift hut, but Jake was having none of it.

"No!" Jake grabbed the back of his coat and dragged him out of the shed. "Give me the keys!"

Jimmy's eyes went wide, but he followed Jake's instructions. In short order, Jake locked the building and popped his ski bindings. It was going to be a pain walking up the hill in ski boots, but it was either that or duckwalk on the blades. With the way the snow was falling, that would be exhausting.

"We have to walk up together." Jake was as calm as he could manage as he regarded January. "And we have to do it now. Things are only going to get worse when the wind starts swirling the snow. It's going to be a fifteen-minute walk up at the very least, and we have to do it as a group."

For a moment, he thought January was going to argue with him. She didn't though. Instead, she popped her own bindings and slung the skis over her shoulder, along with one of her poles. She gripped the other pole in her hand. She was going to need it.

"Let's do this." She was grim.

"Yeah, let's do this."

THE WALK SHOULD'VE TAKEN FIFTEEN MINUTES. It took double that. Between the snow, the wind, and Jimmy's whining, Jake was convinced he'd wandered into some parallel hell dimension, and this was his punishment for some misdeed that he couldn't even remember committing.

During the entire walk, he internally cursed his father for forcing him into this position. Then he cursed January for running out into a storm. He cursed Jimmy for being Jimmy, but his father and January were the ones who got the most curses.

All the while, his skin burned from the wind and snow,

and his pounding heart reminded him that he was responsible for getting January out of the elements. *If you're this cold, she's likely even colder.* Jake couldn't bear the thought, so he kept moving.

When the lights from the summit door finally swam into view, Jake had never been more grateful in his entire life. "We're almost there," he announced. His eyes bounced over Jimmy and landed on January. She was focused on the walk, but she was flagging. He could see it. "Just a little bit more."

"Huh?" January shifted her eyes to Jake and nodded. "I'm okay." As if to prove it, she tried to walk faster. She only made it three steps before she dropped back to her previous pace. "It's really coming down."

"It is," Jake agreed.

Leo was waiting for them at the top. He looked caught between fury and relief at the sight of them. "I was just about to send ski patrol after you," he said. "I was told the three of you were up. I went looking, and when I further questioned Eli in the top lift house, he said it was possible he made a mistake, and you hadn't made it up after all. I threatened to kill him. He didn't seem worried."

Jake snorted. "We're okay. Just cold and tired."

"I want to go home and take a bath," January grumbled.

Because he felt sorry for her—and maybe a little something else he couldn't quite identify—Jake nodded. "I'm taking her to the lodge." He handed his skis to Jimmy and then collected January's skis and poles from her and handed them to Leo. "Can you lock both sets of skis in the main office? We'll return them tomorrow. I'm taking her straight home."

"Absolutely." A small smile played at the corners of Leo's mouth when Jake slipped his arm around January's shoulders. Jake had questions about the smile, like why it was even a thing, but he was too tired to ask.

"Everything else is handled, right?" Jake pressed as he led January to the door.

"We're good," Leo replied. "Just take care of her."

"That's the plan."

JANUARY FELT NUMB IN MORE THAN ONE way when Jake led her through the lodge front door.

"Boots off," he ordered as he flicked the switch to start the gas fireplace. She preferred a wood-burning stove, but those were a fire hazard and had been switched out years before. Only the main fireplace in the lodge still burned actual logs.

January was resentful at his bossy tone, but she was too tired to fight with him and flopped down on the couch. Walking across the parking lot in ski boots had been a chore because there was a layer of ice beneath the snow.

"Everything hurts," she groused as she flipped the buckles. "Like, really, really hurts."

"That's because we're not used to going up the hill," Jake said. He managed to remove his own ski boots and then scooted across the floor to tackle her boots. "Come on, January, let's get these things off."

January made a hissing noise when the boots finally gave way, and then the pain really kicked in. "I think I might be dying." She rolled to her side as her feet were engulfed in pins and needles.

"It's because you were out there for so long." Jake took her feet in his hands and frowned when she gasped. "I need to rub the circulation back in. It's going to hurt."

January didn't say anything, instead squeezing her eyes shut.

Jake muttered a series of dark laments under his breath, his eyes never leaving her face. She knew because every time she opened her eyes, she found him staring at her. When she stopped cringing, he stopped pressing so hard.

"I suppose it never occurred to you to let ski patrol do their job," he snapped finally.

"I was trying to help," she said. "I just ... wanted to help."

"I know." He squeezed both of her feet and then stood. He still had his ski coat and pants on but was agile when shedding them. "Come on." He tugged on her ski pants. We need to get this stuff off you. Then it's under a blanket and in front of the fire for you."

"You're so bossy," she muttered.

"Funny, that's what people say about you."

"That's what people say about women," she corrected, although she shifted her hips so he could tug off the pants. She'd never been this tired. "When a man takes charge, he's formidable. When a woman does it, she's a Karen. Or something worse."

"Yeah. I get it." He tossed her coat and pants on top of his and then snagged the blanket from the back of the couch. "Under," he ordered.

January didn't put up a fight when he tossed the blanket on top of her. When he climbed in next to her and secured the blanket around them both, however, her eyebrows hiked.

"I'm cold too," he said by way of explanation. "We just need to warm up for fifteen minutes. Then everything will be fine."

January wasn't so certain, but she didn't argue. "Okay. Just fifteen minutes."

They both closed their eyes and succumbed to the exhaustion plaguing them. Nobody was paying attention to the time when they slipped under. Nobody was aware enough to realize they'd started cuddling against one another.

ELEVEN

J anuary was warm when she woke. Too warm. For a moment, she thought she'd gotten sick because of her trek up the hill, but then she realized she wasn't sleeping alone.

Slowly—very slowly because her brain refused to fire on all cylinders—she shifted and found herself looking into Jake's sleeping face.

What in the hell?

That was the only thing she could think as she took in her predicament. She was on the couch, which was the last place she remembered being. Obviously, hours had passed, however, because light was filtering in through the shades. She was still dressed—*thank the Lord for small favors!*—and Jake was not only still on the couch with her but also wrapped around her.

What had happened? How had they ended up like this? Was the world ending?

Before she could extricate herself from his embrace—there was no graceful way to do it that she could ascertain—Jake opened his eyes. She held her breath, waiting for him to say something stupid—that was his way after all—but he looked as confused as she felt.

"What did you do?" he asked out of nowhere.

The fear January had been feeling disappeared in an instant, and she glared at him. "That was going to be my line."

"Um ... you're the one snuggling with me." Jake pulled back and struggled to a sitting position. Unfortunately, because they were so close to one another, he accidentally brushed his hand against her breast. January refused to acknowledge it because it was just another layer of trouble she didn't want to sift through.

"I believe you've got that backward," she snapped. She caught a glimpse of her hair in the mirror when she finally managed to get vertical and internally cringed. She looked as if she'd gone through a wind tunnel in the overnight hours. "You're the one who was snuggling with me."

"I very much doubt it." Jake tossed the blanket off and stood. He seemed unsure on his feet as he held out his arms for balance.

"Are you doing interpretive dance or something?" she demanded.

"My foot is asleep," Jake shot back.

"Oh, whatever." January needed to put distance between herself and him. That was the only thing she could think about. In an effort to do that, she stood and almost immediately toppled forward. "Ow!" She made a pitiable sound.

Jake slid her a sidelong look. "What was that?"

"That was me realizing that every muscle in my body hurts." She said it in an accusatory manner, as if he was to blame.

"Oh, don't even." Jake narrowed his eyes. "It's not my fault you're in pain. If anybody should be complaining, it's me. I had to walk up the stupid hill in ski boots—in a blizzard —because you decided to be a hero when it wasn't your job."

"Nobody made you come after me," January reminded him. "I think you were the one who wanted to be a hero."

"Whatever." Jake moved toward the window. To January, it seemed as if the movement took effort. He was grim as he peered out through the glass. "It's still going."

January wanted to look for herself, but she couldn't make herself move. Her muscles hurt too much. "How much snow did we get?"

"We're over a foot now."

"It's supposed to keep going for the bulk of the day. They don't even plan on opening the slopes again until tomorrow."

"Which means we're stuck here." Jake's eyes were thoughtful when they locked with hers. "Together."

January could read the emotion on his face. He wasn't happy. *Well, join the club, bucko.* "I'm going to make breakfast." That wasn't what she thought she was going to say. She had an entire diatribe on the tip of her tongue, one that pointed out he'd been wrapped around her and not vice-versa, but for once she didn't care about winning. She was too tired. And sore.

Good god was she sore.

"Is that an invitation?" Jake asked after a beat.

Was it? January wasn't certain. "Well, if I'm going to be cooking for me, I guess I can cook for you too. You did come after me."

"Like a hero," Jake confirmed on a sly grin. "I swooped in and saved your ass."

"Oh, don't push it." She hobbled into the kitchen, again catching a glimpse of her reflection in the mirror on the wall. She wanted to escape to her bedroom long enough to run a brush through her snarled hair. It was a point of pride that she didn't. "I'm just making eggs and hash browns. There's some sausage links too. If you want something fancier, then you're on your own."

"I was going to have Fruity Pebbles, so I think I'm good."
Jake rummaged in the cupboards without being asked and
came up with three fry pans. One was large enough for the
hash browns. The other two were for the eggs and sausage.
"What do you want me to do?" he asked.

January was surprised by the offer. "You're helping?"

Jake shot her an incredulous look. "Don't act so surprised.
Even I can cook eggs."

"Didn't you grow up with a cook or something?"

"So?"

"I'm just surprised that you know how to do anything
besides order from DoorDash." January shuffled to the refrigerator and started pulling items out. Eggs. Butter. Sausage.
She'd bought a bag of already shredded potatoes for the hash
browns. Was there bread? Now she wanted toast.

"I can cook," Jake shot back. "Well, kind of. I won't starve
or anything if I'm in charge of cooking. Let's just leave it at
that."

For some reason, his response had January smiling. "Well,
then maybe you're not as useless as I always assumed." The
words came out much harsher than she'd intended. "That was
supposed to be a joke," she said when the awkward silence
stretched a few seconds. "I know it was a bad joke, but that's
what I do. I'm not naturally funny, and I try to be funny, and
then it comes across as mean. You should know that's not
what I was going for."

Jake held her gaze for what felt like a really long time.
Then he smiled. "You always were weird. Don't worry about
it. Between last night and this morning, I would be surprised if
things weren't awkward."

"It's not what happened last night," January countered.
She focused on removing the sausage from the package. "I've
always been like this. It's like I'm not comfortable in my own
skin. I'm always the outsider, and I can't stand not being

accepted, so I push things until I make them even worse. That's what I do."

Jake blinked several times, reminding January of a deer caught in headlights. Ultimately, he managed a smile, and to both their surprise, it was genuine. "Have you considered not trying to please everyone?"

January was baffled by the question. "No. I want to be liked."

"Yeah, but the more you try to be liked, the more you're going to turn people off. People can smell desperation, and it's not attractive."

"Well, maybe that's just me," January said primly. "Maybe I'm not attractive."

"No, that's not it," Jake replied.

January snapped her eyes to him. "What?"

It was only then that Jake seemed to realize what he'd said. He could've backtracked. That was what January expected him to do. Instead, he let loose a heavy sigh, resignation pulling down his shoulders. "You're attractive, January. You have a lot of admirable qualities. Are you a bit intense? Yeah. I don't think you want to be though. With you, it's just a knee-jerk reaction."

"I'm unlikable," she said. "You can say it."

"You're not unlikable. You're just ... a lot."

"You mean too much?"

Jake looked puzzled by the question, but he ultimately shook his head. "You need to learn to take a breath. You've always been intense to the point of distraction. I've never understood it. People want to like you. You make it impossible when you become completely fixated on one thing, though, and start barking orders. People don't like being ordered around."

January avoided making eye contact. "I just like things done in a specific manner."

"There's more than one way to do things," Jake pointed out. "Your way isn't always the correct way."

"Sometimes it is though."

"And sometimes it isn't." Jake was firm. "Just take a freaking breath."

Because she didn't know what else to do, January followed his orders in literal fashion and sucked in a breath, holding it for several seconds before letting it out.

"There you go." Jake's smile was soft. "Keep doing it."

"This isn't going to help anything," January grumbled. "I'm still going to be me."

"I don't think you're so bad."

Surprise had January's eyebrows making a run for her hairline. "Since when? You've always hated me."

"That's not true." Jake looked as shocked by the admission as January felt. He barreled forward anyway. "You frustrated me in school. We were always getting paired together on projects because of our names. The teachers showed no originality when assigning partners. I got you fifty percent of the time, and you were way smarter than me."

Now it was January's turn to reel in her emotions. "I'm not smarter than you, Jake. Or, well, I'm not smarter than you on *every* topic."

He chuckled, shaking his head. "School always came so easy for you. It was harder for me. When Jacob Jeffries is your father, you're expected to excel. I didn't excel, and it seemed from a young age that I was always disappointing my parents. Well, my dad more than my mom. Still, though.

"I wanted him to be proud of me, but he never was," he continued. "He would just say, 'I know you can do better than this, Jake. When I was in school, I got straight As. Why can't you do better?' It was too much."

"So you stopped trying," January mused as she handed him the bag of hash browns.

"It wasn't that I stopped trying," Jake countered. "I just refused to focus on the things he wanted me to do and instead tried to branch out on my own. I knew I would disappear in the shadow of the great Jacob Jeffries if I stayed here. I guess that's why I tried so hard to find a different tree to hang my hat on."

January considered the statement for several drawn-out breaths. "I get it," she said finally. "Living up to a parent's expectations has to be a lot of work. You can't give up as a result though. You have to keep trying. Otherwise, you really will fail, and that's worse than trying and not meeting your own lofty expectations."

Jake's mouth dropped open. "That could be the most profound thing you've ever said."

January let loose a hollow laugh. "I don't know whether to take that as a compliment or insult."

"It's a compliment. Trust me." Jake ignored the hash browns and kept his eyes on her. "We all have things we wish we could change about ourselves, January. I wish I wasn't so afraid of my father. I wish I could be a real man for a change. The fact that you wish you were less awkward seems like a small thing when you really think about it.

"Maybe you could start with small changes," he continued. "Like ... maybe you could spend an entire day not caring what others think about you. Even if you do care, pretend you don't."

January cracked a smile. "Fake it until I make it?"

"Something like that."

She exhaled heavily. "I'm just so afraid all the time." It was hard for her to admit.

Jake shifted. He looked as if he was going through some sort of ordeal. "What are you afraid of?"

"Losing everything I've worked so hard to achieve. I can't help feeling it's all going to be taken away one day."

"Why?"

January lifted one shoulder. "I don't know. It's not important."

"It clearly *is* important," Jake insisted. "Tell me."

January had no idea why he was pushing her so hard, but in the moment, she realized she was desperate to open up to someone. It had been a long time since she'd been able to unload the truth on anyone. Was he her first choice? No. Right now, however, he was her only option. They were snowed in together, and it made a ripe breeding ground for vulnerability.

"My mother was never all that together when I was growing up," she said in a low voice.

"I remember your mother." A small smile played at the corners of Jake's mouth. "She used to melt down when she was called to the office when we got in a fight. Like she would fly off the handle and yell at the principal that he was supposed to handle this stuff. It always made me laugh."

"Yes, well, it was never good for me." January didn't even try for a smile this time. "She worked two jobs, sometimes three, just to keep a roof over our heads. She blamed me for it. She said she would only have to work one job if she hadn't had me."

Jake stiffened next to her but didn't say anything.

"When she got called to the school to miss a shift, she was always so mad." January turned to look out the window, so she didn't have to see the pity on his face. "The thing is, even though I knew she would be angry and take it out on me later, I didn't stop fighting with you. Sometimes, those school meetings were the only time I saw her for weeks at a time."

Jake puffed out a ragged breath. "What? How can that be?"

"She always had boyfriends. She would stay with them when she wasn't working. Well, once I was eleven or so and could stay alone. Even when she was between boyfriends, she would remind me that she wouldn't have to pay for the trailer if it weren't for me. She just … hated me."

"January." Jake's voice sounded as if it were scraping across glass. "I'm so sorry. I didn't know any of that."

"Why would you? I worked overtime to keep it secret. It was hard enough to be the girl from *that* neighborhood. I wanted people to see me as something other than what I was."

"What you were was a focused individual who always tried really hard," Jake argued. "I was too young and spoiled to appreciate that, and … I'm sorry." He seemed as surprised as January when the words escaped his mouth.

"What are you sorry about?" January asked. "I was just as mean to you as you were to me."

"Yeah, but you were doing it to protect yourself, and I didn't see that. I never actually considered what you were dealing with in your life, and that's on me."

January waved him off. "We were kids. You're supposed to be stupid when you're a kid."

"That doesn't erase the pain I caused you." Jake edged closer. "Where is your mother now?"

"Why? Are you going to track her down and yell at her? If so, don't waste your breath. She wasn't a terrible mother. I survived. And now, she doesn't remember any of it."

"Meaning what?"

"She's in Radcliffe Downs over in Traverse City," January replied. "I know I said I hadn't seen her in two years, but that was sort of a lie. She's there. She's just not herself and hasn't been in a long time."

"I'm not familiar with Radcliffe Downs. Is that a rehab?"

"It's a long-term care facility. She has dementia."

"Oh. I'm sorry." His tone made January wonder if he meant it.

"She'll be there until she dies. She doesn't remember me

most days when I visit. That's actually a godsend. She's nice when she doesn't remember me. She just thinks I'm some random woman who stops in to visit her occasionally."

"I'm so sorry." Jake slid his arm around her back. "I'm just so sorry. I have no idea what to say to you right now."

"You don't have to say anything." January swiped at the tears that she hadn't even realized were falling. "I just need you to understand that I'm rigid about this job for a reason. I can't afford to lose it. My mother worked three jobs for me. I need to make sure she stays in a good home. If I lose my job, she'll lose her place at Radcliffe."

"I won't do anything to cause you to lose your job, January," Jake promised. "I swear. It's not just about you either. It's about me. I think I'm ready to start being an adult."

"Well, then maybe we can help each other." January forced a bright smile that didn't touch her eyes. "I'm great at being an adult. I have zero charm to spare though. You have tons of charm and need to learn to be an adult. If we're going to be fake married for a few weeks, maybe we can help each other, so it's not a total loss."

"I can get behind that." Jake flashed an impish grin, and it looked genuine. "I'm great at making everybody but my father love me. I have a gift."

January chuckled. "And I'm great at making your father love me, so maybe we really can help each other out."

"That sounds fun." To both of their surprise, Jake tightened his grip until he was hugging her.

Her initial reaction was to pull back, but he refused to let her escape.

"Give in to the moment," Jake ordered. "You need a hug, and I might actually melt down if I can't offer you some form of solace."

"Is that the charmer in you?"

"I think it might be."

"Huh." Because she was helpless to escape the moment, January rested her cheek against his chest. "This isn't so bad."

"No, it's not bad at all," he agreed as he ran his hand down the back of her head. "It's going to be okay, January. We'll figure it out. Together. I won't cost you your job, and you won't make me look like even more of a dumbass in front of my father. It's a win for us both."

"Maybe this will work."

"It will. I'll make sure of it."

TWELVE

J ake's expression was dark when January told him his assignment the next morning.

"And here I thought things were going so well between us," he groused as he slipped the wedding ring onto his finger. He was starting to get used to it, although he wouldn't admit that out loud.

"I'm sorry, but we both have to do things we don't want to do today," January replied primly.

"Yeah, but Maxwell's daughter?" Jake made a face. "You know she's going to be weird."

"I don't *know* that," January countered. "She could be perfectly nice."

"She probably will be nice. That doesn't mean she won't also be weird." Frustration was a gurgle in Jake's stomach as he debated if he had enough time to grab breakfast at the main resort before meeting up with his partner for the day. "I don't want to answer invasive questions."

January fixed him with a stern look, reminding him of high school. While that memory would've been a bitter pill to swallow weeks before, for some reason—and he was certain it had something to do with their conversations from the day before—Jake felt nostalgic about it now.

"What?" he asked defensively, holding out his hands.

"Just stick to the story," she admonished. "We're almost to the main event. It's basically two more weeks of this, and then you can be done with me."

Jake had no idea why the statement bothered him so much. "Do you plan on quitting or something?"

She looked taken aback by the question. "Of course not."

"Well, I'll be here at the resort for the foreseeable future, so I very much doubt we're not going to see each other."

"I just meant we wouldn't be living together. Or pretending to be married."

"Oh." Jake touched his thumb to the wedding ring. "Yeah. Well, let's not focus on that." He forced a bright smile. "We can get through this."

"I know we can get through this. I wasn't the one complaining about today's assignment, if you remember correctly."

He scowled at her. "I'll have the daughter eating out of my hand in twenty minutes flat." Something occurred to him. "What are you doing today?"

January's lips curved down. "Maxwell's son."

Jake waited for her to expand. When she didn't, he made a "come on" motion with his hand. "What are you doing with the son?"

"He wants a rundown of all the plans, so I think I'm going to be stuck with him for the duration of the day."

"Do you know which son?"

"Edward." January's expression got darker.

"Have you met him before?"

"Yeah. He's a little obnoxious."

"Meaning what?"

"I don't know. He just makes me uncomfortable. I can't explain it."

Jake wanted to explore her feelings on the subject more—and what a foreign feeling that was—but he knew they didn't have time. "You can use me for an excuse if you want to get away for lunch," he offered out of nowhere. "We can say we want to spend time together as husband and wife if we need a break."

January laughed. "Would that be a break for you? I thought you hated spending time with me."

Jake didn't like her assumption. "Let's just say there are worse things than having lunch with you, huh? I think we're about to experience one of them."

"Normally, I would say it will be fine. I'm not so sure though. The entire family is weird. I mean, I get faith and worship. I understand it and think it's a lovely ambition. This is a step beyond though. It almost feels like..." She trailed off.

"A cult," he finished.

"You said it, not me."

He smirked. "This feels like forced religion. Like the kids have no choice but to live their lives a certain way. I get it, and I'm right there with you."

January couldn't help being relieved. "Well, I'm sure it will be fine. If you need an escape, though, text me for lunch, and I'll escape with you."

He smiled as he watched her head toward the door, a strange floaty feeling momentarily flooding his heart. "I just might do that."

EDWARD MAXWELL WAS IN WHAT JANUARY HAD taken to calling the War Room. She'd lined dry-erase boards across one side of a huge conference room, and each task that would be necessary to carry out the Winter Extreme

Games without a hiccup was outlined on at least one of the boards. It was easier for her to tackle each task when it was separate from the others.

Some people called her anal retentive because of her attention to detail. It was simply easier for her to operate when she could focus on one thing at a time.

"Edward." She extended her hand to shake his while approaching. "It's good to see you again."

Edward let loose a gregarious laugh when he saw her and bypassed her business-like approach so he could hug her. "Oh, come on! We're much friendlier than that." He pulled her in for a bear hug—something she was not comfortable with— and pressed her against him so tightly she suddenly felt claustrophobic.

"There it is," he said when she tried not to stiffen. "We're family." He beamed at her as he pulled away.

January had news for him. He was barely an acquaintance. She certainly didn't look at him like he was family. Despite that, she didn't frown. This had to go smoothly. "Were you at the party the other night? I can't remember seeing you there." She wanted to keep the conversation friendly.

"I was there," Edward confirmed. "I wanted to talk to you, but you were with some guy I didn't recognize. I asked my father, and he said that it was your husband."

January swallowed hard. Edward's tone wasn't outright accusatory, but there was an edge to it she couldn't quite identify. "I forgot you guys haven't met yet. I'll have to fix that."

"I didn't realize you were married," Edward insisted. "We started these meetings more than a year ago, and you never mentioned it. I brought up my wife, but you never mentioned your husband."

"Oh, well, I wasn't married a year ago." She and Jake were pretending they were newlyweds to cover themselves if anybody who had known them when they were younger expressed surprise and blurted out the wrong thing in front of one of the Maxwells.

"Yeah, but you must have been engaged."

"Oh, not really." January kept her smile in place, but it took work. She didn't like lying, even to someone who made her uncomfortable.

"I'm confused."

He wasn't the only one. After spending thirty-six straight hours with Jake and waking up with him wrapped around her, "confused" was an emotion she knew a little too well. The deep conversations they'd shared the previous day—and *all* day because there was no escaping one another—were not something she'd expected. They'd ended the day somehow closer, and it was entirely unexpected.

"We knew each other in high school," she replied easily. They'd formulated their story to stick as close to the truth as possible to what had really happened so they wouldn't accidentally slip up. "Actually, we've known each other our entire lives. We always used to fight when we were younger though."

"Oh." Edward winked and bobbed his head knowingly. "You guys fought because you were really attracted to one another. I get it."

January didn't want to agree—the statement was starting to hit a little too close to home—but she had no choice. "Well, we were six when we started fighting. I don't know if I would go that far."

"Maybe your six-year-old selves realized you were destined to be together forever and freaked out."

"Maybe." January smiled because it was expected of her. "Anyway, we've known each other our entire lives. Jake is Jacob's son, so he's constantly stopping in at the resort when not traveling. He tends to hang out in the ski area rather than the lobby area, so we didn't see each other often. On one of those trips, by accident, we ran into each other. We started laughing about the way we acted around one another when we were younger. One thing led to another, and now we're married."

"That sounds about right." Edward laughed as he bobbed his head. He didn't appear to doubt the story in the least. "I can totally see that happening. They say there's a thin line between love and hate. If you care enough to hate someone, that usually means something else is there."

Is that true? January was bothered by the comment. Still, she was a professional. She matched his smile. "I'm sorry I missed you at the party the other night. Jake had never been to one of those parties—he just got back into town from another trip a few days ago—and we were catching up on our weeks apart."

"I get it. Being in the same space with one another is different than constant phone and Zoom calls." Edward let out a sigh. "I'll admit it's a little disappointing. I thought you were single."

January was confused. "Why is it disappointing?"

"Because I thought you were single, and perhaps open to hanging out. When my father told me you were married, I was shocked. I had a big plan to … spend time with you when I could get away from my wife." He shot her a rueful look. "I guess that's not happening now. It's a total bummer."

January had news for him. That was never going to happen regardless. He wasn't her type, even if he wasn't already married—did she even have a type?—and she would never risk dating a sponsor. Still, Jake was a buffer, and she was happy to use him. "Well, I'm sure you'll find someone else to woo," she said with a forced laugh.

"Yeah, but I had my heart set on you." Edward held her gaze for another beat, and then he sighed. "So, show me what we've got going on. My father wants me to be the liaison between you and him when things are active. It's going to be a lot of action every day, and it's going to have a lot of moving parts."

"Absolutely." January was happy to talk about work things with him and led him to the first dry-erase board. "This is the food situation. The resort restaurant is going to be the fanciest offering, for obvious reasons. We'll have options for those eating on a budget though.

"For starters, we've completely emptied the retail side of the pro shop and stored everything there," she continued. "We've expanded the restaurant side with more tables. The food available there—because the kitchen is much smaller—will consist of things like burgers, quesadillas, etc. There's a full bar over there too."

"My father doesn't like a full bar."

January swallowed. She'd forgotten that tidbit. "We won't have happy guests if they can't get a cocktail."

"Oh, I didn't say I didn't like a full bar." Edward winked at her in disconcerting fashion as his hand landed on her back and immediately started sliding lower. "Just watch what you say in front of my father. He gets weird about cocktails."

January was frozen in her spot. Edward's hand was very obviously slipping ... right toward her ass. "Um..." She wasn't the type to panic, but she was suddenly very close to doing just that.

"There are other places to eat too, right?" Edward prod-ded. He didn't seem to have a care in the world.

The second his hand hit pay dirt and cupped her rear end, January took an exaggerated step to her left to escape his touch. "We will also have the area that's reserved for skiers set up for various food options," she confirmed, keeping a firm eye on his hand in case it decided to start wandering again. "I can show you the location. They're in the process of setting it up right now."

"I would love to see the location." If Edward was bothered

by what he'd done—or January's reaction—he didn't show it. He acted as if he didn't have a care in the world. "I would absolutely love to see everything you have to offer."

January had no doubt that was true. "Yes, well, let's start with the food."

JAKE MET ZOE MAXWELL NEXT TO THE INDOOR pool on the far end of the summit resort. He had no idea why she'd insisted on meeting him there, but she seemed gleeful as she studied the space. They'd shut down the indoor pool for several days so they could rearrange the chairs and give the area a spruce. They were almost done, which meant the pool would be ready and available when the first Winter Extreme Games guests arrived.

"I love the smell of chlorine," Zoe enthused as she grinned at Jake and rubbed her hands together. If Jake had to guess, she was twenty-two at the most, and she seemed somehow different from the other Maxwells. Although he hadn't yet been able to put his finger on why.

"Oh yeah?" Jake was amused despite himself. "That's a specific kink." He realized what he'd said when it was too late to take it back and scrambled to do damage control. "Not in a weird way or anything." He cringed when Zoe slid her green eyes to him. It was impossible to read her expression.

When the young woman burst out laughing, some of the tightening pressure in his chest dissipated.

"I'm sorry," Jake offered automatically. "I wasn't thinking when I said that. It wasn't very professional."

"It's okay." Zoe waved off the apology. "Trust me. I get it. My father has a specific reputation. It causes people to walk on eggshells around him—and us by extension—and I don't necessarily think it's fair."

Jake pursed his lips, considering. "I just don't want to say the wrong thing," he said finally. "The games are very important to the resort, to the town, and to my family specifically. I don't want to be the cause for strife."

"I'll let you in on a little secret." Zoe's grin was playful as she leaned closer to him. "My father might like to bluster a lot, but it's too late for him to pull out as a sponsor. If he did, the story would explode nationally, and it wouldn't reflect well on him. He avoids that type of media coverage as much as possible. There's no way he can pull out now."

The news was welcome to Jake, although he didn't show it. "Still, I know he's particular about certain things."

"You mean the sex stuff? Yeah. You need to be careful about it in front of him. He's wound a little tight." Zoe giggled and then shook her head. "It's fine. I don't happen to be as uptight as him."

Jake couldn't help being relieved. "Was it hard growing up in your family? There's a lot of conjecture about how religious your father is, so I figured it was probably difficult."

"Oh, it's not religion." Zoe shook her head. "I wish it was. I love when we go to church as a family. I love singing. I love the pomp and circumstance of it all. I am a true believer. My father takes it a step too far, though, each and every time."

Jake suddenly felt sorry for the young woman. She looked so wistful. "You're expected to get married, right?"

"Yup, and only a member of the church will do." Zoe's smile disappeared. "I only have a few more years to do it too. You're basically put out to pasture in our family if you don't get married by the quarter-century mark."

Jake was horrified. "Seriously?"

"Yeah. It's sad too."

"You could break from your family." Jake felt guilty even suggesting it, but the young woman made him feel bad. He wanted to protect her for some reason. She ... well, she reminded him of January, although he was having trouble admitting that, even to himself.

"Oh, I can't do that." Zoe vehemently shook her head. "I'll have nothing if I do. I'll be out in the real world, alone, with no education. I don't have a choice but to do what he wants."

"You always have a choice," Jake insisted. "You can be whatever you want to be."

"I'm not so sure." Zoe gnawed on her bottom lip. "I've always been told what I'm going to be. I was never given a choice."

"That didn't stop you from dreaming though, did it?"

"No. I dreamed a lot when I was a kid." Zoe let loose a little giggle. "I wanted to chuck the whole thing and join the circus. I saw a television show I wasn't supposed to see. It was on HBO, which I wasn't supposed to be watching because of all the sex. Of course, that just meant I snuck on to watch it whenever my parents were out of the house. I couldn't help myself."

"And you watched a circus show?" Jake was baffled.

"Yes. If I remember correctly, it wasn't even a current show. It was older and set back in time. That's not the important part." Her eyes sparkled when they landed on Jake. "I liked that you could be whoever you wanted. You could love whoever you wanted. You could travel and not be beholden to other people."

"You liked the idea of the freedom," Jake mused.

"Yeah. I don't think I'll ever be free." Zoe was quiet for several seconds. "You travel a lot, right? It's great, isn't it?"

For some reason, before he could answer in the affirmative, January's face popped into Jake's head. It had him reassessing his answer.

"Travel is great for a while," he confirmed. "The thing is, eventually, the idea of home and having something stable is pretty appealing. Have you considered talking to your father? Maybe he'll let you travel for a year, and then you can think about marriage when you've gotten all the wanderlust out of your system."

"Oh, that will never be an option." Zoe looked sad now. "It's great that you managed to do both though. Now you know what it is you really want, and you can embrace it."

Did he? Jake wasn't so certain any longer. He bobbed his head in agreement all the same. "It is great to have options. I'm sure you'll figure it out."

"Maybe, but I think I'm doomed to inherit my mother's life." She looked genuinely unhappy about it. "It is what it is."

Thirteen

"They're weird." January kept her voice low as she sat across from Jake in the resort restaurant. Neither of them thought they would use their get out of jail free card for lunch as they'd discussed, but when Jake texted to feel her out, she'd jumped at that chance.

"They're very weird," Jake agreed, leaning back in his chair. "I felt kind of bad for the one I was with though."

"How come?" January had opted for vegetable soup and a grilled cheese sandwich, which looked like a paltry haul compared to his shrimp linguini.

"She was sad but didn't want to admit she was sad. Her father has her on a tight leash. She's not allowed to do anything she wants to do."

"What does she want to do?" January was honestly curious.

"Join the circus."

"Excuse me?" January leaned closer. "Are you messing with me?"

Jake's lips quirked. "That's what she said. As a kid, she

dreamed about joining the circus. She also seems to have a yen for travel because she asked me a lot of questions about the places I'd been."

"Huh." January's forehead furrowed. "That makes me sad, although I get wanting to travel. I've dreamed about traveling for as long as I can remember."

"How come you didn't do it?"

"Um ... money."

Jake frowned, his cheeks flushing a curious shade of red. "I'm sorry. I didn't even think about that."

"It's fine." January lifted one shoulder. "Maybe one day after ... well, after."

"You mean after your mother passes away."

January felt as if she were under a microscope, but for some reason—her trust in Jake was starting to grow, and it wasn't something she could explain—she opted to tell the truth. "I don't want her to die. You shouldn't think that."

"Of course you don't," Jake said easily. He planted his feet on either side of hers under the table, something that instantly comforted January, even as she desperately tried to push aside the warmth crawling through her chest. "I don't think you want her dead. I get it."

"It's just a lot." January glanced at the clock on the wall. "In fact, I'm due to head over to see her this afternoon."

"You don't look like you want to do that."

"Oh, I don't." January was rueful. "I have a schedule though."

Jake shocked her when he started laughing, his voice carrying several tables over to where his father and Jim Maxwell were eating lunch together. January's cheeks felt as if they were on fire when she darted a look in their direction, but to her surprise, she found Jacob smiling as he watched them.

"Why is that funny?" she asked when she turned back to Jake.

"Because your schedule was legendary in high school. People made fun of it—that you had a study schedule—but secretly people were jealous because they couldn't do the things you could do. There's a reason you graduated at the top of our class."

"Yes, because if I didn't, I wouldn't have gotten any scholarships, and college wouldn't have been an option."

Jake's smile disappeared in an instant. "I never thought of that either." He looked genuinely contrite. "Your life was a lot harder than I ever imagined back then."

"Everybody has problems," January pointed out. "Just because you had money, that doesn't mean your life was perfect."

"No, but I'm starting to see that I had everything I needed to succeed at life given to me on a silver platter, and I still failed. You, on the other hand, had to work for everything, and you succeeded despite the fact that nothing was given to you."

January didn't know what to say, so she focused on her soup.

"It's pretty impressive, January," he said in a soft voice. "I mean, look at our lunches. It never even occurred to me not to get the expensive entree."

"It looks good," January said quickly. "There's no reason you shouldn't get it. Your meals here are comped."

Jake jolted. "Are you telling me you have to pay for your food here?"

"I get a discount."

His eyes narrowed, and he darted a look toward his father, who was deep in conversation with Jim and paying no heed to them. "Well, as my wife, I believe that entitles you to comped meals too," he said finally.

"It's not a real marriage," she reminded him. "The only people who think we're really married are the Maxwells, although that knowledge certainly didn't stop Edward from grabbing my ass." She frowned at the memory.

Jake, who had been in the middle of chewing a forkful of linguini, practically choked on his food. "What?" he sputtered after he'd managed to swallow.

"It was a quick thing," January assured him. "That happened three times." She looked disgusted with herself. "The first time I thought maybe it was a mistake. The other two times though..." She trailed off, looking uncertain.

"Did you say something to him?" Jake demanded.

January shook her head. "No. I don't want to be the cause of something bad happening to the marketing partnership. He's Jim's son."

"So what?"

"So who do you think your father is going to side with if I make a complaint and Edward denies it?"

"Um, you." Jake shook his head as if it wasn't even a question.

"Oh, right," January scoffed. "Be serious. If the Maxwells pull out of the sponsorship, then the games will fail. Your father will have to figure out a way to save them. The money will come out of his pocket. It will be a whole big scandal. It's so much easier just to quietly fire me and say I caused the problem."

Jake gripped his hands into fists on top of the table. "I won't let that happen to you." He was obviously furious.

"You can't stop it, Jake." January looked at him in such a way it reminded him of when he was five and his mother treated him like an adorable moppet. "Your father is trying to teach you a lesson. He's not going to listen to you. Although I do appreciate the offer. I just have to get through the next few weeks. It's not a big deal."

"It *is* a big deal," Jake insisted. "You shouldn't have to put up with some asshole putting his hands on you without invitation." He momentarily looked like a vengeful angel to January. "I'll handle it."

"No." January reached across the table and snagged his shirt sleeve, as if expecting him to hop to his feet and rush off. "Don't. It will reflect poorly on me."

Jake searched her face, as if seeking the answers to life's greatest mysteries, and then sighed. "Fine. I don't want to upset you. You won't have to be alone with him again. I'll make sure of it."

The promise made January grin. "I have to be alone with him later this afternoon. We're still not done going through all the white boards."

"Oh no." Jake was firm when he shook his head. "You're coming with me this afternoon."

"Where?" January was baffled. "You have work to do too."

"Yes, and my work consists of taking the runs over by the north ski lift. The instructors were supposed to do it, but they got tied up with a surprise class from Mancelona. Someone forgot to write it down, so they asked me to do the runs. You're coming with me."

"I am?" January looked both delighted and worried. "What about Edward?"

"I'll handle him." Jake's gaze darkened again. "I'll send Leo to deal with him."

January was taken aback. "The head of security? What's he going to do?"

"He's smart. He can follow your charts and maps. Trust me."

January was convinced Jake was holding something back. "It's not his job."

"No, but he can have a discussion with Edward about wandering hands without it being so pointed Maxwell Junior will freak out. Leo knows what he's doing in a situation like this. Trust me."

January hesitated. "It's my job though," she said finally.

"Oh, will you loosen up?" Jake looked pained. "I've got this, January. Just trust me. Please."

He looked so desperate for her to do just that, she couldn't deny him. "Okay," she said finally. "If I get in trouble, though, I'm totally blaming you."

"I would expect nothing less. It will be like high school all over again."

"Here's hoping you don't try to lock me in the band room for the weekend this go-around, though, huh? I don't fancy having nothing but clarinets to talk to."

Jake cringed. "I forgot about that."

"It's fine." She faked a sunny smile. "Mr. Childers had to come back to the class because he forgot his glasses, so I was only there alone until about eight o'clock that night."

Jake's face drained of color. "Did you have to tell me that? Now I feel like even more of a douche than I already did."

"It was nice," January insisted. "I took a nap. My mother didn't even notice I was late. It's good he came back because otherwise I would've gone the entire weekend without anybody realizing I was gone."

"Oh, geez." Jake abandoned his dinner and gripped her wrist. "Stop telling me these stories. They make me want to die."

"I don't want you to die." January was surprised to find she meant it. "I was fine. Look." She flashed a smile. "No harm done."

"Yeah, we're going skiing. You need an afternoon off. The least I can do is send Leo to handle the Edward problem. We can ski and be the first ones to take the Winter Extreme Games routes. It will be fun."

He looked so hopeful all January could do was nod. "Okay, but if I get in trouble, I'm going to be really mad."

"You won't get in trouble. I promise. It's going to be fun."

For the first time in—well, she couldn't remember how long—January wanted to embrace the fun. "We need to change and get our skis then. Let me finish my lunch. I don't want to waste food."

"You're such a Girl Scout," Jake teased.

"Yes, well, if you'd ever gone a weekend only having one can of Campbell's to survive on, you wouldn't waste food either."

Jake slapped his hand to his face and shuddered. "I need you to stop telling me horror stories from your childhood."

"It's not a horror story. It's just a story. I obviously survived."

"I really do want to die when you tell me these stories."

"You'll survive too." She beamed at him. "Give me five minutes, and then we can go over and get bundled up. I'm kind of looking forward to hitting the slopes."

Jake managed a soft smile. "You're not the only one, January. It will definitely be fun."

JAKE FOUND HE WAS IRRATIONALLY—or was it rationally?—angry at what January had told him. He wanted to track down Edward and touch him with his fists until he acknowledged that he understood touching January was not allowed. Instead, he forced himself to remain calm as they bundled up to head out.

The walk to the Raptor hill took them a good ten minutes in their boots. They chatted the whole time, and Jake found he couldn't stop looking her up and down in her black ski pants and slate blue jacket. She'd tugged a blue cap down on her dark hair, and it matched the color of her eyes.

"Let me go first," he said as he snagged tickets for their coats from the lift operator at the top of the hill. He grinned at her frown as he attached the metal hook through her zipper hole. "You think I'm being a misogynist, don't you?" It wasn't really a question. He could read the expression on her face and the emotions attached to it.

"I didn't say that," she said hurriedly. "It's just that I've been skiing since I was a kid. I can handle myself."

"I didn't say you couldn't. I just want to make sure the run is safe."

"You don't think I can handle myself?"

"Oh, I think you can handle yourself in almost every situation. I just don't want you to fall and injure yourself. We're going to be in a world of hurt if you break an arm or a leg. You're the one who is keeping this operation running."

He didn't miss the way her chest momentarily puffed out, pride rippling over her features. She was pretty—something he had seemingly noticed for the first time that night when they were in college—but she was wound so tight that she often didn't allow herself to relax. Today, she looked relaxed, and he wanted to keep it that way.

"I've never played hooky from work," she admitted as she gripped her ski poles. "I mean, never."

"You're the type who doesn't use your sick days when you're feeling well, aren't you?" Jake tried to keep the censure from his voice.

"I don't use my sick days when I'm sick," she admitted. "I work from home, so I don't put anybody else at risk."

He rolled his eyes. "You need to live a little."

"I know it's impossible to actually be the sort of person who is considered necessary for the day-to-day operations of this place, but that's what I want to be." Her lips were bright pink against her skin, and Jake found himself focusing on them.

"Nobody can be everything to an operation this big," he said finally. "You're pretty close to being impossible to replace though. Let that be enough."

"I just want to be successful."

"Oh, January, you are successful. I wish you could see it. The people who work here, they always go to you right away when something goes wrong. That's because they know you're the one who will fix it. You don't always have to be the *only* one though."

"It's nice being needed." She didn't meet his steady gaze, instead looking out on the slope. "I never was before your father hired me here."

It was like a gut punch, and Jake had to calm himself with two steadying breaths before he responded. "I don't think you have a very good view from your position on top of the heap, January. You were always needed, even if your mother didn't say it."

"Maybe." January flashed a smile. "I don't want to focus on that though. If I'm going to play hooky, I want to do it right."

"That is the most January thing that you've ever said." He let loose a laugh. "If you have fun, then you're doing it right. Relax."

She nodded. "That's the plan."

"Good." It was only when he slid back on his skis that he realized how close he'd gotten to her. If he'd leaned in there at the end, he could've kissed her. Why he wanted to do it was a mystery, but he managed to refrain. This wasn't a real marriage after all. If they could come out of this arrangement being friends, however, he would be happy with the outcome.

Either way, he knew he would never look at her the same way again. He'd gotten a glimpse inside the woman behind the hard shell, and he wanted to make things better for her. It was an emotion he wasn't familiar with, and he didn't want to dwell on it. "Let's get going."

Jake was the first to hit the hill. He looked over his shoulder long enough to make sure January was keeping up—

she might not have been fancy on her skis, but she was good—
and then he headed toward the moguls. He was deft when
schussing through them, and then he stopped midway down
the hill to watch her follow.

There was a grace about her he'd never noticed before.
He'd always loved the fluidity of skiing, and January had that
in spades. She might not have considered herself athletic—and
he cringed when he thought about her playing soccer or
volleyball—but she looked so happy when going through the
moguls, it stole his breath.

She's not for you, his inner voice warned.

I know that, he silently yelled back.

For a moment, though, he let himself wonder. Was it
possible that the irresponsible son and the most responsible
person in the world could be good for each other? Could he
help her lighten up enough to enjoy living life? And, more
importantly to him, could she teach him about being the
person his father so desperately wanted him to be?

January was laughing when she came to a hockey stop next
to him. "That was fun. The moguls are tight though. Are they
supposed to be that tight?"

Jake forced himself out of his reverie. He was thinking
things that were better left hidden in the darkest reaches of his
mind. Nothing he was imagining would work. It *couldn't*
work. They could be friends though. He could bolster her self-
esteem—and he desperately wanted to do that.

"These are for professionals," he reminded her. "The runs
are supposed to be more difficult because they're for a higher
caliber of athlete than us."

"True." Her grin was so wide it lightened up her entire
face, and Jake found he was focused on those pink lips of hers
again. "Is it just me, or is it more fun to ski when you're
supposed to be doing something else?"

"Oh, it's not just you." Jake winked at her, determined to

keep things playful. "Just let loose and enjoy it, January. Leo is right now handling your problem with Edward. Don't think about work. Think about fun."

"I'll do my best."

"That's all I ask."

Fourteen

"Let's go!"

Jake stood outside January's bedroom and incessantly knocked because he knew it would annoy her. For once, however, he was hoping it would annoy her in a good way. Since their afternoon of playing hooky together, they'd somehow managed to reach a new relationship height. They could mess with each other, and nobody freaked out or exacted bloody revenge. It felt like some sort of miracle.

January's eyes were on fire when she threw open the door. Her dark hair was polished and in place, but she had a towel clutched to her front, and her bare shoulders told Jake she wasn't completely dressed yet.

"Um..." His heart skipped about seven beats in a row.

"What are you doing?" she hissed.

"We have a meeting with my father," he reminded her, willing himself not to look below the towel line. If he did, he knew he would regret it. Seeing her bare legs might be too much. And wasn't that a sobering thought? When did this happen?

"It's not until nine thirty." Her irritation was palpable.

"Yeah, and that's in fifteen minutes." Jake shifted from one foot to the other and darted a look toward her legs. His breath came out in a whoosh when he saw that she was wearing pants. What a relief that was. Why, though? He couldn't figure it out.

"Fifteen minutes?" January looked over her shoulder at the clock on the nightstand. That allowed Jake to get a look at her bedroom—a place he was steadfastly trying to avoid—and he swallowed hard when he saw the frilly bra lying across the bottom of the bed.

Of course she would have something frilly. That was so January. Then his gaze drifted to her bare back. Her skin was smooth and creamy, and there was a trio of small moles near the small of her back that he was suddenly interested in licking.

What is wrong with me? The only response Jake could come up with was that forced proximity was making his brain go on the fritz. He wasn't allowed to look at another woman as long as the Maxwells were prowling the grounds in the run-up to the games. He knew that and would never risk ruining anything for his father. And January. He was desperate to protect her too. That was the only explanation he could come up with.

"Crap." January's face drained of color. "I didn't realize it was so late. Give me two minutes." She held up two fingers when turning back. "I'm so sorry."

"It's okay." Jake's response came out in a croak. "It's perfectly okay. Don't worry about it. Not even a little. Um, yeah, I'll be in the living room."

January's eyebrows moved together. "What's wrong with you?" She didn't look especially concerned as much as suspicious.

"Nothing," Jake replied way too fast. He forced himself to

keep his eyes on her face and not her dipping towel. "I'm fine. Why wouldn't you think I'm fine?"

"I have no idea," January replied. "Maybe it's because you're acting like an idiot. We don't have time for that either. Two minutes, and we're out the door. Time me."

Jake remained rooted to his spot when January shut the door in his face. The instant there was a barrier between them, he let out the breath he was holding and braced his arms on the doorframe.

He was having some sort of meltdown. Maybe it was a stroke. It had to be that. There was no other explanation. He certainly wasn't interested in January. They'd had one drunken night together a million years ago. It had been good —*really good*—but that didn't mean it could be repeated. They had been kids when it happened, barely adults. Now they were older and getting involved would be a mistake for both of them.

You would ruin her. His inner voice was brutal today. He didn't disagree with it. If he got involved with January—for a fling, nothing more—then people would judge her. They would assume she'd hooked up with him simply because his father owned the resort. They would call her a gold digger and a slut and maybe a few other choice words. She didn't deserve that.

Are you listening to me? he silently demanded of his penis. *You are not to think of her that way. Not even for a second. Just ... no.*

To his surprise, his penis answered. *You know we would have fun.*

Jake did know that. *What did I say?*

She would have fun too. Maybe that's what she needs to lighten up.

Jake knew better than to listen to his penis, but he

couldn't stop himself from entertaining the possibility. *A fling might be fun.*

Totally, his penis enthused. *She would relax. She'll have a heart attack before she hits forty if she doesn't take a breath. You'd really be saving her life. Don't you want to save her life?*

Jake was still considering it when January's door popped open.

"What are you doing?" she demanded. "Do you think mentally screaming at me from the other side of the door is going to make me move faster?"

Jake was relieved she believed he was trying to be annoying rather than the other option. If she let herself think about the second possibility, she would castrate him in his sleep. And that was if she was in a good mood. Things could go worse if she was in a bad mood. "Hurry," he said on a dry mouth. "I've been good all week. I don't want to be late for a meeting with my father."

It wasn't frustration in January's eyes when she patted his arm. It was understanding and, well, solidarity. "I've got it. You can hold my arm, so I don't slip when we run across the parking lot. We won't be late. I promise."

Jake held out his hand after she'd shrugged into her coat. He was too hot to bother with his own. "Let's go."

"Don't you want your coat?" she asked, clearly confused.

"Nope. I don't need it today."

"It's fifteen degrees out."

"It's fine. The cold will toughen me up."

January didn't look convinced, but she nodded all the same. "Okay. You're the boss." She paused after saying it. "Wait, I'm the boss. Don't be getting ideas."

His penis whispered again. *We should let her boss us around in bed.*

Jake was at his limit. "Let's go." He gripped January's

hand so hard he worried he might snap her fingers off. "We can't keep my dad waiting."

JACOB WAS ON THE PHONE WHEN THEY entered his office, which allowed them enough time to get coffee. Jake could feel his father's eyes on his back as he poured two mugs and handed one to January. Then, when he handed January the only chocolate cake doughnut in the box, Jacob's eyebrows migrated toward his hairline.

"What?" Jake asked his dad when the elder Jeffries had hung up the phone.

"Nothing," Jacob replied, although there was a small smile playing at the corners of his lips. "I don't expect this meeting to go long. I just want to touch base with you two. The opening ceremony is in two nights. I want to make sure everything is set."

"It is," January assured him as she whipped out the binder she'd taken to carrying everywhere with her.

That's not hot, Jake silently admonished his penis in his head. *That's not remotely hot.*

Speak for yourself, his penis barked back. *That is totally hot. All she's missing is that pencil she sticks in her bun when she pulls her hair back.*

Ugh. Jake wanted to strangle someone. Maybe his penis. Why was he thinking about that stupid pencil now? It was prissy. He didn't like prissy.

You do like how responsible she is, his penis replied. *More, you like how responsible she's making you. It's more fun than you thought.*

Oh, well, that was a sobering thought. Jake rubbed his forehead, earning a curious look from his father. That had him straightening. January was running through her report. She'd worked hard on it. He couldn't disrespect her by not listening.

Okay, that's less hot, his penis said. *Maybe she's turned into the hot one, and you're now the weak link in this relationship.*

Was that possible? Was January suddenly hot and Jake was not? How was he supposed to react to that? More importantly, what if he was making a mistake. What if he wasn't attracted to her because they were living on top of one another? What if it was something more?

Suddenly, he felt sick to his stomach. What was happening to him?

"HOW ABOUT LUNCH?" Jake asked January when they were finished with the meeting. He couldn't say she wasn't thorough because the meeting had gone on for two hours, and she hadn't stopped talking for the entire duration.

"Sure." Her smile was easy, as though she'd gotten a super-power charge from going through her ridiculous list. "That sounds good."

"I need Jake to stay for a few minutes," Jacob interjected before they could leave. "I won't keep him long. It's a family discussion."

"Of course." January bobbed her head. "I'll grab a table and wait for you."

"Thanks." Jake watched her go, his heart pittering and pattering all over the place. Thankfully, his penis had stopped talking. That was something at least.

"What's going on with you and January?" Jacob asked when the door fell shut, locking father and son inside the huge glass office alone.

"What do you mean?" Jake's brow was furrowed when he turned back to his father. "I'm being nice."

"I noticed." Jacob folded his arms across his chest and regarded his son with the sort of speculation that made Jake's ass sweat. "Are you two ... together?"

Jake had no idea where the question had come from, but he didn't like it one little bit. "Well, I guess that depends on who you ask. I mean, we are supposed to be married. I've had to lie to people I've known since kindergarten about the nature of our relationship since I got back home."

"I don't care about that." Jacob waved his hand as if swatting at a pesky fly. "The majority of the kids you went to school with are idiots."

Jake couldn't really argue. Sure, he still had some close friends in the area. He wasn't sorry about falling out of touch with the bulk of the people he'd graduated with though.

"I want to know what you think the status of your relationship with January is," Jacob pressed.

"We don't have a relationship," Jake replied automatically. Just saying it had his stomach constricting. "I mean, we're getting along. That's what you wanted, right?"

"It is." Jacob's expression was impossible to ascertain, even for the son who thought he knew every expression in his father's arsenal. "You seem calmer than you were when you came back to town."

"Well, to be fair, I wasn't certain I was going to make it back to town that day," Jake reminded him. "It felt somehow miraculous to be back home."

"No, that's not it." Jacob shook his head. "I've heard stories."

Jake swallowed hard but kept his shoulders squared. "What sort of stories?" Hopefully, his penis hadn't learned how to use a phone without his knowledge. That would be bad.

"Leo, for one," Jacob replied, apparently oblivious to his son's inner monologue.

"Leo?" Jake was confused. "I've been good. I haven't seen Leo since the day of the blizzard." That wasn't true, he realized after he'd said it. He'd tracked down Leo to admonish Edward.

His father wouldn't know about that, however. Leo would make sure of it.

"I didn't say you were acting up, Jake," Jacob argued. "I just said I'd heard stories. That doesn't necessarily mean they're bad."

"No offense, but our entire relationship history would indicate otherwise."

For some reason, that made Jacob grin. "I guess that's fair. What I'm saying is that Leo told me January took off on a pair of skis to make sure everybody was off the mountain that day."

"She did. She's a moron."

Jacob continued as if his son hadn't spoken. "He said that the storm was getting bad, and January wasn't back yet. There was mention that you went after her."

Jake wasn't certain how he should respond. What was his father looking for here? He opted to tell the truth. "I was worried about her. I've never skied with her before. I had no idea if she was competent or not. That was a big storm."

"Uh-huh." Jacob didn't look convinced. "Jerry over at the ski shop said you asked about ordering a pair of specialty skis."

"So? I didn't order anything. I asked. I'm not spending your precious money."

Jacob's lips twisted into a scowl. "He said you were looking at pink skis. Some special brand that's made for women, and you mentioned that January had been looking at them in a catalog. That she had them circled, and you were curious."

Jake scowled. "Jerry has a big mouth."

Jacob barreled forward. "Cathy in the dining room said that you checked in with her to make sure that all January's meals were being comped, went so far as to say you would cover them if there was some sort of problem you weren't aware of."

"Cathy has a big mouth too," Jake snapped. "As for the meals, everything should be comped for her here. Do you have any idea how hard she works?"

"Of course. That's why she's my assistant. I wouldn't have her as my assistant if I didn't know she was a hard worker. As for the meals, yes, they should all be comped."

"Well, that's not what was happening. She was covering her own meals, and that's crap."

"Uh-huh." Jacob's gaze was shrewd as he looked his son up and down. "It's okay if you have feelings for her."

Jake's mouth popped open. "Why would you say that?"

"Because I've been watching you with her. You walk to work together every morning now. You walk home together every night. You're always laughing. You even take her for drinks at the bar before you leave most nights."

"She's high-strung. She needs a drink."

"All your work has come in absolutely perfect," Jacob continued. "On the rare occasions when it's not perfect, you come back and correct it. Your work is different. You're different."

"And you're blaming January for this?" Jake demanded.

"I'm not blaming January for anything. In this particular instance, however, I would applaud if I thought it was all her."

"If you have something you want to say, say it," Jake pressed. "This conversation is going in circles, and I don't know what you want."

"I don't want anything," Jacob countered. "I was simply asking a question."

"And what question is that?"

"Do you have feelings for January?"

Jake's response was a knee-jerk reaction. "Of course not."

Jacob stared hard and then lifted one shoulder in a shrug. "Okay, then. Just know, if you are getting something off the ground with January, it wouldn't be the worst thing in the world."

"Well, that's not what's happening." Even as he said it, Jake recognized he was lying. He had no idea what he was feeling for January, but it was definitely something, and it might be the sort of something that couldn't be ignored.

"Okay." Jacob managed a smile, although there was a glint of mischief in his eyes. "Just know, if something is going on, you should tell me before your mother hears about it. She's not going to be nearly as open to the possibility as I am. She's ready for grandchildren, but your history with January will give her pause."

"And why is that?" Jake demanded.

"Because she still remembers the time when you were thirteen and January convinced you that rubbing a jalapeño pepper on your penis would make it grow."

Jake cringed at mention of the incident. "Yeah, that hurt." He wasn't nearly as bothered by the memory as he would've been two weeks before. "That was pretty funny. How stupid was I?"

Jacob's eyebrows hopped. "It wasn't your brightest move."

"Mom needs to get over it," Jake insisted. "January and I did horrible things to each other. Some of the things I did to her were so terrible, I'm lucky I'm not in jail."

"I would rather not hear about those things," Jacob said. "Your mother likes January now. As a worker at least. She's not going to like her as a potential girlfriend for you. That means you need to be careful."

"Well, there's nothing going on between January and me, so there's nothing to be careful about."

"Fair enough." Jacob managed a smile. "That's all I wanted to talk to you about. You can head out to your lunch."

"Okay." Jake let out a breath when he turned and then paused when his hand was on the knob. Normally, he would've exited as quickly as possible. That didn't happen today. "January deserves a raise," he said out of the blue. When he turned back to his father, it was with determination in his eyes. "I know it's not my place to say that—and I have no idea what she makes—but it should be more."

"You sound pretty convinced of that."

"I am. She's the best worker you have here, and when I say that, I mean that she's better than you."

Rather than be insulted, Jacob chuckled.

"She's also taking care of her mother," Jake continued, sadness crawling over his features. "I don't get the feeling her mother was ever good to her, and now she's in a home because she has early onset dementia. January pours every cent she has into that home to keep her mother comfortable. A little financial peace of mind would go a long way here."

Jacob was taken aback. "I didn't realize her mother was in a home."

"She doesn't like to talk about it."

"But she talked about it with you."

"Yeah, well, we're sharing a roof. We can't always talk about the horrible things we've done to each other." Jake managed a sheepish smile. "Just consider it, okay? Pay her what she's worth."

"I'll consider it," Jacob promised. "Thanks for the tip."

"You're welcome." With that, Jake let out a breath. He felt lighter than he had in a long time when he left his father's office.

Seriously, what was going on with him?

FIFTEEN

"What are you doing?"

Jake found January in the living room with a book later that night. The blanket in her hand suggested she was getting ready to settle in front of the fireplace, and he was confused.

"I was going to read," January replied blankly. "I like doing it in front of the fireplace. Is that a problem?"

"Of course not. It's just that they're having a bonfire over by the summit village shops."

January blinked. "Who is?"

"The workers. The people we went to high school with. You know, the people our age."

"Oh, well." January pursed her lips and didn't respond further.

Jake folded his arms across his chest. "That's all you're going to say?"

"I don't see where there is much more to say," January admitted. "You should totally go. I know they would love to see you."

Jake cocked his head. "But you don't think they want to see you?"

"They don't like me."

"That's crap."

"They don't," January insisted. "I'm not fun. I get it. The workers don't find me fun because I'm the one who tells them what to do and has to correct them when they do something wrong. As for the people we went to high school with ... well ... they always took your side for a reason. They find me shrill. Actually, I think the term most often used was 'tight-assed.'" She managed a smile. "Isn't that what you used to call me?"

Jake's stomach did a somersault. "I shouldn't have called you that."

"It's okay. It's true. In the grand scheme of things, that's one of the nicer things you called me."

Exasperation had his insides coiling, but he snagged the blanket from her anyway. "You're coming with me. Opinions from high school don't count. If they did, the girls would still be throwing themselves at me because they heard I could do magical things with my tongue."

January snorted out a laugh and then sobered. "Wait. Is that not true? That's horrifying. I liked that story."

Jake didn't like the way her smile disappeared. "Oh, it's true." He was at his flirty best when he winked. "If you want a firsthand demonstration, that can be arranged." The words were out of his mouth before he thought better of them. He was instantly mortified when he realized what he'd said, however. "I mean, no." He shook his head. "I shouldn't have said that. It was a knee-jerk response. That was wrong."

"The tongue part or the me part?"

Jake's cheeks flooded with color. "Neither. I mean, they were both right, but I shouldn't have said it."

January tilted her head and waited.

"You know what? We're not going to focus on me putting

my foot in my mouth for a change. We're going to have fun."
He gave her arm a light tug. "Get dressed. Make sure you'll be
warm, but you won't need your ski pants or anything. I'll
wait.'"

January was flustered. "But what are we going to do if they
ask about us being married?"

Jake hadn't thought that far ahead, and he stilled. "Don't
worry about that either," he said finally. "If they ask, we'll tell
them it happened fast and to mind their own business. They
don't get to comment on our relationship."

January made an incredulous sound in her throat. "It's like
you don't even remember them."

Jake laughed. "Come on. Two nights from now is the
opening ceremony of the Winter Extreme Games. That
means, for the next two weeks, we're not going to have time to
breathe let alone have a beer with friends. You need a night to
unwind."

"I don't really do that. Unwind, I mean."

"There's a first time for everything." He pleaded, "Come
on, January, there's no reason you can't have fun for a
change."

"I don't really do that either."

"Well, you're doing it tonight. I want to go out, and you're
going with me."

"I don't remember agreeing to those rules."

"They're in the Fake Marriage Handbook. You have no
choice."

Finally, January conceded the argument. "Fine, but if I'm
uncomfortable, I'm coming back here to my book."

"You won't be uncomfortable."

"How can you be sure?"

"Just trust me."

"Fine. Give me ten minutes."

"I'll be waiting."

. . .

JANUARY WAS A NERVOUS WRECK AS THEY MADE their way across the parking lot. She was fidgety by nature, which was why she kept straightening the knit cap she'd pulled on to keep her ears warm. When she reached up to mess with it for what had to be the tenth time, Jake grabbed her gloved hand and kept it in his as they continued to cross.

"They've never liked me," January insisted. It was something that had bothered her greatly when she was younger— that was probably one of the reasons she chose to fight with Jake on a regular basis, she realized—but she was okay with it now. She was comfortable in her own skin. Well, mostly. She didn't need to wedge herself into groups that didn't want her.

"They're idiots then," Jake replied. His gaze was focused forward. "You're great. What's not to like?"

The statement threw her and made her heart rate ratchet up a notch. "You think I'm great?"

If he was bothered at being put on the spot, he didn't show it. "I believe that's what I said."

"Since when do you think I'm great? Because, if our history is any indication, that's a relatively new opinion."

"You can't hold the things I did to you when I was young and dumb against me." Jake sounded practical for a change. "Kids are stupid. They can't vote for a reason. Let's just say I've gained a new appreciation for what you do now that I've been working with you."

"You're the only one," she muttered. She could feel Jake's eyes on her profile and figured he was going to keep arguing with her—or, worse, say something that wasn't true to bolster her confidence—so she changed tactics. "When they ask why we got married in secret, what are we going to tell them? They're going to have questions."

"We'll just tell them we eloped because we didn't want to

wait," Jake replied. He still had hold of her hand. "It's really none of their business."

"That won't stop them from asking questions."

"It will be fine. Just stick close to me. I'll handle it."

January opened her mouth to tell him she was used to being the one to handle things at the resort, but then she shut it. She'd never been a follower. She would never be a follower. Letting Jake take the lead on this one thing felt like the right thing to do, however. In fact, when she made up her mind to do just that, her insides unclenched for the first time since, well, they'd played hooky for the afternoon and gone skiing. She'd been relaxed that day too. Before that, though, she couldn't remember the last time she hadn't been wound tight enough to shatter into a million pieces at a simple touch.

"There he is!" a male voice boomed into the darkness, shattering the reverie January had found herself in. "It's about time."

January's natural instinct was to shrink back when the huge group of people sitting around the bonfire pit looked in their direction. Jake was having none of it. He kept her hand firmly in his and pulled her forward.

"Hey, Kent," Jake said in that easygoing voice of his. "Long time no see."

"I was just about to say the same thing to you." Kent Maloney was well over six feet tall, and he still had the same broad shoulders he'd boasted in high school. As far as January could tell, he was still drinking the same beer he'd imbibed in high school as well because he had a can of Busch Light in his hand. "How have things been?" Kent's eyes drifted to January, speculation rampant, and then he smiled at Jake again. "Seems you've been holding out on us."

January braced herself for the onslaught of questions she knew would be coming.

Why did you marry her?

Did you get drunk and accidentally knock her up?
Is your father making you do this?

Jake surprised her when he took the bull by the horns and tackled the obvious questions head-on before they could start spilling out. "What? I've always had a crush on her. You know that. Why are you so surprised that we ended up together? Or, wait, are you jealous because you're still at the point where your hand is your only regular date on Friday nights?"

A ripple went up through the crowd.

Pansy Lincoln was the next person to speak. "What do you mean you've always had a crush on her? You guys hated each other in high school."

"Well, you know that saying about there being a fine line between love and hate?" Jake's eyes twinkled. "I know it's wrong to teach girls that boys punch them and snap their bra straps to show affection at a young age, but in my case it was true. I didn't know how to express what I was feeling, so I acted out. January has been nice enough to forgive me."

It took everything January had to refrain from registering shock. *He's so good at this*, she realized. People loved him. He didn't care what they thought, so they didn't beat him down with their opinions because it didn't affect him.

I wish I could be like that.

"Are you guys really married?" Pansy looked shocked. "I thought it was a joke when someone told me."

"I don't know if they're really married, but they're sure as shit living together," Danny Graham volunteered from next to the fire. He had a Molson in his hand and looked amused at the entire thing. "I saw them out on their patio a few nights ago, and I swear if it had been a little warmer, I would've gotten a show because they were practically pressed together for the entire world to see."

"I heard he raced down the mountain on skis to save her the afternoon of the blizzard," Shelly Harrison offered.

"Someone said he turned into Rambo, he was so intent on saving her."

"Hey!" January stirred. "I didn't need saving that day. I had everything under control."

Jake chuckled as he released her hand and slung his arm around her shoulders. "Can we not talk about the race down the mountain? She's still irritated, and whenever I think of the walk we had to make up the slope in that snow, it's not good." He made a big show of shivering. "Thankfully, we had a fireplace to warm up in front of when we got back."

"That's it?" Chris Cooper asked when Jake didn't add to the story. "We're just supposed to accept that you guys always liked one another, and that's why you did the horrible things you did when we were kids?"

Jake shrugged. "You don't have to accept anything. I don't really care what you believe. I just know that it's cold, we want a place in front of the fire, and I want something to drink that isn't Busch Light." He gave Kent a dubious look. "Seriously, dude, we are not in high school any longer. Pick a better beer."

The crowd broke out into raucous laughter, and the anxiety January had felt building in her gut disappeared in an instant. When she looked at Jake, it was with awe.

"What?" Jake asked when he realized she was staring at him. "Too much?"

"People just really love you," she said on a sigh. "You can win over a room in five minutes flat. It's like a superpower."

"Yes, I'm like Superman, in a way," he agreed on a grin. "I can leap tall judgements in a single bound."

"You don't know how amazing that ability is. I would give anything to be able to talk to people that way."

"You *do* talk to people that way," Jake insisted. "Maybe not these people, but other people are in awe of you." He paused a beat. "I wish you could see yourself like I see you."

"And how is that?"

"You've done amazing things, January, and you've done them without a financial cushion to fall back on. I had everything given to me and did nothing with it. You're amazing."

"I don't feel amazing."

"Well, get over it because you're definitely amazing." Jake took her by surprise when he pressed a kiss to her temple. It was friendly, not romantic in the least, and yet her heart started making unfamiliar demands the second their skin touched.

"I need a drink," she croaked when she was reasonably sure she could speak without making a fool of herself.

"You read my mind." He squeezed her shoulder. "Find us two chairs, and I'll get us something to drink." He paused after he'd taken three steps and looked over his shoulder to offer her a wink. "Don't let anybody take my seat."

"I'll do my best."

"You always do."

JAKE THOUGHT HE WOULD HAVE TO FIELD MORE questions about his relationship with January, but his former classmates were surprisingly open to the shift in his personal life.

"I always knew," Kelly Seaholm said smugly as she sat in the chair to Jake's right. They'd been at the bonfire two hours at this point, and he was ready to call it a night and head home. Their shifts started earlier than normal the following day because they had to run through a lengthy checklist to make sure everything was ready for the opening ceremonies. They were a big deal.

"You always knew what?" Jake asked as he sipped his Molson. Even though he was talking to Kelly, his attention was on the other side of the fire, where January was talking with Kent. He had no idea what they were saying to each other, but his insides were tight enough that he recognized he wanted to pull her away and take her home before the conversation progressed much further. Kent had her laughing, and Jake found he wanted to be the one to make her laugh.

Was he jealous? He was rarely honest with himself, but he was starting to realize that there was more going on than a fake marriage and a history of hating one another. Perhaps their feelings for each other as children had been more complicated than either of them realized.

"I always knew you would end up with her," Kelly replied, not missing a beat. "I saw it back when we were in high school."

"Most people saw us being horrible to one another," Jake pointed out.

"Yes, but you don't spend that much time plotting horrible things for another person if you don't care," Kelly pointed out. "I mean, you guys came up with some elaborate scenarios. That means you spent hours upon hours thinking about the other person. If you don't care, you don't spend so much time going after them. There was definitely something there."

Jake smirked. "It turns out there was."

"Still, it was quick to get married," Kelly continued. She was buzzed enough that she hadn't stopped talking since she sat down next to him. "Aren't you worried that all you have is chemistry and that your lives won't ultimately mesh well together?"

Jake's eyebrows knit. "Why would you think that?"

"Because you're polar opposites despite the chemistry. I mean, all she cares about is doing a good job. She's so desperate for somebody to acknowledge her as more than trailer trash that she puts her whole heart and soul into this place and her daily tasks. You've never cared about the job."

"That's not true," Jake automatically protested, although

after several seconds, he had to acknowledge to himself that he understood why people believed that. "We're not so different," he added in a lower voice. "I was just too weak to admit that I wanted approval too back in the day. Now that I'm home, well, things are different."

"Whose approval do you want?" Kelly asked.

The easy answer was that he wanted his father's approval. He'd been thrilled when his dad acknowledged the work he'd been putting in during their meeting earlier. It wasn't just his father though. He wanted others to respect him as well, including January. "We're more alike than you realize," he said. "We complement each other well."

"I can see it." Kelly bobbed her head. "If you both have a goal you want to work toward together, I can totally see it."

"You can?" Jake couldn't help being skeptical. Nobody had seen it before now.

"Totally," Kelly said. "You make life fun for her and help get her out of her head. She makes you be responsible even when your head is in the clouds and you're feeling easily distracted. You're actually a really good match, as long as you both want the same thing."

The statement flooded Jake with feelings he didn't know he had. "I never thought about it that way," he admitted.

Kelly made an odd face. "You never thought about it and yet you got married?"

Jake covered quickly. "I just never thought others would see it," he clarified. "I believe it though. You're absolutely right. We can make things better for each other."

The question was, did they want to? This union was starting to feel real to Jake, and he had no idea what to make of it. The fear he would've been flooded with at the prospect two weeks before wasn't there.

Something was definitely happening to him. Was it a good or bad thing though?

Sixteen

"How do I look?"

January was fidgety when she emerged from her bedroom the night of the opening ceremonies. A huge party was overtaking the entire main area of the summit lodge, and she knew she had to look both professional and striking if she was going to garner—and keep—Jim Maxwell's attention going forward. The man was starting to give her a complex because he almost always went around her to get things done. Whether they were small or big things, he preferred going straight to Jacob. January was starting to think it was a man thing and was determined to garner his respect one way or another.

Jake, his hands on his tie as he straightened it, went rigid as he regarded her. She'd opted for a beautiful blue dress—it was almost silver—and the way he looked her up and down told January that she'd either picked a great dress or maybe a terrible one.

"It's bad, isn't it?" She always jumped to the worst conclusion. She couldn't help herself.

"Why do you always lean into the negative?" Jake asked after several seconds. "You're really hard on yourself."

"I don't know." January fussed with her skirt. It had several overlaying pieces in various lengths, and it was designed to flutter as she moved. "I just remember when I went to the winter formal senior year. That's always what pops into my mind. I can't quite forget it."

Jake slipped closer, smirking when her hands automatically came up to straighten his tie despite the fact that he'd already done it. "I don't remember you going to more than a handful of dances when we were in high school."

"That's because nobody ever asked me to dance."

He frowned. "I would've asked you."

January snorted. "No, you wouldn't have. You would've made fun of my dress. I couldn't afford to buy a new dress for every dance, so I had exactly one. That's why I took on a second job for a few months senior year. I wanted to save up for a nice dress. I found one at a dress shop, and it cost three hundred bucks, so I was saving for months."

Jake's frown grew more pronounced.

"Anyway, I paid for the dress and was so excited the night of the big dance." January was talking fast now. "I didn't have a date, but I thought it would be okay. I just wanted one good memory of a dance. You know, so I could hold on to it as an adult."

"I take it that didn't happen."

"No. I never made it to the dance. When I was leaving, my mother had a date over, and they saw me in the dress. It was white and beautiful and reminded me of a snowflake. She started laughing when she saw it, said it was ridiculous, that I looked like a cotton ball. She asked if I was going to throw myself in peroxide and dab wounds at the dance.

"Then she and her male friend—I think it was Carl around then, but I can't really remember because they all start melding together in my mind—started making fun of the fact that I didn't have a date," she continued. "She asked if I was going to try to find one of the guys to have sex with so I could get pregnant and trap him. She seemed to think that was a good idea. I started crying and couldn't stop. And that was the end of that dance."

Jake's hand went to her cheek, surprising her enough that she finally lifted her eyes. All she found there when she looked at him was compassion. Despite that, she said what came naturally.

"You're probably relieved. I would've ruined the dance for you."

Jake was solemn as he shook his head. "No. You wouldn't have ruined anything. I am so sorry."

"What are you sorry for?" January pulled away from him and reached for the coat she'd left on the back of the couch. It wasn't thick but would cut the wind for the walk to the resort. "It wasn't your fault."

"No?" He didn't look convinced. "I made your life hell in high school. I guess I didn't realize everybody else was making your life hell at the same time."

"I made your life hell too."

"Except you didn't. I had a good home life. I had friends. I was never afraid to go to a dance."

"It's fine." January waved off his apology. "I survived."

"It's not fine." Jake grabbed her chin so she had nowhere to look but into his eyes. "None of this is fine."

"Like I said, it's fine. I think I grew stronger because of it."

"Maybe, but that still doesn't make it right."

They stared into each other's eyes for so long January wondered if time had stopped. After a few seconds, she blinked and smiled. "It's okay. Let's just make tonight great, huh? At some point Jim is going to have to acknowledge me as something other than the random woman who irritates him with her lists."

"I didn't realize he was doing that." Jake shook his head. "We'll get through to him, one way or another."

"Here's hoping."

He held out his arm. "Come on." They made it to the door before he spoke again. "Just for the record, you're beautiful, and you look like a glittering snowflake in that dress. You make everything brighter just by smiling."

January's cheeks flushed hot. "I guess I should smile then."

"That would be best."

JAKE TOOK JANUARY'S COAT WHEN THEY ENTERED the summit lobby. He took it to the coatroom and shrugged out of his jacket before emerging into the lobby and taking a look around at the festive decorations. The decorating committee—led by January, of course—had gone all out. Everything sparkled. There were twinkle lights everywhere. Even the garland was perfectly placed.

"Impressive, huh?" Leo asked as he moved to stand next to Jake. He was in his normal suit but had added a splash of red to his jacket pocket.

"I didn't realize you would be here." Jake grinned at him.

"Security is always needed, especially for an event like this. I need to make sure nobody drinks too much and tries to wear the garland as a hat."

Jake snorted. "That happened one time."

"Yes, and you weren't even a teenager when you did it." Leo winked at him. "Where's your date?"

"You mean my wife?" Jake arched a challenging eyebrow. People were still asking about his "marriage" to January, but some of the fervor had died down. Only Leo hadn't questioned him yet.

"I'm aware of that situation," Leo replied evenly. "I had a few choice words for your father over it—if we have to pretend to be something we're not, are we actually winning?—but he basically told me to keep my mouth shut and not worry about it."

Jake pursed his lips. "It's okay."

"It's okay? You're okay being fake married to January Jackson? How did that happen?"

Jake shrugged. "She's not so bad. I think... I think maybe I never looked at her the right way before."

"And how were you supposed to look at her?"

"Like she was a real person. I spent all that time as a kid obsessed with beating her, and looking back, I know that I was at fault."

"Oh yeah?" Leo's tone was breezy, but Jake knew he was honestly curious. "Why do you think that?"

"Because I had everything and always wanted more. She had nothing and was just trying to survive."

"As I recall, she did some pretty dastardly things to you."

"Yeah, and I did worse to her." Jake bobbed his head in acknowledgement. "I don't know who started it. Does it matter? No. We were kids. Kids are idiots. I know darned well that I kept it going though. I was obsessed with beating her."

"I think she might've been obsessed with beating you too. You were her benchmark for success."

"That doesn't make it okay. She was trying to earn something for herself. I was trying to take something away from her. That makes me the bastard."

Leo's look was appraising. "Well, look at that. You might actually be growing up after all. January has been a good influence on you."

"She's a good person." Jake shot Leo a dark look. "Don't go getting any ideas. We're coexisting. She's teaching me to be a better man. Nothing is going on though."

"You don't think that teaching you to be a better man is a little more than nothing?"

"I think that she deserves whatever accolades come from this event," Jake replied firmly. "The fake marriage part feels unnecessary, but we're committed to it now. This will be a stepping stone for her. She's put in more work than anybody. She deserves it."

"Listen to you." Leo huffed out a laugh. "You really are becoming a man."

"About time, huh?"

Leo nodded. "I always knew it would happen."

Jake left Leo to skulk in the corner and watch the punch while he crossed the lobby to January. She had a bright smile as she chatted with Jim and his wife, a dour-looking woman who appeared to be wishing she was anywhere but at the party. Jake slipped his arm around January's waist as if it was the most normal thing in the world and smiled at Jim's appraising smile as January continued chattering.

"I'm glad you like the decorations," she said. "I was going for bright but not too garish."

"You did an amazing job," Jim replied. "You have a fine eye for detail. Perhaps you should be in charge of the resort's decorating going forward."

January's smile didn't falter, but Jake's did.

"She's multitalented," Jake volunteered. "She can do a little of everything. Her organizational skills are through the roof."

"Always an important thing when a woman is going to keep a house in order," Jim agreed. "So, let's talk about more important things. When are you going to have children?"

The question came out of nowhere, and Jake's mouth dropped open before he could stop it. "Um..."

"We're not there yet," January replied smoothly, the charm

Jake never knew she possessed on full display. "We haven't been married all that long. We have time."

"Children are a blessing," Jim encouraged. "It's never too early."

"Yes, well..." January faltered, which provided an opening for Jake to slide in and drag her away.

"I think I'm going to dance with my beautiful wife," he said as he gripped January's hand, ignoring the surprised look on her face. "She looks like a snowflake, and I want to enjoy it. Maybe we'll get a jump on those kids after all, thanks to this dress." He'd meant it as a tongue-in-cheek statement, but the look January shot him suggested she didn't think it was funny.

"Come on." Jake didn't hesitate before drawing her to the dance floor. His arms immediately went around her waist even though escape looked to be her primary goal. "Pretend you love your husband," he ordered when she was stiff in his arms.

January relaxed some, but there was irritation in her eyes when they snagged gazes. "I can't believe you just said that to him."

"What? It's what he wanted to hear."

"You insinuated that we were going to get busy after we were finished here tonight."

"Get busy?" Jake choked on a laugh. "What a weird way to phrase it. For the record, he thinks we're getting busy twenty-four-seven. Haven't you seen the way he watches us? I swear he's doing complicated math problems in his head to see how many kids we can pop out."

"He does seem to be intent on it," January agreed. "If this were an apocalypse movie, he would expect us to repopulate the world without any help."

Jake relaxed as he swung her around the dance floor. "I've noticed. He's intent on it. I wonder what that's about."

"I think he's Quiverfull."

Jake waited for her to expand. When she didn't, he prodded her. "What's that?"

"It's a religious belief that large families are a blessing from God. Birth control and family planning are no-nos."

"I'm fine with having a kid or two down the line, but I have my limits. I'm sure you do too. We'll have to plan accordingly."

January's eyes went wide, and he realized how the statement sounded.

"I didn't mean that as we would have kids together," Jake automatically volunteered. "I just meant it as..." He trailed off. Why was the notion of having kids with January not as preposterous as it should've been? He didn't want kids right now, of course—he was still trying to get his life together—but what once would've seemed ridiculous to the extreme now seemed like a possibility. Granted years down the road but a possibility, nonetheless.

"What were you saying?" January asked when he'd been quiet for several seconds.

"I don't even know." Jake leaned forward, his eyes tracing the line of her mouth. She'd opted for a muted plum color, and he found he was infatuated as she licked the seam of her lips.

"Jake." His name was strangled as he leaned closer.

"*Shh.*" He had no idea what he was doing. It was as if he'd been taken over by an alien invader and was suddenly a pod person who had no control over his actions. "I want to try something."

"What?" January squeaked. "You're freaking me out."

"Honey, I'm freaking myself out." His lips hovered directly over hers. He told himself it was a bad idea. *This is a mistake.* He would regret it if he followed through. He was almost positive that was the case. Not kissing her was worse than anything he could imagine though.

When his lips finally touched hers, it was as if an explosion had gone off in his head. He could only see stars. Or perhaps it was snowflakes because of the dress. At first the kiss was tentative, a simple brushing of lips. Warmth exploded through him as he groaned, and then he went for it.

His tongue swept against hers. She responded. Their lips melded together, and they moaned in tandem.

Jake had no idea how long they stood there on the edge of the dance floor kissing each other. It wasn't the first time they'd lost themselves in each other. He had no idea if it would be the last. All he knew as he slowly became aware that murmurs were flowing around them was that she'd gripped the front of his shirt so tightly she was practically ripping it apart.

When he pulled back far enough to see her face, the wild look in her eyes was like a kick to the gut. Breathing hard, practically panting, they didn't look away from one another.

Then a familiar voice invaded the moment.

"It's a good thing you're standing under mistletoe," Jacob said.

Jake and January flew apart like shrapnel from a bomb, January taking three tentative steps backward as Jake regarded his father with hazy eyes. "I do love me some mistletoe," he said when he was reasonably certain he could speak in coherent sentences.

"Uh-huh." Jacob looked more amused than disturbed. "The Maxwells are starting to talk." He kept his voice low. "He thinks he inspired you to add to your family." Jacob shot a kind smile toward January before focusing on his son. "Perhaps you should take this little show back to the lodge."

January blinked twice and then made a face. "What did he say?"

Jake laughed at her confusion. "He said we should take a walk." He extended his hand to her, a move that felt iffy given the way she'd pulled away from him. "Dinner is done. All that's left is small talk and drinks. How about we do the small talk and drinks back at our place."

Jacob and Jake watch January closely to see what her reaction would be. It was impossible to miss the maelstrom firing in the depths of her eyes. Ultimately, she slipped her hand in his. "Okay." Her voice was so small, he almost didn't hear her.

"Okay?"

She nodded.

"Okay." He gripped her hand and drew her away from the crowd. "I'm sure you'll give our regrets to the Maxwells," he said.

Jacob smirked. "I think I can handle it. Even though you two are apparently on fire right now, don't forget your coats on the way out. It's snowing."

"I've got it." Jake led January to the coatroom and helped her into her thin winter jacket. He didn't bother with his, instead slinging it over his arm. "Come on."

Nobody said anything until they were clear of the building. Even though he was in a hurry to get home—and maybe try that kiss again—Jake didn't rush across the icy expanse. He remained close in case she slipped in her high heels.

"What are we going to do?" January asked finally. "I mean, seriously, what are we going to do? I wasn't expecting that."

Jake wasn't expecting it either. That didn't mean he regretted it. On the contrary, he was pretty eager to pick up where they'd left off. "I thought we could try it again at home and see what happens."

January arched a dubious eyebrow. "We both know what's going to happen."

"We do." Jake had no interest in lying to her or himself. There was no doubt what was going to happen when he got his hands on January when there was nobody to interrupt. "How do you feel about that?"

"I don't know. How do you feel about it?"

"As if it's inevitable."

Apparently, that was enough of a response for January because she bobbed her head. "Yeah, let's see what happens. It can't possibly get any weirder, right?"

Jake wasn't so certain. All he knew was he didn't care. He had to get another hit of January's lips. The feeling that he might die if he didn't wasn't going anywhere. If anything, it was getting stronger.

And stronger and stronger and stronger.

SEVENTEEN

What happened was sex.

They both knew it would when they crossed the parking lot, their hands clamped together as they studied each other with intense eyes. The second they walked through the door, they were on each other. Hands, tongues, arms, legs—it was hard to tell where one of them began and the other ended. January wasn't even sure whose room they ended up in until she woke the next morning and recognized her ceiling fan.

It wasn't shame that flooded her when she registered the warm body next to hers. The memories of what they'd done—and in three different rooms, no less—had her cheeks burning hot. In the bright light of day, however, she had questions.

What were they going to do now? Was this a one-time thing? Now that they'd scratched that itch, would they pretend nothing had happened? Did she want that? Did she want more?

Her stomach threatened a revolt.

"Get out of your head," Jake murmured as he slipped his arm around her waist and tugged her closer. The way he gripped her meant she had no choice but to rest her head on his chest.

Up close and personal, his morning stubble on full display, January couldn't believe she'd ever hated him. It seemed impossible. He was a giving individual, easily moved and always there when he thought she might need him. Had he always been that way? Had he somehow really been a terrible child and yet somehow grew into a good man?

She lodged her chin on his chest and studied his profile for so long, she was surprised she didn't burn a hole in that strong jaw. When he finally opened his eyes, they were full of mirth as they locked with her terrified gaze.

"We need to talk about you sleeping in at least once a week," he supplied.

That was it? No witty banter? No wandering hands other than the one lightly trailing up and down her back in an effort to lull her? They couldn't just ignore everything that happened. Did he expect her not to talk it to death?

"Um..." She licked her lips and dragged a hand through her hair, frowning when her fingers got tangled. Bedhead was the worst, and she'd forgotten to wash her makeup off the night before. She probably looked like a raccoon.

"We're going to talk," he assured her as he cuddled her close. "I'm not an idiot. I know there's no way there won't be a talk. We don't need to have it right now though."

We don't? What were they supposed to do if they didn't talk?

"January, close your eyes," Jake ordered. "Enjoy the morning. Don't start freaking out about what comes next. Bask in the moment. We'll worry about the future in an hour."

The future? Did he think they were going to have a future? Was this supposed to be more than a one-night stand? She was so confused.

He was quiet for several minutes, eyes closed and mouth

relaxed. When she didn't melt against him and remained stiff, he forced one eye open. "You're not going to relax, are you?"

January considered lying, but given how far they'd come, given the fact that they were in bed together, that didn't seem fair. To either of them. "I have questions," she whispered.

His lips quirked. "I'm sure you do."

"Don't you?"

"I have thoughts," he replied.

"I would like to hear those thoughts."

"Do you want to hear them here or in the kitchen?"

Before January could answer, her stomach let loose a ruthless growl.

"I guess that answers that question." Jake pressed a kiss to her forehead. It was more chaste than sexy. It was actually friendly. When he smiled, though, there was a wolfish quality about it. "Okay, we can get up. I'll cook you breakfast. We'll talk."

January nodded. "I think that's for the best."

He chuckled before leaning in to give her another kiss. It was soft and sweet. "You don't even know how the talk is going to go. I'm glad that you're feeling upbeat about it."

Upbeat was not the emotion January would've assigned to herself. Still, she smiled encouragingly. "I think it's still for the best."

"Fine." Jake looked reluctant as he rolled out of bed. He was naked—gloriously, ridiculously naked—and he stretched his arms over his head as he stared down at her. "I'll make pancakes. How does that sound?"

January clutched the blanket to her chest, which was ridiculous because he'd already seen everything that was under the covers, and nodded. "I could eat pancakes."

"Good. I'll see you in the kitchen in ten minutes. I'll be the one with your coffee and carbs, two things I'm certain we're going to need for the talk you have planned."

January was certain he was right. Still, when he exited her bedroom, she let loose a breath. She was both relieved and a little sad. How could she miss him already? He was still under the same roof.

"This is going to be a shit conversation," she muttered.

"It was your idea," Jake called out from somewhere in the hallway, proving he'd been listening. "Get up. Because you refused to relax, now we're having this conversation whether you like it or not."

She wasn't sure she did like it. That didn't change the fact that it was necessary. "I'm coming."

JAKE SIPPED HIS COFFEE AND STOOD IN THE middle of the kitchen, wearing nothing but boxer shorts and a smile, when January emerged fifteen minutes later. She'd taken the time to brush her hair—and likely her teeth, if he had to guess—and she'd washed her face. She'd pulled on a T-shirt and wore a pair of flannel sleep shorts, and her smile was friendly but not intimate as she edged into the kitchen.

"That coffee smells good," she said as she eyed the machine.

Jake took another sip of the life-giving elixir. "It's delightful," he agreed. "Would you like some?"

"Yes."

"You'll have to come over here to get it." He didn't move away from the pot. Instead, he was firm when luring her in. "I promise I won't bite. At least until after we've finished breakfast."

"I'm not afraid of you." The set of January's jaw was defiant as she moved in front of him to pour her own mug of coffee. He caught a whiff of something that smelled like marshmallows and leaned close so he could sniff the back of her neck, which was bare because she'd pulled her hair back in a ponytail. "What is that?" he rasped, his body responding in such a way that he was going to have to pull away from her sooner rather than later if he didn't want to lose himself and lift her onto the counter. Pancakes be damned.

"What's what?" When January turned, her eyes went wide. His proximity had obviously thrown her. "Um ... what's what?" she squeaked.

Damn, she's cute. Jake couldn't understand how he'd ever missed it. She was freaking adorable. And that scent—it was going to be the ruin of both of them if he didn't get it together. "You smell amazing," he gritted out.

"That's my body spray. I haven't showered yet."

"Maybe we can do that together later, and then you can put on the body spray again. I think I might like that."

January's mouth dropped open. "We have exactly two hours before we have to be over at the resort. The events start today."

Jake blinked several times in rapid succession. *Events? What events?* That was when reality slapped him across the face. The Winter Extreme Games kicked off today. It wasn't a full schedule, but that didn't mean they could play hooky and spend the day in bed. The old Jake, the one who traveled on his parents' dime and loathed the idea of a nine-to-five job, might've tried to convince her to go back to bed regardless. This new-and-improved Jake knew better. They were both needed at the resort in two hours. That didn't mean they couldn't have a bit of fun before then.

"Right." He backed up and moved to the refrigerator so he could grab milk and eggs to make the pancake batter. "I guess that means we should get this conversation out of the way first thing."

"That would probably be best," January agreed.

Jake kept his back to her as he grabbed the Bisquick from the cupboard. "Why don't you start?" When he turned, he found January's mouth hanging open in comical fashion. "Do you have a problem with that?"

"Why do I have to start?" she demanded.

"Why don't you want to start? You always have something to say. I figured now would be as good a time as any for you to get it all out."

"Because you want me to admit I like you? Are you going to say you just want to be friends if I say I kind of want to see where this could go? Or do you want me to say the opposite, so it frees you to call last night a fling and walk away?"

Jake wasn't sure how to respond. Somewhere in the back of his mind, he realized she'd been shit on so many times in her life—and many of those times by him—that it was going to take a bit of work to make her feel secure. He wasn't opposed to doing the work. In fact, he was looking forward to it. He still had to be conscientious of the things that had happened. As much as he enjoyed spending time with her, she was still getting her feet on the ground emotionally.

"I'll go first," he said as he retrieved a bowl. "Can you get the pan out? I would like to streamline the pancakes, so we still have time before we have to get cleaned up and head over."

"Time for what?" January retrieved what he was looking for, her brow furrowed. "What is it you think we're going to do?"

"I have a few ideas." That smile of his was back and firmly in place. It didn't slip, even when she scowled at him. "Here's the thing," he said as he braced his hands on the counter and organized his thoughts. He wanted to do this the right way, for a change. She needed it. He did as well, but not to the same degree. "I would like to see where this goes."

Surprise registered hot and fast across January's face, but she shuttered it quickly. Jake didn't miss how her cheeks turned pink, and unless he was mistaken, it was pleasure he saw reflected back at him. "You do?" He could barely hear her voice, but the emotion attached to it was unmistakable. She was relieved.

"I do," he confirmed. "I've been ... *feeling* ... things for a few days now. It might actually be longer than that." He dumped the Bisquick mix into the bowl, added the eggs and milk, and started beating the batter. "I don't know when it happened, but I feel something when I look at you."

"Disgust?"

"Don't," he warned, his eyes flashing with annoyance. "It's definitely not disgust."

"You weren't happy when you came back and found out we were going to be living together. What changed?"

"You weren't happy either," he reminded her.

"Well, obviously." A hint of a smile appeared as she lowered her eyes. "I remembered you one way. It's possible that you're no longer that way."

And that was the biggest compliment she ever could've given him, he realized. He wanted to leave the boy behind and embrace the man. "I want to believe I was never that way, that I was never so bad I hurt you. I know that's not true though."

"We were kids." January turned her back to him so he couldn't see her face. "It's fine. I forgive you."

"No." Jake's fingers were gentle when they wrapped around her arm and turned her. He saw nothing but open trust in her eyes, and yet he knew that she would remain wary for the foreseeable future. He needed to push past that. She deserved some peace. "It's not okay. I was a jerk."

"I was a jerk too."

"Yes, but I'm starting to wonder who acted like a jerk first. It doesn't matter. I don't want to be a jerk any longer. I like spending time with you."

"You do?" The pleasure that spread across January's face made him weak in the knees, punching hard against his ribs as he tried to keep breathing evenly.

"I do. I know I was angry when my father said we had to pretend to be married, but I'm not angry any longer. Being fake married to you is the best thing that's happened to me in, well, a really long time."

"I've enjoyed it, too, although it's not easy to admit." January was sheepish. "I'm worried that you're only feeling the things you're feeling because we're on top of one another. What happens in two weeks when I move back to my place, and we're not forced to spend inordinate amounts of time together?"

"I'll probably go through withdrawal," Jake replied, not missing a beat. "What? Don't look so surprised. I need multiple January fixes a day."

January pressed her lips together, her eyebrows moving toward her hairline. The resulting face was so adorable he thought his chest might burst.

He couldn't stop himself from leaning in and giving her another kiss. It was supposed to be a simple touching of lips, reassurance that he meant what he said. Their tongues got involved much faster than he was anticipating, and he was breathless when he finally came up for air.

"I think we need to be careful," he cautioned, his chest heaving. "We're going to be dealing with crap from all sides. My father obviously knows something is going on."

"Do you think he's mad?" January asked. Her cheeks were so red she almost looked windburned. Jake found the color appealing.

"Actually, I don't think he's mad." Jake let loose a low chuckle. "He looked amused more than anything else last night. He's probably hoping you'll be a good influence on me."

"I'm hoping that too."

"Of course you are." Jake dropped his forehead to rest against hers. Kissing her again was dangerous, but resistance was futile where she was concerned. He wanted to get the rest of it out before then though. "I think some of the workers have caught on that we're faking being married."

"You mean Leo."

He laughed. "Oh, Leo definitely knows. I'm not concerned what people think. I am worried that if they pick up on the fact that we're really together, they're going to start gossiping."

"And you don't want people to know," January surmised. The wariness was back in her eyes, and Jake didn't like it.

"Actually, I'm not worried about that," Jake replied smoothly, his fingers moving to her cheek so he could touch the soft skin there. "It's not that I don't care what they think —although I don't—as much as it's that anybody would be proud to have you on their arm." He meant it and was gratified when she relaxed a bit.

"My concern is that they're going to open their big fat mouths in front of the Maxwells," he continued. "If they say the wrong thing because they can't stop themselves from gossiping about us..." He trailed off, his mind working overtime.

"Oh." January bobbed her head as realization dawned in her eyes. "If the Maxwells overhear the other workers making a big deal about us hooking up, they're going to have questions."

"And we're in deep now," Jake confirmed. "This could blow up in my father's face. I'm still not happy he put us in this position, but we need to be careful for the next two weeks."

"That makes sense." January let out a breath, and Jake had to stop himself from groaning when it tickled his chest. "We'll just have to act normal at the resort and keep the other stuff for when we're here."

That wasn't what Jake wanted. In fact, it was the opposite

of what he wanted. He would've preferred taking her skiing on lunch breaks, perhaps even finding an empty banquet room to enjoy here and there when their schedules permitted. He didn't want to ruin anything, though, for his father or for January.

"Are you okay with that?" he asked after several seconds.

"Of course." Her answer was automatic. "This could mean big things for the resort."

"I'm not really okay with it because I would prefer being able to take you out whenever I feel like it, but I don't see where we have a choice."

"It's only two weeks," January pointed out. "I'm sure it will be fine."

Jake could only hope that was true because the more time he spent with January, the more time he wanted. "How do you feel about skipping the pancakes and grabbing breakfast sandwiches when we get up to the resort?"

Mischievous energy rippled over January's face. "What are we going to do with the time we'll free up if we do that?"

"I thought I would show you." He was already leading her back toward her bedroom. "It will lose something in the telling."

"Well, who am I to deny such a charming offer?"

"I was hoping you would see things my way."

Eighteen

January was nervous when she emerged from her room. She'd purchased new thermal pants from L.L. Bean and had paired them with a pretty blue sweater for inside and a nice new cream-colored jacket for outside. Jake was in his normal clothes when she joined him in the living room, and he looked her up and down appraisingly.

"I like the pants," he said on a wolfish grin. "They fit you really well."

January was taken aback. "Are they too tight?"

"They're just tight enough." He reached out to touch the smooth material and grinned. "I don't want you to think I'm sexually harassing you or anything, but it's going to be pretty hard for me to keep my hands off your butt in those things."

January's mouth dropped open. "Should I change them?"

He frowned. "That was flirting."

"Oh." January's forehead creased in confusion. "I guess I'm not very good at it."

"We'll practice." He took her hand as they left the lodge, and she couldn't help sending him several shy smiles as they crossed the parking lot.

"I thought we were keeping our new relationship under wraps."

"We're holding hands. I'm not mounting you in public."

"Luke is over there." January watched Jake closely to see if he would suddenly drop her hand. He didn't. "You really don't care?" she queried.

"Why would I?"

"Luke is your friend."

"So?"

"So aren't you embarrassed?"

Jake made a growling sound deep in his throat. "I don't like it when you say things like that. Why would I possibly be embarrassed?"

"I don't know." January squirmed. "I didn't grow up on the same side of town as you."

"At the risk of sounding like a broken record, so?"

"So people have always looked down on me for that. They'll look down on you for it, too, when they find out."

"I don't happen to believe that." He sucked in a breath and then let it out. "January, I don't want to minimize your feelings. I get it. Kids can be real assholes. I was a real asshole. I never really thought about where you lived though. I fought with you because you fought with me, and apparently, I liked it, although I only recently put that together."

She laughed. "Yeah. It seems twisted when I look back at how I was convinced I hated you. Hindsight is a terrifying thing."

"You were warm for my form, and you know it." He winked at her and then sobered. "You have a right to feel what you feel, and those feelings are valid. I don't think you should let it define you. People don't see you the same way you apparently see yourself."

"You can't tell me that your friends haven't been questioning you about the time we've been spending together. I know they've been making jokes."

"Well, jokes are what they do, but the jokes aren't aimed at you. They're aimed at me."

"Because, on paper, we make no sense." She was suddenly troubled.

"Actually, on paper, I think we make a lot of sense. You're exactly the sort of person I need and want in my life. That's neither here nor there though. The jokes I've been hearing have been about me settling down. They're not aimed at you."

"Really?" She let out a pent-up breath. "Is that true?"

"Yeah." He chuckled. "I get that you were teased for things you never should've been teased for. It's not okay. Kids are cruel. I promise you that nobody sees you that way now. In fact, everything I've heard from the people around the resort suggests they all respect you more than just about anybody else."

"Oh, now you're just trying to appease me. Wait. Is this you flirting again?"

He laughed so hard she was afraid he might choke. "Yeah, we definitely need to work on the flirting because I'm either really bad at it or you're simply blind to it. We'll play that game later though." He squeezed her hand. "People here respect you. Sure, some of them complain about you, but that's because you're their boss." He slowed his pace and brushed her hair away from her face. "I wish you could see yourself as others see you."

"I thought I was." Her answer was simple, but he shook his head all the same.

"We need to work on your self-esteem." He leaned in and rested his forehead against hers. "Just in case you're wondering, you're great."

She went warm all over. It was exactly what she'd always wanted to hear—and not just from him. Still, there was a niggling bit of doubt in the back of her mind that she couldn't shake. It was always there. "You didn't think that when you first came back."

"When I first came back, I was in a bad place. I was in a foul mood because the deal I thought would finally impress my father had fallen through. I was trapped in Vegas and angry at myself because I had no way home without his help. I wanted to pout when I got back, but that wasn't an option. I didn't mean to take it out on you."

January raised her hand and rested it against his cheek, their foreheads still pressed together. "Maybe we both need to let go of the past and try to move forward with a clean slate."

"I think that sounds like a great idea." He kissed the tip of her nose, grinned, and then gave her a longer kiss on the mouth.

"Get a room," Luke yelled as he passed on his way to the summit shopping area. "You guys are grossing me out. This isn't high school."

January's cheeks burned as she pulled back, but with something akin to wonder she watched as Jake shot his friend the bird. "You're just jealous. And stop ruining my good morning," he barked. "Now she's going to be focused on work, and there will be no kissing her. You totally just screwed me over."

"Then my work here is done." Luke offered up a saucy salute and kept walking. "They're all down on top of the bunny hill, by the way," he called over his shoulder. "All the bigwigs. Everybody is smiling, but they seem tense."

That was enough to rocket January back to reality. "We should get going."

"Yeah." Jake smoothed his hand over her hair. "We'll talk about the clean slate and your lack of flirting skills later, when it's just the two of us."

"I'm looking forward to that." January found she meant

it, which somehow felt like a miracle to her. "Maybe we can practice the flirting."

"See, now you're thinking."

JAKE WAS WARY AND PREPARED AS they approached the group on top of the bunny hill. He knew that January would be worked up for the duration of the day. She was far too diligent to react any other way. Rather than try to calm her down—something he knew would be impossible— he decided to plan a relaxing evening for them in the hot tub after the day's events were finished. He figured rewarding her for a job well done was better than trying to get her to take a breath when so much was at stake.

"What's going on?" he asked his father as he drew even with him. The Maxwells were grouped together about twenty feet away, and whatever conversation was occurring looked intense.

"They saw a woman wearing ski pants they consider lewd," Jacob replied in an annoyed voice. "They're wondering if they should keep their kids away from the events just in case they see anything that shatters their fragile minds."

Jake didn't have to ask his father's opinion on the subject, but his eyes automatically went to January's ridiculous ass in her new ski pants. His smirk was instantaneous.

"Oh, you're unbelievable." Jacob shook his head, but there was a smile on his face. "You two are together, aren't you?"

"We're working on it," Jake replied. He was careful when choosing his words. "January doesn't want it getting out until after the event. We're not talking about anything serious until the Maxwells are gone. Don't ask her about it and make her uncomfortable."

"I have no intention of embarrassing her. You're another story though."

Jake didn't want to laugh—it would only encourage his father—but he couldn't stop himself. "We're still trying to figure things out. Our past history adds an extra layer of drama, as we've discussed. We need time to get everything in order."

"Have you ever considered that you only did those things to each other because you liked one another?"

"Actually, we've both come to that conclusion." Jake's smile slipped. "Does that make us sick?"

"That makes you kids," Jacob replied. "Let's not pretend you were in love with each other in fourth grade. You probably did have issues with each other, and I'm not a psychiatrist so I can only theorize what those issues were. By the time you got to high school, though, I saw it. I just didn't say anything because your mother was convinced she was trying to ruin you."

Jake was taken aback. "Mom doesn't like January?"

"Oh, look at you." Amusement cascaded across Jacob's refined features. "Son, your mother cares about protecting you above all else. When she assumed January was trying to hurt you, she turned into a rabid animal.

"As for liking January," he continued, "she recognizes January is a good worker and unbelievably smart. Do I think there's going to be some pushback when she realizes that you two are together? Probably. She won't be able to resist that smile of yours, though, so it will be fine."

Jake had no idea what to make of that. "I'm not smiling," he said finally.

"You've been smiling for days. You're definitely smiling this morning. Given how you and January were acting last night, I don't have to ask why, and I never want to know the details."

"I like her." Jake's voice was soft. "I didn't realize how much. Part of me thinks that I should've known after what happened when we were in college, but she was so mortified the next morning. I think I had to harden my heart to her because otherwise I would have to think too hard, and I didn't want that."

Jacob snickered. "I knew about the thing in college. Leo told me."

"How did he know?" Jake was horrified.

"Because some of the people at that party worked here, and this place is thick with gossip."

"I guess." Jake wasn't happy about the news. "What did you think at the time?"

"I was hopeful she would help you get your head out of your ass."

"That obviously didn't happen."

"No, but she's a good influence on you." Jacob let loose a heavy sigh. "Jake, you're a smart boy who never grew into a man. You're finally starting to do that now. It's not all her. She's a miracle worker, but you deserve some credit here. I expected you to come in pouting, which you did. The pouting didn't last though. You pitched in and helped. More importantly, you took the time to listen to what January was telling you. I think the transformation from boy to man is finally happening."

"See, I can't decide if that's a compliment or an insult."

"It's both," Jacob replied. "You stayed a boy for far too long. I think the man is going to do great things."

Jake had no idea how to respond. A warmth had begun spreading throughout his chest as his father spoke, and for maybe the first time in his life, he realized how desperately he needed his father's approval. "I want to be a good man," he said after several seconds.

"I know." Jacob patted his son's shoulder. "You've always wanted to be a good man. You just got lost along the way."

"I think January will help me be a good man."

"I think January is amazing. She can't do it all in two weeks though." Jacob smirked. "Just pay attention to her. She's wound a little tight. She's desperate to do *all* the good things in the world at once. You needed help being a man. She needs help embracing the child she never truly got to be. That's why you balance each other out."

Jake worked his jaw. "You know what's weird? I thought the same exact thing when we were walking across the parking lot this morning."

"You mean when you stopped to make out in the middle of traffic?"

"How do you even know that?" Jake demanded.

Jacob made a snorting sound when he laughed. "What did I tell you? This place is thick with gossip. Leo texted me ten minutes ago with a photo."

"Leo is going to get a foot up his ass," Jake groused.

"Forget about Leo and focus on them." Jacob inclined his head toward the Maxwells. "They're going to be a problem for the next two weeks—and a big problem at that."

Jake sobered. "You're wishing you'd partnered with someone else, aren't you?"

"I thought it would be easier to get one big sponsor," Jacob acknowledged. "Now I realize it would've been better for all concerned to cobble together smaller sponsors. That guy has way too much power, and he's exerting his beliefs on everybody around us."

Jake leveled his gaze on Jim. "I thought you were a 'live and let live' guy."

"I am, but he's not, and that's the problem. I don't care what they believe. If they want to pop out a million kids and have them all work at the same dealership together, more power to them. My problem is that they're trying to force everybody else here to their way of thinking. Do you know that Jim actually approached me last night and explained that

January was old enough that she should have multiple children under her belt by now? He suggested I encourage you to knock her up and get her out of the workforce as soon as possible."

Jake, who had only mildly disliked the Maxwells before, scowled. "Are you kidding me?"

"No, I am not. He's a sick man worrying about other people's breeding habits."

"But there's nothing we can do," Jake surmised. "We're stuck with them for the next two weeks."

"We are, and I blame myself for the situation we're all in." Jacob was grim. "There's nothing we can do now. The contracts are signed. There's no breaking them."

Jake's eyes went back to January, who was standing next to Edward. To his absolute stunned horror, out of nowhere, Edward bobbed his head as January said something and then lowered his hand to her butt. "Did he just...?" Jake's cheeks were on fire.

"Yes, and we're not having that." Jacob tugged on Jake's arm. "You let me do the talking."

The inside of Jake's brain felt as if a curse word bomb had gone off. Every foul word he knew was fighting for supremacy, and they all wanted to be hurled at Edward.

"Does somebody need coffee?" Jacob asked as he moved to stand directly in front of Edward.

The man looked confused, but Jake noted with intense relief that he had removed his hand from January's rear end. "I've already had my one cup this morning."

"Well, perhaps you should drink more," Jacob said as he calmly reached over and tugged on January's jacket to remove her from Edward's vicinity. "I think those hands of yours were looking for your wife."

Edward's cheeks flooded a dark shade of crimson. Jake read mortification there, but it wasn't because of his actions.

No, Edward was angry because he was being called out on his actions.

"I think you're mistaken," Edward replied. "I'm sure if you ask Miss Jackson here, she'll explain that you didn't see what you thought you saw."

Jake hated—*absolutely hated*—that Edward was putting January on the spot like this. She was far too agreeable to throw him under the bus. Even though his father had warned him to keep his mouth shut, he couldn't follow through.

"Mrs. Jeffries," Jake corrected pointedly.

"What?" Confusion wrinkled Edward's forehead.

"Mrs. Jeffries," Jake snapped. "She's not a miss. She's my wife."

The muscles in Edward's face went rigid. He glanced over his shoulder, but his father and siblings had moved several feet down and didn't seem to be registering the conversation. "I think there's been a misunderstanding," he hedged.

"No." Jacob shook his head. "There hasn't. You're to keep your hands to yourself."

"I don't think I like what you're insinuating." Edward turned haughty. "I wasn't doing anything."

"I know exactly what you were doing, and it's not tolerated here." Jacob gently pushed January toward Jake and leaned close enough that only the four of them could hear what he was about to say. "Don't touch her. Don't touch any of the women here. Classroom rules are in effect. Keep your hands to yourself."

Jacob held Edward's gaze for one second longer and then turned to look January up and down. "Are you okay?"

January nodded. "I'm fine. I—" She clearly didn't know what to say and snapped her mouth shut.

"You did a lovely job here," Jacob said when it was clear January wasn't going to continue. "The first event kicks off in twenty minutes. I can't wait."

Jake put his arm around January's waist when his father left and shot a dirty look toward Edward, who didn't have the good sense to drift away from them despite his bold words.

"There's no need to look at me that way," Edward chided Jake. "Nothing happened."

"You're not going to touch her again," Jake growled. "I mean it. You won't like what happens if you do."

"Is that a threat?" Edward demanded.

"Touch her again and find out," Jake replied. "I dare you."

NINETEEN

The first day of events wasn't a full day. That meant things only truly got crazy on the second day. January expected issues—there was no way an operation this big could run smoothly without a single issue—but she had no idea how many fires she would be putting out.

She was exhausted when she returned to the lodge the evening of the second day. It was well after nine o'clock, and she was starving, although she didn't know if she had the energy to chew.

All the weight she was carrying fled when she walked into the kitchen and found the table set with candles and Jake working behind the stove.

"W-what?" Her mouth dropped open when she saw that he'd made a huge dinner for both of them.

"I figured you would be tired." Jake grinned as she circled the table.

"You baked bread." It was a dumb thing to say, and yet it was all she could think.

"No, I went to the main dining room kitchen and stole

their fresh bread," Jake replied. "I just kept it warm here because nothing is better than warm bread."

January couldn't disagree. "What's that smell?" She drifted toward the stove. She couldn't see any food, but she could smell it.

"They had a great seafood pasta in the dining room tonight, so I got that, along with salads, and I stole an entire cake for dessert." He looked gleeful. "It's chocolate."

January was wowed ... and touched ... and feared she might burst into tears. "You did this for me?"

Jake looked taken aback. "Why are you surprised?"

"I don't know." January wrung her hands. "You were as busy as me today. I barely saw you. I just figured I would be coming home to peanut butter and jelly. Well, if I wasn't too tired to put it on bread, that is."

"Oh, my wife deserves more than peanut butter and jelly." Jake winked at her as he took her coat. His gaze was searching as it roamed her face. January had no idea what he was looking for, but she felt exposed under his steady gaze.

"Come on." Jake pulled out her chair for her and hung her coat over the back of one of the counter stools. He dropped a kiss on top of her head as he passed behind her and returned to the stove. "I would like to say I went all out to plate this stuff, but it seemed like a lot of work." He carried the container of pasta to the middle of the table and placed it on a pot holder. Then he went to the refrigerator to claim the salads. "I did pour the wine though."

January laughed and took a grateful swallow of the white wine he'd supplied them with. When he sat next to her, rather than across from her, she smiled. "Nobody has ever done anything quite this nice for me."

"That makes me sad." He ran his hand down the back of her head. "You look tired."

"I'm pretty sure that's not a compliment." She was rueful.

"I had no idea how many tiny things could go wrong in one twelve-hour day. Nothing big happened, but it was a million little things."

"And I'm betting you handled each one of those little things yourself. You know you can delegate, right?"

"But then how will I know it's being done correctly?"

"Ah, the lament of control freaks the world over." Jake sipped his wine before dishing out the pasta. He started with her plate in an effort to be gallant, but when her stomach made a goblin noise, he burst out laughing. "Did you eat lunch?"

"I tried, but there just wasn't enough time. I think I had an apple around three o'clock."

"You're not going to be any good to anyone if you don't take care of yourself."

"I'll try to do better, *Dad*," she teased. "Speaking of dads, yours is proud of all the work you've been doing." January had meant to save the information for when they were both relaxing later, but since he'd gone out of his way for her, she wanted to do the same for him. "He's been checking your work personally, and he's thrilled."

"I kind of want to be mad that he's been checking my work personally," Jake admitted. "That suggests he doesn't trust me. Of course, I haven't done anything to earn his trust."

"I don't think that's true." January opened her salad. The pasta smelled amazing, but she was a rules person, and in her mind, you always started with the salad. "He's smiling a lot this week though. He's been really nice to me."

"I'm pretty sure he thinks of you as his real daughter-in-law now."

"Why would he think that?"

"Because he knows we're together."

January froze with her fork halfway to her mouth. "He does?"

Jake nodded. "It came up right before the incident with Edward yesterday." He frowned at the mention of Jim's obnoxious son. "You didn't have any trouble with him today, did you?"

"I barely saw him. I'm pretty sure that alpha thing you did —you were basically one step away from thumping your chest —scared him off."

"I only wish I could believe that." Jake made a face. "He's the sort of guy who feels he's owed something by the world because that's what life has taught him, thanks to his father's money. I don't trust him to keep his distance. He might've been surprised at what was said to him, but he'll regroup. If he lays a finger on you, I want to know about it."

January waited until she'd swallowed to speak. "You know I'm capable of taking care of myself, right?"

"I *do* know that." Jake bobbed his head. "My problem is that you put the job ahead of yourself. You'll absorb the sexual harassment so as not to rock the boat. That's not fair to you."

January considered the statement. She wanted to argue, but she wasn't certain he was wrong. "I don't want to be the sort of person to absorb sexual harassment."

Jake's eyes gleamed. "What if I want to sexually harass you in the privacy of our own home? Does that count?"

"I don't think it's harassment when it's mutual." She laughed when his smile doubled in size. Then she sobered. "What did your father say? Was he mad we haven't been sticking to work? I know he teased us about being together the other night, but that's all I thought that was. I thought he was fishing and nothing more."

"That is such a you thing to worry about." Jake shook his head. He, of course, had started with the pasta. One thing he'd told January years ago was that the good things in life should never be delayed. "He's fine with it, January. If you want to know the truth, I think he's pretty entertained by the whole thing. He adores you."

"Yeah, but workplace entanglements can get messy."

"Oh, I plan to clean you up in the hot tub later. Don't worry about getting messy."

She practically choked on a tomato. "You're really good at the flirting thing," she said when she'd recovered. "I wish I was as good at it as you."

"You're doing fine." He rested his hand on top of hers. "I think your problem might be that you think about it too much. Just let the flirty words flow whenever they pop up in that busy head of yours."

"Okay." January looked down at her plate. "I was kind of hoping, even though we're both exhausted, that we could sleep in the same room tonight." Her cheeks burned when his gaze landed on her.

"Was that you flirting?" he asked after several seconds.

"Yeah."

"We'll work on it." He patted her hand again, laughing when she lightly slapped his arm. "Don't worry about sleeping in separate rooms. I think the sleeping arrangements will sort themselves out."

"Meaning what?"

"That I already put my sleeping boxer shorts in your room. They look happy next to your flannel pajamas."

"Oh." January brightened considerably. "That sounds nice."

"Yeah, that was me flirting again. It wasn't good though. Apparently, we need to work on it together."

January laughed. "It might make me a geek, but I'm looking forward to it."

"I am too." Jake tapped the side of her plate. "Eat your dinner. Then we'll take the rest of the wine to the hot tub."

"I can't afford to get drunk," she warned. "Tomorrow is going to be just as busy as today."

"One bottle of wine split between us isn't going to get you drunk. Besides, I plan to get you drunk on me."

Puzzlement washed across January's features.

"That was me flirting again," he volunteered.

"Oh." Her smile turned sheepish. "I'll get better at it. I promise."

"I kind of like you awkward."

"Then are you in for a treat tonight." She winked and then froze. "Wait ... did I just flirt?"

"Yes, and that was almost a tolerable attempt."

JAKE WAS NAKED IN THE HOT TUB WHEN January let herself onto the patio. They'd been in the hot tub together since things had turned romantic, but they'd both worn swimsuits because they were nervous, and things hadn't turned romantic until they were safely inside. He planned on changing things up tonight.

"Your wine is over there." He pointed toward the glass he'd placed on the rim of the hot tub.

"Thank you." January sounded mildly nervous as she approached the hot tub. She had her robe cinched around her waist, and the way she clutched at the sash told Jake her anxiety was spiking.

"Honey, don't think about it," he said in a low voice. "It's okay. We *are* married."

To his surprise, that was apparently all she needed to hear. She whipped off the robe as if she were turning into a superhero and climbed into the hot tub naked. Sure, she didn't make eye contact, but it was a bold move.

"Ah." She closed her eyes as she got comfortable across from him. "This is the life."

Jake couldn't form words. He'd seen her naked—and multiple times now—but the way she'd just thrown off the robe had totally titillated him. She'd been bold when doing it, even if nerves had her moving quickly, and Jake was just now realizing that his kink might be a bold January. Who saw that coming? Certainly not him.

"Why are you suddenly being quiet?" January asked when the silence had stretched for more than a minute. "Is something wrong?"

Jake immediately wanted to kick himself. She was still getting used to the fact that he truly did want her. Their situation—all the fighting when they were younger—made her feel vulnerable. It was his job to ease those fears and bolster her confidence. She was halfway there. He just had to get her across the finish line.

"Nothing is wrong." Jake left his spot and moved closer to her, his hands finding her taut midriff and moving over her soft skin. She wasn't the sort of person who went to a gym to work out. The skiing and constant movement kept her fit, though, and he found he was fascinated at the way his hands felt as they glided over her curves. She didn't have a lot of them, but they were in all the right places. "January, I need you to take a breath."

Before she could respond, he dipped in to kiss her. It was a little tease, tongues touching and sighs being swallowed, but when she melted against him, he took it as a good sign.

"I know we're in a weird spot," he said when he pulled back. "All the things we did to each other when we were young, all the things I did to you..." He trailed off. "Honey, I want you to trust me. Although it's okay if you still have the occasional lapse because we have a lot of history."

"I thought maybe you'd changed your mind because you were quiet for so long," she admitted.

"Like maybe I saw something I didn't like?"

"Yeah." She scratched her cheek. "I have issues."

"It's okay." He rubbed his nose against hers, enjoying the emotional intimacy as much as the fact that they were both naked. "The reason I was quiet is because I liked what I saw, and my mind fuzzed up."

"Really?"

The look of hope in January's eyes would've brought him to his knees if he'd been standing. "Really. I really do like you." He grazed his knuckles along the side of her breast. "That's all of you. I need you to start believing that."

"I want to." She blew out a sigh and tentatively raised her fingertips to his cheek. He didn't move because he wanted her to feel comfortable touching him. He was going to be comfortable touching her before it was all said and done, and he needed things to be equal between them.

"It's okay." He closed his eyes and moved his fingers over her stomach. "We have all the time in the world to get comfortable with one another. Heck, the next two weeks is going to be you and me every single night."

She laughed. "That doesn't sound like a hardship to me." Her fingers moved to his chest, and he smiled as she traced the contours of his pecs. He had zero intention of moving until she'd touched everything she wanted to touch.

Everything.

"I want to get to know you," he said, his voice husky. "I want to know what your favorite movie is, what your favorite food is, and what you dream about at night." He moved his hands to her hips and gripped them tightly. "I want to know what turns you on, what turns you off, and if there's anything new you want to try."

She let loose a little gasp. "That sounds ... interesting."

He laughed and moved his mouth back to hers so he could steal a soft kiss. He wasn't ready for the big event—he wanted to drag her to the edge multiple times before embarking on that particular journey, and he hadn't even gotten started—but he needed his fix.

"I want to be with you." He was sincere when he pulled back far enough to look into her eyes. "It's hard to get past what we've done to each other, but I want that for both of us. I think we need to come up with some ground rules."

January's eyebrows flew up her forehead. "You want ground rules?"

"Yup." He didn't hesitate when leaning in for another kiss. He couldn't seem to stop himself. "It's okay to have doubts. When you have them, though, I want you to promise to discuss them with me. I want a chance to talk about what's bothering you before it becomes a thing."

"Do you have doubts?" she asked in a voice so low he almost didn't hear her.

"Not about this." He moved his hands over her legs as he drew close. "If someone had told me a month ago that I would be in here, with you, and there was no place in the world I would rather be, I would've laughed in their face. This is what I want though. You're what I want."

"I guess I'm just afraid."

"I know. I was a real shit as a kid."

She laughed. "It's not that. I know you're not that kid any longer. It's just... I'm afraid to rely on anybody."

And that was when the final piece of the puzzle slipped into place for Jake. "Nobody has ever come through for you." It wasn't a question. It was something he inherently recognized.

"No." Her lashes were lowered. "Nobody ever has."

"Well, I'm happy to be the first." He kissed her again, this time more fiercely. "Just promise me that you'll talk to me about whatever is bothering you. I don't have to be the source of why you're upset. I just want to be there for all of it."

"What about after though?"

He blinked. "After what?"

"After the games are finished. When we're not living together. What happens then?"

"I'm hoping we can go on some real dates. I don't even know where you live."

"I have an apartment on the east side of town. Pendleton Manor."

Jake frowned. "You live over there? Is my father not paying you enough?"

"I need the extra money for my mother's care."

"Oh, right." Jake nodded. "Well, we'll figure it out." He wasn't opposed to her staying in the lodge with him for the foreseeable future. Something told him it was too soon to bring up that possibility. No, that would have to wait.

"January, when the games are over, we'll still be together. We just won't have all this pressure hanging over us."

"That sounds kind of nice."

"It does." He kissed her again. "Do you know what else sounds nice?"

"I'm pretty sure I can feel it against my hip."

He barked out a laugh. "See, you're already getting better at the flirting thing."

"I didn't even realize that was flirting," she complained.

"Yeah, we'll work on it." He kissed her again and then drew her off the bench so she was pressed tightly against him. "I think we should save the flirting class until later. For now, I want to do something else."

"What?" She was breathless.

"I think I'd better show you. It will take too long to tell you."

"I like that idea a lot."

"I was hoping you would say that."

TWENTY

J anuary wasn't the type to sleep in. Winters in Michigan
valued darkness over light, which meant the sun often set
before six o'clock and didn't rise until after seven o'clock
the following morning. She was an early riser, and yet
over the course of the first week of the Winter Extreme Games,
she found herself sleeping later and later.

She never woke alone.

"Where are you going?" Jake caught her naked waist in his
hands and pulled her back against him, snuggling close.

"I was going to make coffee." She was sleepy. They'd been
up late doing, well, each other. She needed caffeine before she
could focus on the work of the day.

"It's Friday."

She blinked, confused by what point he was trying to
make. "So?" she asked finally.

"So you're supposed to sleep in on Friday."

She rolled so she was facing him, which seemed to make
him perfectly happy because he sighed as he leaned in for a
kiss. When had it become normal to kiss like they were a
regular couple? January was still grappling with her new real-

ity. She liked it—there was no doubt about that—but it still felt like some marvelous gift that had been bestowed upon her rather than something that could be her new normal. Eventually, she would have to give serious thought as to why she felt the way she did. For now, she was just enjoying it.

Well, mostly.

"Since when is sleeping in on Fridays a thing?" she asked, her fingers automatically going to his messy hair. Somehow— and it shouldn't have been possible—he was even more attractive with bedhead and morning stubble. In fact, he was so ridiculously hot in the morning, she was convinced it should be against the law.

"It's always been a thing for me." He nuzzled his face in the hollow of her neck. "In fact, I think three-day weekends should be the norm, not a special treat."

Smiling would encourage him to keep at it, something she told herself she didn't have time for, but she couldn't stop herself. "You've had a lot of three-day weekends over the course of your life, haven't you?"

"Yup." He lightly bit the soft spot under her chin and smiled when he opened his eyes. "And I'm guessing you haven't had a lot of three-day weekends."

"Not really." January was rueful. "Even when I was in college, I was one of the few people who purposely scheduled Friday classes."

Jake looked so horrified January could only laugh. "Why would you do that?"

"Mostly because I didn't want to go home on the weekends."

His smile slipped. "Because of your mother."

"She wasn't a bad mother," January volunteered automatically. Jake had been digging for information on her mother for days, and she'd told him what she felt comfortable sharing, but she could always see the disappointment in his eyes when she was finished. On top of that, he seemed desperate to somehow soothe her after the fact. He didn't realize that it wasn't necessary. January was matter of fact about her mother. The woman did the best that she could. Was she limited compared to other mothers? Yes. You didn't get to pick your parents though.

"Okay." Jake smiled as he brushed her hair away from her face. "You don't have to talk about her if you don't want to."

"I was just happier at school," January explained. "The other kids made fun of me because I was studying on the weekends instead of partying, but I met a few other kids like me. They understood, and that was more than I ever had here."

Jake rubbed his hands up and down January's bare back. It wasn't a sensuous move as much as a soothing process. He liked to lull her. And, truth be told, she liked to be lulled. It was something she'd never considered before.

"I was a partier," he said after a few seconds.

January barked out a laugh. "I never would've guessed."

He grinned. "You did what you had to do to give yourself the life you always dreamed about." He was deadly serious. "The other kids never had to struggle like you. You did what was right for yourself, and you're the better for it.

"When I look back at my time in college, nothing specific sticks out," he continued. "We had fun, but I never worked hard in my classes. I worked hard at drinking and carousing, but the actual learning part, well, it was never a priority for me."

January nodded. "And yet we ended up in the same place."

"No, we ended up in the same location. You're way smarter than me. There was a reason my father paired us together, although I didn't see it at the time."

"Punishment?"

He shook his head. "No. He wanted me to understand

that being entitled wasn't the same thing as being driven. I want to be more like you."

January was dumbfounded, and she had to blink to hold off a sudden rush of tears she hadn't anticipated. "You didn't have to say that."

"I meant it." Jake was calm. "You make me want to be a better man."

The statement was straight out of a romance novel, but January went warm all over. "You make me want to be less uptight," she said when she could speak again without her voice cracking. "You make me want to find balance."

"Maybe we can balance each other?"

"That would be nice, huh?" She leaned in for a kiss, but she never got to his lips because on the nightstand, her phone beeped with an incoming text. "Ugh."

"See, I would've gone for the kiss instead of the text," Jake teased as she pulled away to retrieve her phone. "That's just me though."

January pursed her lips as she read the text, feeling all traces of snuggly mirth disappear from her features.

"What is it?" Jake asked, picking up on her mood.

"It's the home where my mother is. They're asking if I can spare the time to stop in this morning. That's usually a bad sign."

"We can go."

January took a moment to register the offer. "What?" Immediately, she started shaking her head. "We're supposed to be at breakfast with the sponsors and athletes."

Jake made a face. "They'll survive without us. I'll text my father and tell him what's going on. It will be fine."

"But I have a job to do."

"You also have a life, January." Jake was firm. "We're going. Get in the shower. I'll text my father and join you."

"Are you sure?"

"Yeah, I've never been more certain of anything in my life. Get moving."

JAKE HAD NEVER BEEN INSIDE RADCLIFFE DOWNS BEFORE. Thanks to January, he knew of the hospital's existence—and in hindsight, he recognized the name because you couldn't grow up in a town the size of Bellaire and not know about it—but he'd never actually crossed the threshold. Nothing inside was as he expected.

"It's so bright and colorful," he noted as he followed January toward the front desk. "It's not what I was expecting. It doesn't really look like a hospital at all."

"That's why I wanted her here," January admitted. She'd been quiet for the ride, and Jake was worried about her mental state. "They're proactive with the patients here. They don't just leave them in their rooms to entertain themselves. They take them on outings and do group activities."

Jake nodded and rubbed his hand over her back. He had questions about her mother's condition, but now was not the time to ask them. "It looks like a good place." He wanted to kick himself after saying it. *A good place?* Her mother had early onset dementia. That could never be considered good.

"Hey, Sheryl." January gripped her hands together as she approached the woman behind the desk. "I got a text that they wanted to see me this morning."

"Hey, January." Sheryl, a fiery redhead in her forties, smiled at January in welcome, but Jake didn't miss the sadness tinging the woman's eyes. Something bad was about to happen. He could feel it. "Dr. Cosgrove wants to see you. I'll tell him you're here." Sheryl's eyes swung to Jake. "I didn't realize you would be bringing someone with you. I think they're expecting just you for the meeting."

"I don't have to be in the meeting," Jake assured her,

although he instantly regretted saying it. What if January needed him? There was no taking it back now. "How about I visit your mom while you're in the meeting, and we'll go from there, huh?" he said to January.

"Or you could do the meeting in Clara's room," Sheryl suggested. "If you're careful, she won't understand what's going on."

January glanced at Jake, seemingly debating, but he was the one who answered.

"Let's do the room thing," he said, sliding his finger through January's belt loop. He had no idea if he should be inserting himself into this particular situation, but one thing was clear. January was worried. He wouldn't let her face this alone—whatever it was—if he could help it. "Let's do that."

"Sure." Sheryl sent him a sunny smile that felt fake. "Go to the room, and I'll send Dr. Cosgrove there right now."

"Thank you," January said in a small voice.

"Yes, thank you." Jake nudged January to get her moving. He didn't say anything as they marched down the hallway. He waited to speak until she turned left and entered a room. "Are you okay?"

"Of course," she replied in perfunctory fashion. "Why wouldn't I be?"

Jake scanned her face for clues and then turned his attention to the woman sitting at the table in the corner. He'd met Clara Jackson before. She'd been called to the principal's office multiple times when he and January got into it as kids. She'd never been what he would call *warm and fuzzy*, and that had always amused him when he was a kid. When Clara threatened January with making her pay for the time she'd lost at work, that had struck him as funny. Now none of it was funny.

"Hello, Ms. Jackson." Jake pasted his friendliest smile on his face when her eyes landed on him. "You're looking as lovely as ever."

"Okay, Eddie Haskell," January drawled, causing Jake to grin.

He kept his gaze on Clara and pointed to the chair across from her. "May I sit?"

Clara smiled at him and nodded. "Are you my new doctor?"

Jake shook his head. It was obvious she was confused. He didn't want to add to it, so he decided to keep his response simple. "I'm friends with your daughter."

"Daughter?" Clara's nose wrinkled. "I don't have a daughter."

Jake froze and darted his eyes to January, who looked inexplicably sad. "January and I are friends." He gestured toward his fake wife, who was starting to take up real space in his heart. How awful for January that her mother didn't even remember her. Was that a regular thing? "We work together."

Clara shifted to look at January, but her gaze was back on Jake within seconds. "I'm pretty sure she's a nurse. I don't know her name though."

Jake felt sick to his stomach. Despite his protective instincts for January, he recognized that pushing Clara was a bad idea. It wasn't her fault she couldn't remember. "Are you doing a puzzle?" he asked, smoothly changing the subject and gesturing toward the pieces she had spread out on the table. "That looks fun."

"It's supposed to help keep me sharp," Clara replied dryly. "I can't remember if I've crapped or not today, though, so I don't think it's working."

"Well, it still looks fun." Jake darted his eyes to the door when a man in a white coat entered. He looked to be in his sixties, and the grave expression on his face told Jake things were indeed about to go sideways.

"Thank you for coming." Dr. Cosgrove extended his hand

for January to shake. "I understand you're busy up at the resort, so I won't take up a lot of your time."

"Is something wrong?" January asked. She gripped her hands together so tightly in front of her that Jake marveled at the white sheen of her knuckles. "Is something wrong? Did you find something on a test?"

Cosgrove shot January a sympathetic look. "Your mother's tests are the same. We've gone over her prognosis multiple times. It hasn't changed."

Jake shot one more look toward Clara, who appeared to have become lost in her own little world as though unaware people were in her room, and got to his feet. He moved toward January at the other side of the room and addressed the doctor in a low voice. "Go over it with me," he instructed. "I want to know what her prognosis is."

Cosgrove's eyebrows winged up. "And you are?"

"January's boyfriend," Jake replied, not missing a beat. He registered her surprise at the declaration but didn't acknowledge it. "I'm going to be helping with this situation going forward, so I need to know what we're dealing with here."

Cosgrove seemed to consider it for several seconds and then nodded. "Okay, well, Clara's dementia is quite severe," he said, speaking quietly. "It's also progressive. She's a young woman to be in this state—and we can only theorize why it might've happened—but it's only going to get worse."

"There are days she remembers me," January said in a low voice. "She gets caught in the past and thinks I'm still a kid." Something about January's expression told Jake those weren't good days.

"Those days are few and far between now," Cosgrove interjected. "It's been at least a month since Clara has remembered you, January. We're starting to get into the phase I warned you about. Soon, she won't even be able to do a puzzle. She'll just be in her bed, staring at a wall or the television, and not registering anything."

January sucked in a breath. "So what do we do?"

"There's nothing we can do," Cosgrove replied. "We can help work her muscles and check on her regularly—we already do that—but there's no stopping the cognitive decline." He hesitated and then continued. "I think now is the time to consider moving your mother into a county facility."

January's mouth dropped open, and Jake immediately leaned forward to lend her his strength. "Why would she want to do that?" Jake demanded. "Are you guys not taking care of Clara or something?"

"Don't be ridiculous." Cosgrove shot Jake a scathing look. "We take care of all of our patients. It's just that Clara is coming to a point in her life where she won't know the difference. Our rates are officially going up, Ms. Jackson." He looked sad as he regarded January. "I mentioned this was a possibility. The board voted last night. If you want to keep your mother in this facility, it's going to cost another two thousand dollars a month."

January reeled back from the doctor and focused on the window. Jake didn't miss the rapid blinks that suggested she was fighting off tears. To him, two grand a month didn't sound like the end of the world. He knew January was already struggling to keep her head above water though.

"Are you saying you're kicking Clara out?" Jake demanded.

"That is not our intention, and we'll certainly try to help January with this moving forward," Cosgrove replied. "I happen to know that she's already struggling to meet the monthly payments, however. She's been late several times."

"Thanks for your compassion, Doc." Jake shot him a sarcastic thumbs-up before moving to January and rubbing her back. He'd never felt so helpless in his entire life.

"The rate increase doesn't go into effect for three months," Cosgrove said. "Until then, the rates will stay the same. If you want your mother to stay, however, we're going to need you to start paying quarterly, and that will be a big chunk of change you need to come up with by the end of the month to reserve her bed."

The way January's shoulders shook told Jake this was her worst possible nightmare.

"I'll get another job," she said in a low voice. "As soon as the Winter Extreme Games are over, I'll pick up a second job. I'm sure one of the restaurants will be hiring."

Jake was dumbfounded. "How are you going to work at the resort and take shifts at a restaurant?"

"I'll figure it out." January was desperate when she stepped closer to Cosgrove. "Don't give my mother's bed away. She has to stay here. I made a promise."

"I'll do my best." Cosgrove looked legitimately sad. "I just don't know what I'm going to be able to do. The edict from the board was very specific."

Jake's heart felt as if it were riding roughshod over a cheese grater, and before he even realized what he was going to say, it was already coming out of his mouth. "Do not give Clara's bed to anybody else."

"I need the down payment," Cosgrove said. "There's nothing I can do without it."

"You'll have it by the end of the day." Jake was firm. "I'll bring you a check by five o'clock."

Confusion etched across January's face. "I can't come up with that money by five o'clock."

"I can." Jake refused to back down, even when she started shaking her head. "Don't." He extended a warning finger. "I've got this, and I don't want to hear a peep from you." He flashed a smile for Cosgrove's benefit. The doctor looked well and truly confused. "Jacob Jeffries is my father. I'll have the money in a few hours. Do not give Clara's bed away."

Recognition dawned on Cosgrove, and it was quickly replaced with relief. "I see. That is very good. I mean, very, very good."

Jake wanted to tell him where he could stick his rate increase, but he didn't want to upset January further. "I'll be back as soon as I can manage it. I might have to do a few things for the games before I can head back. I've got it though." He turned to January. "Trust me. Nobody is getting a second job."

January looked close to bursting into tears. "Jake—"

"No." He was having none of it. "You've done enough for ten people. Let me help you."

January's lower lip trembled, and she managed a nod before he pulled her in for a hug.

Over her shoulder, Jake met Cosgrove's gaze, the two men exchanging a significant stare.

"I'll get a firm number for you from the front desk," Cosgrove said. "You should be all set when you leave."

"Awesome." Jake stroked his hand over January's hair and started swaying back and forth to lull her. "Then I guess we'll just nip this little problem in the bud before the sun sets, won't we?"

Twenty-One

J ake had to drop by his parents' house to pick up more clothes upon leaving the facility. He didn't want to abandon January when she was clearly struggling, but she was determined to get to work. He decided to let her calm down a bit before pushing her on what had happened. If he'd learned one thing about her, it was that she needed to think hard on things before talking them out.

It was better for her—and therefore him—to take a step back, so that's what he did. Since there was another party that evening for the sponsors and workers—to celebrate the first week going so well—he needed to focus on that, which meant grabbing another suit from his closet at his parents' lake house.

"What are you doing here?" Enid seemed surprised when she walked into the kitchen and found Jake rummaging through the refrigerator.

"I need another suit for tonight," Jake replied as he closed the refrigerator door. He was hungry, and yet nothing sounded appetizing. "I'm going to grab a few other things from upstairs too."

"Oh, that sounds nice." Enid smiled at him, but Jake didn't miss the curiosity in her eyes.

"What?" he demanded.

"I didn't say anything."

"What?" he repeated, annoyance building up and crowding his chest.

"You just seem ... upset," Enid replied. "I'd heard you were slipping into your new role at the resort well. I guess those rumors were wrong."

"Work is fine," he assured her. "Work is actually better than fine. That's not what I'm upset about." He hopped up onto the counter even though he knew it annoyed his mother. Irritating her seemed like a minor thing compared to what he'd seen—and heard—at the hospital earlier. "Do you know January's mother?"

Enid's eyebrows hiked up, although there was so much Botox in her forehead, only someone who knew her well could recognize her reaction. "I know Clara," she confirmed. "Why?"

"I just saw her."

"I thought she was in some facility."

"Radcliffe Downs," Jake confirmed. "It's between here and Traverse City. She has early onset dementia. She didn't even recognize January today."

"Really?" Enid cocked her head. "I guess I didn't realize it was that serious. January never mentions her mother."

"I'm pretty sure there's a reason for that." Jake snagged an apple from the fruit bowl and passed it from one hand to the other. "Do you know that January lives in those run-down apartments over on the east side?"

"I didn't know that."

"She spends every spare cent she has keeping Clara in that facility, even though every story she tells me about her mother is a version of that woman being cruel to her."

Enid angled her chin, seemingly debating, and then sighed. "I guess those rumors are true?"

Jake balked. "What rumors?"

"People are saying you and January are a couple."

"Isn't that what Dad wants?" He had no idea why he wasn't confirming it for his mother—he wasn't embarrassed about being with January—but he didn't want some big, emotional conversation when he was trying to figure things out.

"Oh, let's not play *that* game." Enid was stern as she snagged the apple from him and motioned for him to jump down from the counter. "Sit down at the table, and I'll make you a sandwich."

Jake did as he was told, curiosity rippling through him as he watched his mother gather the lunchmeat from the fridge.

"I happen to know that you two have been seen kissing in various parts of the resort this week," Enid said as she set about making the sandwich. "We're talking parts of the resort where the Maxwells wouldn't see you, which suggests to me you weren't putting on a show for them."

"So?" Jake's spine went straight. "What does it matter?"

Enid sighed. "I'm not giving you grief."

"You're not?" Jake couldn't help being dubious. "Since when don't you give me a hard time?"

"Don't push it." Enid scalded him with a serious look. Her expression softened after a few seconds. "I like January."

"You do?" Surprise wrinkled Jake's forehead. "That's not what Dad said."

"Your father doesn't know everything." She pulled a tomato out of the fruit bowl and started slicing it. "I will admit that I was a bit leery when she first started working for your father. All I remembered of her were those instances in the principal's office when the two of you were growing up."

"That wasn't entirely her fault."

Enid's lips twitched. "I'm well aware."

"You are?"

"Of course. I'm not one of those parents who believes my baby boy is always perfect. I know you antagonized her as much as she antagonized you." Enid took a breath before continuing. "I also know that girl had no business growing up to be as together as she is now. Clara was ... not a present mother. January basically raised herself."

"Maybe that's why she's so strong."

"Maybe," Enid agreed. "The thing is, in hindsight, I can't help but feel that we as a community failed January. We should've done something to help her. Half the reason she was acting out against you is because she was a sad, lonely, neglected little girl."

Jake was surprised to realize his eyes were burning. He wasn't a crier in the least. He blinked twice to force himself to remain calm and then filled his mother in on the rest. "The facility where January is keeping her mother is raising the prices. She won't be able to afford to keep paying the monthly fees unless she gets a second job."

Enid looked taken aback. "That is horrible."

"It's not fair," Jake insisted. "The bulk of her money goes to Clara, who doesn't even remember her."

"If the rumors are true about the way Clara treated January when she was growing up, that might be a good thing."

"January won't let her mother be moved to a county facility. She feels it's her duty to keep Clara in that hospital, and she's willing to work herself to death to do it."

Enid stopped what she was doing long enough to study her son's face. "Something tells me you're not going to let that happen," she said after several seconds.

"I'm not." Jake was firm. "I'm still allowed to take some money out of my trust every year, right?"

"Your father doesn't want you touching the principle on that trust your grandfather left you until he's certain you won't blow it," Enid acknowledged.

"I don't want to touch the principle. I want to take the money I'm allowed to take out and use it for Clara's care."

Enid's mouth dropped open. "What now?"

"Don't give me grief." Jake extended a warning finger. "This is what I want to do. January needs to breathe. She can't breathe as long as this is hanging over her head."

"I see." Enid rested her palms on the counter, her expression unreadable. "Does January know this is your plan?"

"Oh, she's not a gold digger, so get that out of your head right now." Adamance squared Jake's shoulders. "She needs to feel as if the walls aren't constantly closing in on her. I can pay for the next two years with one withdrawal from my trust. That's what I want to do. I need you and Dad to sign off on it."

"Which is really why you're here," Enid surmised.

"I need a suit. I don't want to wear the same one again. January's dress tonight is purple. I saw it hanging in her room. I have a pocket square that will match it."

Enid was quiet for so long that Jake started feeling self-conscious. "What?" he demanded.

Her smile was soft and warm. "Nothing." She wiped off her hands on a towel. "I'll talk to your father. He'll agree."

"You were thinking something," Jake insisted.

"I was thinking that your father was right. There was always a good man buried under that playboy exterior of yours. I didn't realize January was going to be the one to expose that man, but somehow, given your past, it feels right."

"I just don't like the idea of her living in constant fear," Jake explained. "She's wound really tight, but when she relaxes, she's a completely different person. I need her to relax."

"I'm fine if you want to help January. What I'm not okay with is you trying to change her. Wanting her to be able to breathe is a good thing. You can't change her though. She's still going to be uptight, even when she no longer has to worry about her mother. That's simply who she is. If you expect her to suddenly be happy-go-lucky—"

"That's not what I want," Jake assured her. "I like her uptight. I'm starting to think that's my kink or something."

Enid frowned. "I don't think I needed to know that."

Jake snickered. "She's an organized individual, and I've always been driven by chaos. I want her to rub off on me."

"And in turn, she wants you to rub off on her," Enid mused.

"It seems to be playing out that way."

Enid was quiet for several seconds and then nodded. "Okay, well, I can float you a personal loan until we can clear the money from your trust. That will take a few days."

"Won't Dad have a problem with that?"

"You leave your father to me." Enid went back to preparing his sandwich. "Tell me about the facility where Clara lives. My charity ladies have been looking for a new cause. Maybe we can start volunteering some time—and resources—there."

Jake let out a breath. He hadn't realized how worried he'd been that his parents would shoot him down until his mother readily agreed to help him. "Thank you, Mom."

She nodded. "I want to help her too. She's a good girl."

"Yeah."

"She's the only girl you've ever acted this way over."

Jake's expression darkened. "Oh, I know what you're doing." He wagged his finger and made a tsking sound with his tongue. "Don't get ahead of yourself. We have to figure out if we can make this work between ourselves before you're going to even get a whiff of grandchildren."

Enid was the picture of innocence. "Did I say anything?"

"I know the way your mind works." Despite himself, Jake grinned. "Maybe one day though."

"That's all I want to hear."

"Yeah, somehow I knew that would make you happy."

JANUARY WALKED INTO THE PARTY BY herself shortly before seven o'clock. She'd been expecting to walk over with Jake, but his father had called an hour before and asked Jake for help with some family issue—apparently, there was some banking thing that needed to be done—and she'd been left to her own devices. That meant crossing the parking lot in boots because she didn't want to risk falling and carrying her shoes.

"Classy," Leo said when he saw her slipping behind the front desk so she could change out her shoes. "I think you should keep the boots and lose the heels."

"Oh, if only," January said on a laugh as she shoved her boots into the office. Her heels were so uncomfortable she grimaced as she slipped into them. "The price we pay for fashion, huh?"

Leo smirked. "You look lovely." He held out his arm for her. "How about I act as your escort until we find that husband of yours?"

January made a face. "You don't have to tease me about the husband stuff. I know darned well that you've been informed about the specifics of that arrangement."

"I have," Leo agreed. He looked dapper in his suit. "That doesn't mean I don't recognize the real thing when I see it."

January almost tripped as he led her toward the dining room. He had to grip her arm tighter to keep her on her feet. "What?"

Leo was a kind man—she'd always known that—but he

looked more amused than sympathetic this evening. "I think it's best you don't try to lie to me."

"I would never lie to you," January sputtered.

"Not lie like that." Leo shook his head. "Sweetheart, I'm not trying to upset you. I just..." He took a breath and seemingly regrouped. "You're a good influence on Jake. You're making him the man we always knew he could be. That's a good thing. That's all I was saying."

To her surprise, January felt the need to stand up for Jake. "You guys are purposely hard on him. He's always been a good man. He's just been prone to flights of fantasy while doling out that good."

Leo gave her a sidelong look. "Is that so?"

"It is." January bobbed her head. "He's always been a good person. You guys just had unrealistic expectations for him."

"Were those expectations unrealistic, or was he just slow getting it together?"

"I think they were unrealistic." January averted her gaze. "It doesn't matter. He's a grown-up now. Isn't that the important thing?"

"Uh-huh." A small smile curved Leo's lips. "I like that you're loyal to him. He's always needed that. You're loyal to the man and not the money. That's always been his biggest fear."

"I don't see money when I look at him," January replied. "I only see the man."

"Keep it that way." Leo squeezed her arm and then grinned when something caught his attention on the dance floor. "I think your husband wants you."

January jerked up her eyes, a wide smile taking over her features when she saw Jake trying to entice her to join him on the dance floor. "I guess I shouldn't leave him waiting," she said when her heart had stopped sighing in delight at the sight of Jake in his suit.

"Definitely not." Leo released her, and she could feel the smile on his face rather than see it. She was too busy looking at Jake to bother glancing at the security chief.

"You look nice," January said automatically when she reached him. "Like, *really* nice."

"You look beautiful." Jake smoothly slid his arms around her waist and pulled her in for a dance. "I'm sorry I couldn't walk you over. My father needed me to sign some paperwork, and we had to get it out of the way today."

"It's fine," January assured him. "Although it wasn't something bad, was it?"

"Nope." Jake pulled her flush against his chest, his eyes only for her. "Part of me doesn't want to tell you what I was doing because you're going to make a big deal about it, but the other part feels I need to explain because you'll freak out otherwise when you get the news from Dr. Cosgrove."

January froze in his arms. "Did my mother lose her spot?"

"No, baby." He shook his head. "Your mother's spot is secure for the next two years. All her bills have been paid during that time, in fact."

January thought she might fall over. "What? How?"

"I pulled my interest check from my trust and took care of it."

"But you can't do that!" January's cheeks flushed hot, and she was legitimately worried she might pass out. "That's not your responsibility."

"January, it's not about responsibility. That's my money to do with as I please. I want to take care of your mother."

"But..." A tear slid down January's cheek.

Jake caught it and pulled her tightly against him. She couldn't see his face now. All she could do was feel him, and he felt so right. Nothing had ever felt better—and that terrified her on every level imaginable.

"It's done," Jake said in a low voice. "I needed my parents to sign off on it. That's what I was doing when I had to head across the parking lot early. My mother cut me a check because it will take a few days for the trust money to be available. That money is going to your mother's care as soon as I can transfer it."

"Jake, I don't know what to say."

"I don't want you to say anything." He pulled back far enough to see her face and then pressed a kiss to her forehead. "I don't want you freaking out over this. I just want you to be able to breathe and maybe move out of that craphole you live in."

"I'll pay you back," January insisted.

"No, you won't." Jake adamantly shook his head. "I want to do this. You're not paying me back. Also, I hate those apartments where you live, so I think we should find you something else."

"You've never even seen my apartment."

"I don't care. I've seen other apartments over there, and they were run-down ten years ago. I know for a fact they haven't funneled money into them to make them better in that time. I have an idea on that when the games are over. We can talk about it in a week."

January wanted to feel uneasy, but she didn't. Instead, she melted into Jake's arms as he swayed back and forth. "I don't know what to say."

"You don't have to say anything. Just be with me. Have fun. Take a breath. Maybe have a cocktail or two."

"What about after?" she asked. "What about when we're not living a fake life in a lodge? What happens then?"

"We figure it out."

"What if we can't?" January realized that was her biggest

worry. It was no longer her mother. It was losing this feeling that had been slowly taking her over.

"We will. Have a little faith."

That was what January wanted more than anything. Faith. Security. Him. Was she falling in love with him? She had no frame of reference, but it certainly felt that way. "Fine. I'll have faith."

"Good." His lips brushed against her cheek. "I think the plan should be to put in a good showing here—I'm thinking forty-five minutes—and then we'll take our faith and a bottle of champagne back to the hot tub."

January giggled. "Don't you think we'll be missed?"

"Live a little."

"Fine, but I'm blaming it on you if we get caught."

"I think that's more than fair."

Twenty-Two

Only a handful of events were planned for Saturday and Sunday. They were big events but spread out. Unfortunately for January and Jake, they had parties to attend both nights, and being social was starting to grate.

"Why can't we just be home in our hot tub?" Jake complained as they danced in the dining room Sunday night.

Home? The word threw January. They'd certainly made it their home, but it was a temporary arrangement. In a week—maybe they could stretch it to a week and a half—she would be returning to her apartment. Then where would they be? Was this all a result of forced proximity? She couldn't help but wonder. Despite her worries, she was determined to enjoy the time she had with him no matter what.

"We could sneak out again," she suggested.

Jake slid his eyes to her. "Oh yeah?" He looked intrigued. "What did you have in mind?"

"I was thinking we could grab a bottle of wine and hit the hot tub."

"Sold." Jake surprised her when he planted a firm kiss on the corner of her mouth and pulled away.

January managed a sputtering sound, and then her eyes went wide. "We have to be smooth about it. We can't just race off together. People will talk."

"So what?" Jake's reaction was bland. "We're married. Why wouldn't we take off with each other?"

January pinned him with a dubious look. "We have to be smart about it." She tapped the side of her head. "That means we have to hobnob with the Maxwells before sliding out one of the side doors without anybody noticing. We want people to assume we're still here, just mingling."

"That's very devious, but I like it." He squeezed her hand and appeared to be thinking hard. "Okay, here's what's going to happen," he started. "We're going to hit the big dogs. That's King Maxwell himself, his closest three kids, and my father. You're going to start for home before me because it will take you longer to get across the parking lot." He paused a beat. "If you think you're going to slip and fall in those shoes, wait for me down at the end of the sidewalk, and I'll carry you."

January made a face. "I'm more than capable of walking across a parking lot."

"Do not fall and hurt yourself." Jake was stern. "I'll be mad if you do. I have plans for you." He leaned in and gave her a sweet kiss, apparently not caring in the least that people might be watching. "I'll handle the wine. Luke is working the bar."

January's eyes shifted in that direction. "Okay. So, thirty minutes, and then we meet back at the lodge?"

"Thirty minutes, and I'll have you naked in our hot tub," he readily agreed.

January giggled at his enthusiasm—she so wasn't a giggler —and nodded. He left her breathless, which was something she couldn't wrap her head around. She'd never considered herself to be the sort of woman who would lose her head over a man, but it was happening. She was both exhilarated and terrified at the prospect.

"I'll see you then." She squeezed his hand but didn't lean in for another kiss, even though she desperately wanted to. If she did, she was afraid that they would lose themselves in one another right on the dance floor, and there would be no coming back. She wanted time alone with him, and she was prepared to make it happen.

She was calm while cutting through the crowd. Despite her anxiety, she was good with people. They trusted her to get the job done. She made sure she was seen talking to Maxwell and his wife. Then she took a few moments to chat with his children, including Edward, who continued to make her distinctly uncomfortable despite the scene with Jake days before.

Her last stop was the front desk to talk to the night manager and make sure he understood about cleanup efforts after the party. He was diligent, so she wasn't overly worried. When she turned, prepared to take off and beat Jake to the lodge so she could light some candles around the hot tub, she found Enid watching her.

"Mrs. Jeffries," she blurted, internally cringing at how shrill she sounded. "You look amazing tonight," she added, hoping the woman wasn't suspicious about what she was doing.

"You look lovely too," Enid said, her lips curving. "That blue dress is flattering on you. You almost look like a snow queen."

Confused, January glanced down at her dress. It wasn't ostentatious or designed to make her stand out. "Thank you," she said finally.

"You make simple things lovely, January," Enid continued.

"I ... um..."

"You also seem to have grounded my son," Enid added.

January's cheeks caught fire. She wasn't embarrassed about her relationship with Jake—the opposite, actually—but talking to his mother about what was going on between them felt somehow surreal. "I don't know what you mean." She avoided making eye contact.

"Let's talk a second." Enid took January's hand and led her away from the front desk, tossing a significant look in the night manager's direction should he try to eavesdrop. When they were away from the crowd and standing in front of the huge Christmas tree, Enid fixed January with a soft smile. "I know that you and Jake are still figuring things out," she started.

"He told you?" Horrified disbelief burned through January's chest.

"My son is a bit of a mama's boy," Enid confirmed on a grin. "He always has been. Even if he wasn't, though, I would've known. You two look at each other in a very specific way. You always have."

January was floored. "Did you feel that way when we were constantly being called into the principal's office as kids?"

Enid chuckled. "When you were very little, I wasn't quite certain what was going on with the two of you. You clearly bristled like fighting cats whenever in the same space. I started suspecting it was something more when you were in middle school. By high school, I knew what it was. I simply didn't know what to do about it."

"It's a cliché, right?" January queried. "You always fight with the one you ... like."

Enid nodded. "I don't like dealing with clichés, but there was always a spark there when you were younger. I don't think the two of you would've put as much energy into torturing one another as you did if you didn't care. Still, that didn't necessarily mean you would be able to figure things out."

January's voice was soft when she responded. "I don't know that we've figured anything out."

"You're well on your way to it," Enid argued. "I see it." She let her shoulders drop and turned plaintive. "You don't have to figure it all out now. It's perfectly fine to not know everything, January. You're allowed to figure things out on whatever timetable you want to embrace."

"I'm afraid for when the games end," January admitted, surprising herself. She liked Enid, however, and since she'd never had a female role model, she was happy to look up to Jake's mother. "When I go back to my place, and we're not forced to be so close to one another..." She trailed off and lifted one shoulder. "I just don't know how it's going to turn out."

"I think you two are going to be fine. In fact, you'll be better than fine." Enid absently patted her arm. "The two of you are under a lot of pressure right now. I'm glad you have each other to get through it."

"Yes, well, it's a lot, but we seem to be coping." January darted her eyes toward the front door.

"And I'm keeping you," Enid said out of the blue. "I'm guessing you and Jake are trying to slip out again without anybody noticing. You should get going. It will take you twice as long to get across the parking lot in those heels as it will him."

January was floored. "You knew that we left last night?"

"I'm not an idiot. Of course I knew." Enid let loose a laugh. "Don't get worked up about it. I don't think the Maxwells knew. Even if they did, it's none of their business."

"We need to keep them happy," January argued. "What if we need them for a future sponsorship or something?"

Enid hesitated and then held out her hands. "Those things work themselves out. Don't fret. Let Jacob handle that part.

You just take some time to be happy. That's all anybody wants for you."

"Thank you, ma'am."

"Call me Enid."

January wasn't certain she could manage that. "I'll do my best," she said after several seconds.

"That's all I can ask."

JAKE HUMMED TO HIMSELF AS HE APPROACHED the bar. Luke was busy making holiday drinks—something with pomegranate—and he only briefly glanced up when Jake appeared.

"What's up, man? You want a beer? I was told that I had to keep it fancy. Wine and cocktails tonight, but I might be able to hide a beer in one of those weird Christmas steins they bought."

"Under different circumstances, I might take you up on that," Jake replied. "I want a nice bottle of wine though."

"You want a whole bottle?" Luke laughed. "Are your parents driving you crazy or something? That's a lot of wine to drink by yourself. Are you going to hide in a closet and drink straight out of the bottle?"

"Actually, I don't want an open bottle of wine. I want a fresh bottle to take with me."

"Oh, yeah?" Luke arched an eyebrow before placing two cocktails on a tray. He waited until one of the servers picked them up before speaking again. "Hot date?"

Jake didn't want to smile—it would only encourage his old friend—but he couldn't seem to stop himself. "Something like that."

"Oh, yeah?" Luke's smile was easy. "What's her name? Oh, wait, I know. It's Samantha, isn't it? She's the new server over there. I've seen her watching you. She seems to like what she sees. I bet she's wild in bed." Luke waggled his eyebrows, causing Jake to frown.

"I don't know who Samantha is," Jake shot back. "I'm not dating her."

"Oh." Luke barely missed a beat. "Is it Ginny with a G?"

"I don't know who that is either."

"That's how she introduces herself. 'I'm Ginny with a G. Would you like to play with my double Ds?' I added that last part, but you can totally tell she's thinking it when she introduces herself."

Jake's scowl was pronounced. "I'm not dating Ginny with a G either. I'm ... married." Saying it wasn't as ridiculous as he would've thought. Yes, he knew that he wasn't really married, but he wasn't as frightened at the prospect as he would've been weeks before.

"You're fake married," Luke countered.

"Shh." Jake pressed a finger to his lips and glanced around to make sure no Maxwells were within hearing distance. "Are you trying to get me in trouble? Keep your voice down."

Luke chuckled. "Sorry. Everybody knows you're not really married."

"How does everybody know that?"

"Because word has spread. Everybody was confused when the gossip started up about you guys living together at the lodge. Then some people were saying you were married. It all started to make sense when the Maxwells appeared on the scene. They're a bit rigid with the religious stuff."

"They certainly are," Jake agreed, glancing over his shoulder to where the Maxwell patriarch stood with his children. "I don't like him."

"What's to like? He's a judgmental prick."

"He's a judgmental prick with a lot of money."

"Which is why we have to put up with him. It's only another week. Then January can move out of your lodge, and you can get your life back. You must be thrilled about that."

Slowly, deliberately, Jake swung back to face his friend. "Why would I be thrilled about that?" His voice was tremulous when he spoke, throwing him for a loop. Was he about to cry? He didn't think so. Why did he sound like he was then?

"Because she's January Jackson," Luke replied, not missing a beat as he checked another incoming order and started mixing a drink. "Everybody knows she's an anal-retentive pain in the ass.

"I mean, she's hot, don't get me wrong," he continued, seemingly oblivious to Jake's rising fury. "I never realized how hot she was when we were in school. I looked at my yearbook a few days ago, and she's definitely hot in the photos, but I never saw that when we were kids."

"What did you see?" Jake asked, his voice deceptively mild.

"Well, she was a tattletale, wasn't she? She's the one who got us in trouble that time we decided to get stoned in the auto shop classroom."

"You mean the time we decided to operate heavy machinery without Mr. Nixon present?" Jake challenged. "Yeah, she's the one who made sure we didn't lose any fingers."

Luke continued as if Jake hadn't even spoken. "Remember the time we went up to the second floor to skip class because we didn't want to sit through another bad *Romeo & Juliet* movie? We weren't supposed to go up there because they said there was asbestos or something. She caught us and reported us then too. We got a week's detention out of that one."

"So?" Jake's eyes flashed with annoyance. "We shouldn't have been hanging around with asbestos. Give me a break."

Luke's lips quirked. "Still, you have to be excited to get rid of her. Only one more week, buddy." He clapped his hand against Jake's shoulder, his eyes going wide when Jake grabbed his wrist and squeezed. "What?" he asked blankly. "Did I say something? You don't really like that anal-retentive priss, do you?"

"Don't call her that," Jake growled. He was barely hanging on to his temper. If he lost it in front of everybody, his father's disappointment would need its own zip code by the time he was finished tearing Jake a new one. "You don't even know her."

"I know she walks around here with a to-do list every single day," Luke countered. "She's got a stick up her ass."

"She's organized. That doesn't make her a bad person."

"Dude, she's just your fake wife, not your real one," Luke offered in a conspiratorial whisper. "It's okay. You can talk shit about her."

That did it. Jake grabbed the front of Luke's uniform shirt and dragged him halfway across the bar. He no longer cared if anybody was looking. "Don't say one more word," he growled.

"What seems to be the problem?" Luke asked blandly.

"You don't know anything about January," Jake seethed. "You have no idea what she's been through. The fact that she's managed to do the things she's done, given her home life, given how her mother broke her down every single day, is nothing short of a miracle."

Jake gripped his left hand into a fist and fought the urge to plow it into Luke's face as he kept hold of the man with his right hand. "She's a freaking miracle. She did everything on her own. That's *everything*. She had no help.

"So what if she's organized?" he continued. "So what if she likes things neat? She keeps this entire place together and running smoothly. I don't want to hear another word about her."

"Because you're falling in love with her?" Luke demanded.

"I..." Jake blinked several times and slowly released Luke as realization washed over him. Did he love January? He wasn't certain. It was too soon for that. At least that was what he told himself. He knew one thing beyond absolute certainty though. He could fall in love with her, and he was very close to that precipice. One more solid push, and he would tumble over the edge. It wasn't the scary proposition he would've assumed.

"There it is." Luke calmly removed Jake's fingers from his shirt. "Everybody knows your fake relationship with January is way more than that now," he said in a low voice.

"We're going to try to make it work," Jake admitted. "Once this is over, we're going to make an honest go of it."

"Because you like her."

"Yeah." Jake managed a grin. "I really do. She's fun and soft, and I like that she's organized. She leaves lists all over the lodge, and I read all of them, for some reason."

Luke chuckled. "That's a very weird kink you're developing, man."

"Maybe." Jake bobbed his head. "I like spending time with her. It's only been two weeks, but it feels longer than that."

"Maybe because you and January have been building up to this since you were five and you broke her orange crayon."

"Maybe." Jake let loose a breath. "I just know that my favorite part of the day is when I wake up and she's there, usually already working on a list. My second favorite part of the day is when I go to bed and she's there, likely thinking about what she's going to put on her list for the next day."

Luke barked out a laugh. "What's your third favorite part of the day?"

"Watching her mark things off her list. I can't explain it. It's baffling."

"As long as you're happy, that's all that matters." Luke rummaged underneath the bar and came back with a bottle of wine. "I'm glad you admitted it. I've been watching you, and it's obvious. I wasn't certain you realized it though."

"She makes me happy," Jake said. "More than that, she makes me content. For the first time in my life, I don't want to be anywhere else. I don't want to get on a plane and head out. I just want to be here, with her."

"I think that's what people call forward progress."

"Yeah."

"You might want to tell her what you're feeling, just in case she needs to hear it."

"Yeah." Jake managed a smile. "I think I might do that."

"Awesome. I still want to hear the details when the games are over. Just because I'm a good friend, that doesn't mean I'm not a gossip too."

"I'll consider it."

"I'll take that as a win, at least for tonight."

TWENTY-THREE

Married life was treating Jake very well. Some mornings, he cooked for January. The other mornings, she cooked for him, or they caught a quick bite in the resort dining room together. Always, they woke up cuddled next to one another and spent a full hour whispering and kissing. Sometimes the encounters led to sex. Other times, he was just as happy to hold her close and settle. That was how he thought of it in his head. He wasn't settling, but he felt settled. His mind was no longer in turmoil.

That was another miracle to him.

"What's on the agenda today?" Jake asked January as she doled out scrambled eggs and sausage onto two plates.

"Well, it's the mid-Monday," she said. She'd pulled her hair back in a simple bun and looked professional. For some reason, her business attire kicked Jake's hormones into overdrive. Her insistence on being put together and prepared was definitely turning into his kink. It was baffling to him.

"Meaning what?" Jake asked, forcing himself to focus on the important things of the day. He could make her pretend to take dictation later and play a little game when they were alone again, he told himself. He chose to make that the dream and work the reality. At least he hoped he could pull it off.

"Meaning that there will be meetings." January carried the plates to the table and sat across from him, her smile at the ready. "I'm going to be out watching the three races we have going this morning. I was hoping you could take the meeting with your father and Edward." She didn't make eye contact when she said it.

Jake's eyes narrowed as he regarded her. "Has Edward been giving you a hard time?"

"No." January emphatically shook her head. "Not even a little. It's just—" She didn't finish what she was going to say, and that bothered Jake even more.

"Tell me," he prodded in a soft voice. "Has he touched you again?"

January fixed him with a stern look. "No, and don't do anything weird. We just need to get through one more week."

"If he's putting his hands on you, I want to know about it."

"He hasn't," January insisted. "He's just ... been weird."

"Yeah, I'm going to need more than that." Jake didn't bother digging into the food she'd provided him with. He'd suddenly lost his appetite. "Tell me what's going on."

"He just says things." January gripped her hands together on her lap. "He asked questions about our relationship. At first, I thought it was because he didn't believe we were married—and I was worried that he was going to say something to Jim—but I don't think that's it. It's almost as if he's trying to feel me out in case I want to have an affair or something."

Jake's eyes were narrow slits of disgust. "Well, I don't like that."

"I don't either, but it's literally just one more week. If you take the meeting today, then I might not have to see him for the rest of the time he's here." She almost sounded pleading.

"Baby, you don't have to worry about taking the meeting," Jake assured her. "I'll take it." *And I'll make sure he knows harassing my wife isn't allowed.* He barely registered that he'd called her his wife and that it felt real. "Don't worry about it, okay?" He held his hand across the table for her.

"Okay." She managed a soft smile as she linked her fingers with his.

It was Jake's right hand, which he needed for eating, but he decided to make do with his left hand because he didn't want to let her go. "What else is going on today?"

"Um, I'm not sure." If January thought holding his hand while eating was weird, she didn't show it. "First up are the races. After that, I'll probably do a run-through of the resort to see if we can improve on anything from last week. We have a lot of guests who checked out yesterday and more coming in today."

"Okay, well, after the meeting, I'll find you," Jake said. "I'll help with whatever you need help with."

"Whatever I need help with?" she asked, a teasing glint in her eyes.

Jake smirked. "Maybe we can visit one of the empty rooms this afternoon. You know, just to make sure it's clean and everything."

She laughed, as he'd intended. "Don't you think messing it up would be counterproductive?"

"Not if we put it back together."

She arched an eyebrow, considering, then nodded. "Good point."

"I knew I would bring you around to my way of thinking."

.   .   .

JAKE PRESSED HIS LIPS TOGETHER AS HE LET himself into his father's office. Things were going well. So well, in fact, he couldn't ever remember being this happy. It was a humbling thought, one that should've felt alien to him. It didn't, though, and he was genuinely baffled at the turn his life had taken over the last three weeks.

"You seem happy," Jacob noted as he met his son at the coffee cart. "Since when do you sing Christmas carols?"

"I was humming," Jake replied. "There's a difference."

"Only in your head, son." Jacob glanced at the door, as if assuring himself that nobody was entering, and then focused on his only child. "How is January?"

"She's good." Jake's smile was soft. "She's got a list of things she wants to get through today."

"Doesn't she always have a list?"

"Yup. I like helping her finish the lists. She gets really excited when every single item has been marked off."

Jacob made a face. "I don't think I need the details."

"I figured. I do have a question though." Jake followed his father back to his desk. "What's the status on the chalets out here?"

Jacob clearly wasn't expecting the question because his eyebrows hopped as he sat. "I'm not sure. Why?"

"How much would it cost to buy one? Like, how much would I need for a down payment?"

"It depends on which one you want. They range in price from sixty to three hundred grand. Why do you want to buy one?"

"Because I think it's time I own my own house, don't you?" Jake demanded. "I'm almost thirty, and I've never owned anything."

"Okay." Jacob stretched out his answer. "You know you can stay at the lodge, right?"

"Yes, but that belongs to the resort. I want something that belongs to me."

"And January?"

Jake hesitated and then shrugged. "Maybe. I don't think we're there yet, but I would like to have something to work toward. You know, a plan. January lives in those really crappy apartments over by the park."

"I only recently found out about that." Jacob frowned. "Renting the way she does is like throwing money out the window, but only after setting it on fire. I'm surprised she hasn't tried to buy a house yet. Even if she couldn't afford to live in Bellaire, Mancelona is only fifteen minutes away, and the houses there are cheap."

"Yeah, we're not living in Mancelona if we can help it," Jake said.

"I like how you assume you'll be living together."

Jake hadn't realized he was making that assumption until he'd already done it. "I want to be with her," he said simply. "I think that requires a plan."

"Okay." Jacob seemed more than happy to help. "I can arrange for you to borrow the down payment for one of the chalets from us. One of the nicer ones just came on the market." He hesitated but only for a beat. "I could give you the down payment, make it high so you have no problem hitting the monthly mortgage payments, and give you favorable terms on paying me back at the same time."

Surprise ricocheted through Jake's chest. "You would do that?"

"I would."

"I thought you were cutting me off."

"I didn't want to cut you off, Jake. I just wanted you to find a purpose. I felt as if you were meandering."

"And suddenly, three weeks later, you don't think I'm meandering any longer?"

Jacob held out his hands. "I think you seem to be finding your focus. I don't want to dissuade that. If you want to buy a place for you and January, I'm all for it. Although you haven't been dating that long."

"No? Weirdly, it feels as if we've been gearing up for this our entire lives. I have no idea what that says about me, but it just feels right."

Jacob chuckled. "You two have always had an interesting relationship. Just for the record, I know you're in the honeymoon phase, but the arguments will return at some point. I'm sure they won't be as frequent—or as fraught—but you aren't going to go through the rest of your lives without arguing."

"Oh, I'm well aware." Jake dusted off the lazy smile he was famous for. "I'm actually looking forward to our first fight."

"Is January?"

"I don't know. It's not happening until after this week. I know that for certain. She's wound a little tight with everything that's going on."

"I can see that." Jacob leaned back in his desk chair and drummed his fingers on top of the desk. "Do you want me to check into buying the chalet?"

"Just the basics," Jake replied. "I need to know how it would work. Then I need to talk to January. I don't want to frighten her by moving too fast."

"But this is what you want."

"I want her." Jake's reply was simple. "She makes me want to be better, and she makes it so it's not so scary when I try."

Jacob grinned. "That could be the schmaltziest thing you've ever said. I like it though."

"Oddly enough, I like it too."

"I figured."

. . .

FATHER AND SON HAD TURNED THE conversation to sports by the time Edward showed up to join the meeting. The Maxwell heir was all smiles as he went to the food cart to grab a coffee and a scone, and when he sat in the chair next to Jake, he acted as if he didn't have a care in the world.

"Things appear to be going well," he said, biting into the scone and continuing to speak without swallowing. "My father is very pleased about most everything that occurred over the week."

"Most everything?" Jacob prodded.

Jake settled in. He expected Edward to unveil a laundry list of teeny things that bothered him. Instead, he went for one big thing—the one thing that had Jake wanting to throw punches.

"Our only problem is January Jackson," Edward replied evenly. "We were led to believe that she was not only efficient but also chaste. Her insistence on leading me on suggests we were misled on that front."

Jake's body went rigid. "What did you just say?"

Jacob lifted one finger in warning to keep Jake at bay and didn't shift his gaze from Edward's face. "I think there must be some sort of error."

"That's what I thought the first time it happened, but it turns out, that's simply who she is." Edward turned a feral smile toward Jake. "I'm sorry to be the bearer of bad news, but your wife isn't nearly as devoted to you as she pretends."

Jake didn't believe that for a second. Sure, he and January weren't really married. He knew her though. There was no way she was flirting with this man. This was all about him hitting on her and her not reciprocating. "Listen here," he started on a growl.

"Jake, I've got this." Jacob's words were laced with warning as he pinned his offspring with a quelling look. "We'll definitely look into your accusations," he said to Edward when he was done glaring at his son. "I'm sorry if you've felt led on. I think the easy solution to that problem is to make sure you don't work with January any longer."

"He can work with me," Jake said pointedly.

Jacob nodded in agreement. "There's the fix." His smile was wide, but there was an edge to his voice.

"What about the others?" Edward sounded mournful. "I mean, if she did it to me, what's to stop her from doing this to others? I would hate to see some poor man be dragged down, his reputation ruined, because someone is bored and playing a game."

Jake gripped the arms of his chair so tightly it was a miracle he didn't snap and turn into the Hulk.

"I'll talk to January," Jacob said, his smile never diminishing. "She's worked for me for years. I've also known her since she was a child. That doesn't sound like something she would do."

"Are you calling me a liar?" Edward's voice was as cold as ice.

"Certainly not." Jacob didn't miss a beat. "I would never suggest anything of the sort. Your reputation is also stellar. As I said, we'll simply keep the two of you apart."

"My father isn't going to like the idea of you keeping someone on your staff who might serve as a distraction to some fine man who is trying to raise a family," Edward insisted.

"Well, your father doesn't have to worry about it this week," Jacob said. "I'll handle it." He kept his smile firmly in place, but the challenge in his eyes was directed squarely at Edward. "Is there anything else?"

The meeting continued another ten minutes, but nothing of importance came up. The second Edward left Jacob's office, Jake was on his feet.

"You cannot believe him," Jake growled. "There's no way January led him on. In fact, he's been making her uncomfortable for days. He's the reason I'm here for this meeting in the first place."

"I have no doubt."

"You—" Jake broke off. "Wait, you don't believe him?"

"Of course I don't. I know January. Even if she wasn't involved with you, she would never be anything but professional with him."

"But why didn't you just say that?"

"I did, in a roundabout way."

"In a roundabout way?" Jake's temper fired up again.

"Son, we have one week left with these people. I've already told you that I don't plan on doing business with them again. I would really appreciate it if you didn't cause a scene that will extend their time in our lives."

"But it's not fair to January. She shouldn't have her name besmirched."

"Nobody who has ever met January is going to believe it."

"I don't care. I don't like that guy."

"I'm fairly certain that nobody likes him," Jacob said. "It doesn't matter though. We'll keep January away from him until the end of the event. There's no reason to even tell her what Edward said."

"I don't know." Jake's stomach twisted. "I'm not comfortable lying to her."

"You don't have to lie. Just don't bring it up."

"No." Jake shook his head. "I'm not starting my relationship with her on an omission."

"And what good will telling her do? She'll get anxious if you do and try to fix things. She's not going to fix this. That man's ego was bruised when she showed no interest in him. He's out to hurt her now. I think it's best you don't let him."

What his father was saying made sense. That didn't mean Jake had to like it. "I'll think about it. I'm not going to lie to her. If she doesn't ask, I may let it slide, although part of me thinks she should know to stay away from him."

"You yourself said she was uncomfortable being around him. It's not as if she's going to seek him out."

"Maybe."

Jacob's pent-up breath escaped on a heavy gust. "Jake, don't let this get to you. There are millions of people in this business, and not all of them are good people. You're going to cross paths with more good than bad, but the bad are still out there."

"I don't want him being left alone with January," Jake said out of the blue. "He'll terrorize her because he thinks he has the upper hand. She's dealing with enough stuff without adding him to the mix."

"Then we'll keep her away from him." Jacob was matter of fact. "Don't dwell on this, Jake. I know he's lying. The other workers will know he's lying if he says anything. In a week, they'll be gone, and we won't ever have to see them again. Let's keep the peace until then."

Jake understood what his father was saying. He didn't have to like it though. "I'm going to keep my eye on him. I don't trust him."

"I think that's totally fair. Just don't get in his face. You two throwing punches isn't going to make anything better."

"I promise to try to keep things civil." That was the best Jake could do. "If he moves on January, though, all bets are off."

"Well, let's hope it doesn't come to that."

"Yeah, let's hope."

TWENTY-FOUR

J ake woke up five minutes before his alarm went off on Wednesday. Multiple days of working in lockstep with Edward to save January from finding out what the man was saying about her had left him surly. He wasn't used to being so regimented with his time. Surprisingly, he found he didn't hate that part of it.

He just hated Edward.

He grabbed his phone from the nightstand and killed the alarm before it could jolt January awake. She was asleep next to him, her hair fanned out around her face. She made soft sighing noises in her sleep—something he found endearing— and he shifted to his side so he could watch her.

She looked like an angel when she wasn't fretting about something, he decided. When her features were soft and unguarded in sleep, she touched places inside him he didn't even know existed. That didn't stop him from thinking about their *wars* when they were younger. He simply looked at them in a different way now.

As if sensing him watching her, she shifted. "What time is it?" she murmured.

"We still have a few minutes." He brushed her hair away from her face and grinned as consciousness fully claimed her, thanks to the small nightlight illuminating the way to the bathroom.

She ran her hands up and down his arms as he brushed her hair away from her face. "Is something wrong?"

The question bugged him. Maybe it was because she'd asked it multiple times over the past three days. To him, it signified she was worried, and that was the last thing he wanted.

"Nothing is wrong," he assured her.

"Then what are you thinking?"

"Honestly?" A small smile played across his face. "I was thinking about the time we were juniors, and you were wearing that pink skirt."

January's forehead puckered. "I don't know what you're talking about."

"You had this pink skirt you always wore on Thursdays."

"I remember the skirt." She puffed out a laugh. "How did you know I wore it on Thursdays?"

"I honestly don't know. It just popped into my head."

"I used to wear all of my decent outfits once a week. I was hoping nobody would notice I only had enough school clothes to make it through a week."

He couldn't see it, but he knew her cheeks were flooding with embarrassment. "Baby, it's not something I noticed back then."

"Obviously you did if you committed it to memory."

"Fine, but it's not something I consciously recognized. I never talked about it with anybody else."

"Because you didn't want them to know you were paying that much attention to me?"

Jake cocked his head, considering. "Good question. I'm

starting to think I was obsessed with you and didn't even realize it."

"You were obsessed with besting me."

"No, I was obsessed with you in general, but the only time you ever paid attention to me was when we competed. Even negative attention is attention, right?"

Her giggle warmed him to his very toes. She didn't often giggle, although she was becoming more comfortable with him, and the instances were growing in frequency. He loved the sound more than just about anything, he realized.

"I've been starting to wonder the same thing," she admitted.

"Just think, if we'd gotten our heads out of our asses back then, we could've been together all this time." He leaned in and nuzzled his face against her hair. "Think of all the things we've missed out on." He was genuinely bereft when he spent too much time pondering what could've been.

January, however, had another take on the situation. "Do you really think we could've made things work as seventeen-year-old morons?"

"I happen to think I've always been a genius."

She giggled again, and he wanted to cocoon himself in the sound. "And I think I wasn't in the best frame of mind back then."

"You were in a better frame of mind than me."

"No." Her smile disappeared. "Back then, my mother was bringing home a new boyfriend every six weeks, moving them into our trailer, and basically ruining my life at every turn. I had to lock myself in my room every night just in case."

The reality of her words was like a brick to the face. "What? Are you saying her boyfriends—?" He couldn't even finish the question, he was so horrified.

"No," she said hurriedly, shaking her head. "That never

happened. I was convinced it could happen though. Some of them used to look at me a certain way."

Jake wanted to hate her mother—so very much—but the woman he'd met in the hospital couldn't be held accountable for what happened to January. The woman from back then, however, had earned his ire and then some. "You could've moved in with me."

She laughed so hard she almost choked. "Oh, right."

"I would've found a way. My parents aren't as bad as you think. Plus, they both love you."

"Now. They didn't love me back then."

That was true, but he was still bothered. "We could've been Romeo and Juliet," he insisted. "It would've been romantic."

"You were not into romance back then, and let's be honest, I was too focused on getting an education. I needed to get out of here for a bit." She was deadly serious. "I learned a lot in college. I know I'm still a bit rigid but having so many things out of my control for those four years was a good thing."

"Did you think that at the time?"

"No." She giggled yet again. "I thought I was being perse-cuted. I needed a reality check though. I'm sure you needed something too."

"At the time, I thought I just needed to get away from my parents," he admitted. "Now I know I needed more than that."

"What did you need?" Her fingers traced the contours of his bare chest, and for the first time, it hit Jake really hard what he needed.

"I needed you."

"Me? How do you figure?"

"I needed someone to pay attention to me. I mean *really* pay attention. You do that. You listen to me. You offer suggestions without being overbearing. You want to help me be the best man I can possibly be."

January looked floored. "I think that might be the nicest thing anybody has ever said to me."

"Yeah?" Jake's smile turned wolfish. "Well, I mean it. I was lost for a long time."

"Do you think you're found now?"

He hesitated. Pretending that his old bad habits didn't continue to threaten to sneak in despite his best intentions wasn't possible. "I think I'm getting there." He pressed his lips to hers and pulled her tight against him. "I'm getting better."

"And what happens when this is all over with?"

His heart seized before he realized she was referring to their current living situation. She wasn't talking about the relationship ending. No, she was talking about putting the games behind them and having to embrace an authentic life. Right now, they were living in a bubble, and like him, she was terrified of what would happen when the bubble burst.

"I don't know. I have some ideas."

"Oh yeah?" Intrigue lit her eyes. "What ideas?"

"I don't want to talk about them now. I want to wait until this week is over with and we can both breathe again."

"Okay. That sounds fair." She happily snuggled against him. "As much fun as we're having, I'm looking forward to the games being over. The Maxwells make me uneasy, and it's only getting worse."

He stiffened. "What do you mean? Has something happened?"

"They're just weird. I feel bad for some of the girls, like Margie. I can tell she wants more than she's getting from life, but she's afraid to break away from the life her father demands of her. It's a big leap to walk away from all that money."

"You didn't have the money to fall back on, so it was easier for you," Jake mused. "I'm more like Edward. I never had to worry about leaping without a net."

"You were just searching," January countered. "You were never afraid of leaping. You were afraid of the fall. Now you've realized that the fall is part of the journey."

"Oh, that was almost poetic, baby." He pulled back far enough to allow her to see his face. "I want my next leap to be with you. I don't want you worrying otherwise."

"I'm not worried."

Staring into the fathomless depths of her eyes, Jake believed her. Was it simply because he wanted to believe her? That was the question. He refused to let fear dictate his life though. He was happy—truly happy—for the first time he could remember in a very long time.

"It's only a few more days," he whispered. "We can make it. Then afterward we'll start making some decisions on how the real world is going to work."

"That sounds good." She let loose a little sigh. "I'll make breakfast this morning. We shouldn't be late. I've managed to avoid Edward all week, thanks to you running interference. I want to keep up the streak."

That's what Jake wanted, too, because if she found out what Edward was saying about her, things would explode.

That was the last thing he wanted.

JANUARY HUMMED TO HERSELF AS SHE stopped in the housekeeping department to get an update from Emma Eubanks. She was a former classmate, and January liked her a great deal because she was efficient. When she walked into the storage room that led to Emma's office, however, she didn't see anybody milling about. Given the time of day, that was odd. It wasn't until she was cutting between two aisles of cleaning products that she heard voices.

"So, it's all a scam?" a female voice asked.

January slowed her pace. She recognized the voice. It belonged to Dakota Krause, one of the newer members of the cleaning staff. She'd also gone to Bellaire High School, but unlike with Emma, January had no friendly feelings toward her.

"That's the rumor," another voice said. This one belonged to Cally Michaelson. January was almost positive. "I heard that the father forced it on them because that Jim guy is apparently allergic to hanging around anybody who isn't married."

"Well, *that* explains it," Dakota said. "I couldn't figure out what someone as hot as Jake would see in her. Now I know."

January's stomach twisted. Was that what everybody would think about them when they finally took things public? Sure, everybody at the resort was talking—that was to be expected—but what about the other people in town? Would Jake constantly have to stand up for her? How long would it take before he found it too grating to deal with?

January was so lost in thought she didn't realize somebody had arrived at her side until she saw a hint of movement out of the corner of her eye and jolted. Emma, a clipboard in her hand, looked furious as she stared in the direction of the office.

Because she was uncomfortable, January cleared her throat to buy a bit of time. Emma shook her head before January could utter a single word.

"Let me handle this," Emma said as she started toward the office.

January remained rooted to her spot, watching as Emma made her presence known.

"Are you guys done with your work?" Emma demanded.

From her position behind the shelf, January couldn't make out the other two women. She could hear them scrambling, however.

"Almost," Dakota replied. "We were just talking."

"Yes, I heard what you were talking about. I wasn't the only one either." Emma's tone was severe. "I believe you guys have stocking that needs to be done. You'd best get to it."

"It was just five minutes," Cally whined. "I don't see what the big deal is."

"We're looking for dirt on Jake Jeffries and January Jackson," Dakota said in a conspiratorial whisper, obviously not picking up on her boss's mood. "Do you know anything about it? You went to high school with them."

"I know that it's none of your business," Emma fired back.

"Oh, come on," Cally complained. "People say they really hate each other and it's killing them to have to pretend to like one another."

"Is that what people say?" Emma drawled. "Well, if the gossip mill says it, then it must be true."

"You were there," Dakota insisted. "I know you went to high school with them. Jake is ridiculously hot. There's no way he would actually marry January. It has to be an act."

"I don't know anything about that part, and it's none of my business," Emma replied. "I will say this though. Anybody who knew them back when we were in high school wouldn't actually be surprised by this. Oh, they might be at first, but not for long. January and Jake were all up in each other's business back in the day. They were drawn to each other like magnets. Like magnets of destiny, actually."

January was floored by the statement but didn't move. Not to leave or enter the office. Instead, she chewed on her bottom lip and listened.

"I heard they were drawn to each other because they liked to torture one another," Dakota argued. "I think that's different."

"Really? Because I don't." Emma let loose a low chuckle. "Those two have always been fixated on one another. If you truly hate someone, you don't bother wasting your time on them."

"But—"

"Get to work," Emma ordered. "I'm sick of you guys hanging around doing nothing. You're not here to gossip."

"We're great multitaskers," Cally teased.

"Get to work."

January remained hidden behind the shelf and was thankful Cally and Dakota exited through the opposite aisle. When she stepped through Emma's open office door, she was grateful and maybe a little curious. "Did you mean that?" she asked in a low voice.

"The part about them driving me crazy with the gossip? Yes." Emma offered up a rueful smile.

"I meant the part about us being magnets. Jake and me."

"I meant it." Emma lowered herself into her chair and surveyed January with probing eyes. "You seem upset. If you want to talk about it, I'm here. I won't be contributing to the gossip train because that's not my way."

January let loose a little wheeze and then rubbed her forehead. "They're right. I don't know what he sees in me."

"They're not right, and I know what he sees in you. Unfortunately, you don't have a rock-solid picture of yourself. I don't really blame you. Things were rough for you in high school. I always knew there was something there more than the bickering though."

"I didn't know that. How could you?"

"Because it's easier to see the whole picture when you're on the outside looking in. I'm still on the outside, and unlike the gossipy twosome, I've actually seen you and Jake together over the last few weeks. I know exactly how things are playing out."

"You've seen us? Where?"

"Mostly in the parking lot. I'm a big fan of how he pushes

you across the ice in your flats, him behind you so there's no chance you'll fall. You guys laugh the whole time."

"He's carried me a few times too," January admitted.

"I know. I've seen it." Emma let loose a sigh. "You guys are adorable together."

"We're in a bubble," January admitted. "This started as something manufactured. It wasn't real. They were right about that."

"It doesn't matter how it started," Emma replied. "It matters what it is now, and I'm telling you right now, there's nothing manufactured about the two of you from what I saw last night."

January's mouth dropped open. "What did you see last night?"

"I saw you holding hands as you crossed the parking lot. Nobody was watching but me. There was nobody to impress. You swung your hands like teenagers in love, and you talked the whole way across the parking lot. If that's not real, then you guys missed your calling and should be actors."

"It feels real. Maybe it feels too real. I keep waiting for the other shoe to drop."

"I know it's normal to feel fear when you're just starting out, but I don't think you have anything to worry about."

"What if I do?"

"You don't." Emma sounded certain. "I can see it when he looks at you and when you look at him. Some things are meant to be. I hate to break it to you, but I think all that fighting you guys did in high school was foreplay."

"Doesn't that make us sick?"

"It just makes you imaginative."

"I wish I could believe that. I just... I feel like something is going to go wrong. I'm going to be crushed when it does too."

"Or maybe you'll get everything you ever wanted when

things don't fall apart," Emma said. "Have you ever considered that?"

"No." January let loose a small laugh. "Maybe I should start focusing on the good instead of the bad."

"I think that is the exact right thing to do."

TWENTY-FIVE

"Do you want to ski with me this weekend?"

January looked up from the schedule she was studying and arched an eyebrow as Jake leaned against the counter sipping his morning coffee and watching her.

"You want to go skiing?" January couldn't contain her surprise. "I would think, after the past two weeks, that skiing would be the furthest thing from your mind."

"You mean the games?" Jake put his coffee down long enough to pour a mug for January. He grabbed the flavored creamer she favored from the fridge, added the exact right amount, and then delivered the mug to her.

January nodded, her insides warming at the fact that he'd not only gone to the trouble to pour her a mug of coffee, but he'd also taken the time to memorize how she liked it.

"We haven't been skiing since the day we played hooky. Before that it was the blizzard," he reminded her. "And that didn't really count."

"I don't know." She smiled at the memory. "It was kind of a catalyst for us. Who knows? Maybe if we hadn't gotten stuck at the bottom of the hill, none of this would've ever happened."

"Oh, some things are destined to happen." He let loose a low chuckle.

"Do you believe that? In destiny, I mean?"

"I do."

"What else do you believe in?" January sipped her coffee and watched him over the rim. It was the last day of the games —although they had a closing ceremony to get through the following day—and she was anxious to put the Maxwell family in the rearview mirror. She was also worried about what the future would hold. No matter how much they talked about it, how much he reassured her, she was terrified that the bubble bursting would change everything.

"You mean like ghosts?" Jake grinned as he sat next to her. They still had thirty minutes until they had to be at the resort, and he didn't look worried about the snow that was starting to fall.

"Actually, that's not what I meant. Although, do you believe in ghosts?"

He cocked his head and then lifted one shoulder in a shrug. "I'm honestly not sure," he admitted after several seconds. "I think questions regarding eternal souls make my stomach upset. I would like to believe in ghosts, but I've never seen one or anything."

"Do you believe in soulmates?" January felt like a bit of a dolt asking the question, but she couldn't stop herself.

"Like, do I believe that there's only one person for everybody?"

She nodded.

"I don't know. What do you want me to say?"

"The truth."

"Are you sure?" Jake didn't look convinced.

"I'm sure. I would always prefer to know a hard truth rather than absorb an easy lie."

He nodded, as if agreeing, and then let loose a breath. "I find it hard to believe there's only one person for everybody simply because there's a great big world out there, and what are the odds of everybody being located close to their one person?"

January smirked. "That's a very pragmatic response."

"I'm not done." He held up a finger to still her. "Instead of believing that there's only one soul out there that's a perfect fit for your soul, I think it's more like there are multiple souls that connect perfectly but finding that perfect fit feels like a miracle. It's still hard. It still takes work. But it's worth it."

"Huh." January was both elated and flummoxed by his response. "That's interesting," she said finally. "I kind of feel the same way."

"Yeah?" Jake grinned.

She nodded. "There's a moment when it feels like things lock together. It's like Legos fitting. Or a puzzle piece, like you said. Fitting them together the wrong way means that things will never feel exactly right."

"And how do you feel now?" Jake's question was asked in a soft voice.

"Are you asking if I feel like we fit perfectly?" January felt put on the spot, but she didn't back down. He was going out of his way to make her feel safe and coveted these days. He deserved honesty in her response.

"Yeah."

"It doesn't feel like we're trying to wedge ourselves together when we don't fit," she replied, her cheeks warming under his bright grin. She wanted to make him happy. She couldn't ignore the flutter in her stomach though. "I'm still afraid."

Jake looked pained. "What are you afraid of?"

"That you're going to change your mind. That this only worked because we were forced to be on top of one another, and once you get a chance to breathe again, you're going to realize I'm too much work."

"Do you think you're too much work?"

She shrugged. "According to my mother, I've *always* been too much work."

Jake frowned. "January..." He trailed off, clearly debating his response. When he moved toward the table, he had his coffee in hand and a sad look on his face. "I don't want to talk badly about your mother," he said as he sat next to her.

"You can. I talk badly about her all the time." She let out a hollow laugh.

"Maybe, but part of you still loves her." Jake took her hand and pressed it to his chest. She wasn't even certain he realized he was doing it. To her, it seemed like an automatic response, and that just made her more uncomfortable.

Here was this man. This once-in-a-lifetime man. He was willing to offer her things she'd never been offered before. What did she do in response? Whine. She was always whining. How could that possibly be considered attractive?

"Whatever is going through your head, I want it to stop right now," Jake warned in a low voice. "It's unnecessary."

January pressed her lips together and nodded, not a single sound escaping.

"As for your mother, I know I'm not supposed to rail on someone who's in a position where she can't defend herself, but your mother is a total bitch."

January made a sputtering sound when she sucked in a breath. "Tell me how you really feel," she said on a half laugh.

"That is how I really feel." Jake gripped her hand tightly. "I know that your mother is in a position where she can't defend herself, and I don't want to attack the woman in the hospital. She is clearly not to blame for what has happened. I would never be cruel to her, and I want to help you take care of her. Don't ever doubt that."

January could do nothing but nod. She had no idea where he was going with this, but she wanted to hear him out.

"I think it's likely that your mother didn't have a great home life when she was younger," he said. "You never mention your grandparents. Where are they?"

"I've never met my grandparents on my father's side," January admitted. "I know they're out there, but they've never tried to get in touch with me, and I haven't seen a reason to get in touch with them. It's not as if they can help me."

Jake nodded.

"As for my grandparents on my mother's side, well, I don't know a lot about them," she continued. "I know my grandmother is over in Alden. My mother never mentioned her much. She would go over there looking for money about once a year, but my grandmother would always shut her down. I never got to spend any time with her. I just saw her from the car when my mother was inside."

"And your grandfather?" Jake leaned forward and brushed her hair away from her face.

"He's Fred Bix."

Jake's shoulders jerked, and January could practically hear the gears of his mind working.

"You mean the fire chief?" Jake asked finally.

January nodded.

"Brian and Brenda Bix's grandfather is also your grandfather?"

"He and my grandmother never got married," January explained. "They were going to, but it never happened. They had my mother, my grandmother raised her alone, and my understanding is that Fred never really saw her.

"I'm sure my mother went to him a few times for money and was shut down," she continued. "I did catch him watching me at one of the festivals downtown when I was about twelve. My mother made me wear shoes that were a size too small because she didn't want to go shopping, and I was giving my feet a rest because the shoes hurt a lot, and he came over to see if I was okay."

Jake leaned in and pressed his forehead against hers. "I hate this story," he growled.

January understood that. She continued anyway. "He asked about the shoes. I didn't know who he was at the time. I just thought he was a nice man trying to help. There was nothing he could do about those shoes, but the next day, a new pair of shoes showed up on the front porch. I knew who they were from."

"What did your mother say?"

"I didn't tell her. She would've sold them. If I remember correctly, she was with Meth Head Mike at the time and was selling anything that wasn't nailed down. I tossed the box and kept the shoes in my school bag."

"God, I really hate her now," Jake complained as he stroked his hands over the back of January's head. "I'm so sorry."

"Why? You didn't do it." January was practical to the point of pain when it came to stuff like this. "Besides, I survived."

"I still hate her," Jake growled. "I just ... what a piece of crap. I can't understand how you turned out as well as you did. It feels like a miracle."

"Are you sure I turned out well?"

The question obviously caught Jake off guard because incredulity swamped his handsome features, to the point where he was bordering on angry when he pulled back. "Why would you ask that?"

"Because sometimes I think that I have some of her inside me," January admitted, her heart rate picking up a notch. "I think that ending up like her is inevitable, and I've been fooling myself that I can be more. She always said that I was snooty, and it would come back to bite me. What if she was right?"

Jake couldn't bite back his annoyance. Not this time. "You listen here." He caught her chin in his hands and stared directly into her eyes. "I want to say your mother never had a chance, but that's not true. She could've done a million things differently. She didn't, and that's on her.

"You're not her," he continued. "You're some other-worldly gift from the gods. Yeah, you have a few quirks. We all do. You're not her, though, and I need you to understand that. You'll *never* be her."

"I don't want to be her. My entire life, that's been the ultimate goal. *Just don't be her. You can get away from her. You'll be better than her.*"

"And yet now your life is still about her," Jake mused as he tugged January closer. "Most people would've abandoned her to the county hospital, January. The fact that you haven't, well, it's amazing. If she were my mother, she would've been cut loose a very long time ago."

"I don't think that's true. You're too good of a person."

"No, *you're* too good of a person." He moved his lips to hers and graced her with a kiss. It was nothing more than a soft brushing of lips, but it was all he had to offer in the moment. "I need you to listen to me for a second," he said when he pulled back, his eyes clear. "Can you do that?"

January nodded. Did she have a choice?

"Your mother was hobbled by things in life. I'm guessing nothing was ever easy for her. She had a reason to be mad at the world. So did you, though, and you turned your hardships into triumphs."

January let out a wobbly laugh as she fought off tears. "I think that's a bit of an exaggeration."

"It's not." Jake was firm. "Your mother was terrible to you. She did her best to bring you down. It's a parent's job to exalt their child. You're supposed to build them up. You didn't have that, and yet here you are."

"Here I am, with my fake husband." She laughed, relaxing a bit when he joined her. "I want to put what happened with her behind me. I want to be the bigger person when I'm visiting her. I have all these feelings when we're together though. I can't tell her what she did to me because you're right, the woman in that hospital is not the one who put herself ahead of me all the time."

"You can't change what happened." Jake was calm. "I don't know that bottling everything up inside is good either. Maybe it's okay to tell her how you feel. Even if she doesn't know why you're angry, it's okay. You have a right to your feelings."

January balked. "I can't hurt her just to make myself feel better."

"Baby, she won't remember it after fifteen minutes anyway. Maybe it's time to worry about what you need. It's okay to put yourself first, even if it's just for a moment."

January squeezed her eyes shut and nodded. "Maybe. I'm not sure I can bring myself to do it though."

"That's okay too. There are no wrong responses here. You just need to feel what you feel." Jake pulled her out of her chair and settled her on his lap, wrapping her tight. "I want to protect you from everything that hurts, but I don't think that's possible. Instead, I'm going to prove that I'm here, and I want to be your sounding board when you need it."

"We just need to get through these games." January rested the back of her head on his shoulder. "Everybody is tense because we're near the end. Nothing truly terrible has happened. We're so close."

"We're going to make it," Jake assured her, and January

had to wonder if he was talking about the games at all. "I promise. Everything is going to be okay. Tomorrow night, as soon as the closing party is finished, we're going to mix cocktails, get naked in that hot tub, and do absolutely nothing but each other all night."

January's laughter bubbled out. "It sounds like you have a plan."

"I do. We're going to get through tomorrow. After that, we'll figure it out without so much pressure hanging over us."

In the bright light of day, with Jake wrapped around her, January wanted to believe him. She couldn't completely disregard the niggling feeling haunting her though.

Something bad could still happen, and if it did, she wasn't sure she was strong enough to put the pieces back together again. She hoped she was that strong, but what if she wasn't? What if her mother was right?

"Let's just get through today first," Jake said. "We have four races left. Tomorrow is a party. After that, I'm taking you skiing and for a nice dinner that's not at this resort. Come Monday when the world turns real again, we'll take it one step at a time."

"Okay." For once, January wasn't the one who had to organize everything, and she was grateful. "That sounds like a plan to me."

Twenty-Six

J ake bobbed his head to the music blasting from the speakers as he readied himself for the final race of the games. He'd been excited when he first heard they were being held at Sylvan Slopes. He figured he would spend his time hitting on snow bunnies and learning the business while having a great time. Things had somehow changed over the last month. He was settled, and that was something he'd never realized he wanted.

"I bet you'll be glad when this is over," Jacob noted as he drew closer to his son. Jake thought he could recognize every expression in his father's arsenal, but the one currently on display was a mystery to him.

Jake shrugged. "I don't know. Part of me will be glad. The other part, I'm not so sure."

Jacob pursed his lips and then nodded. "And how are things with your lovely wife?"

Jake made a face. "If you're about to be difficult—"

Jacob raised his hand quickly to cut off a potential argument. "I'm being serious. How are things with January?"

On a sigh, Jake held out his hands. "The real world is right around the corner."

"And that makes you nervous."

"I would be lying if I said I wasn't concerned," Jake acknowledged. "She's a ball of nerves. We're so close to this being finished—and without casualties—that she can't see beyond it."

"Have you considered that she's simply afraid of what the beyond looks like?" Jacob asked calmly.

"Only every moment of every day."

Jacob's lips swished. "She's been a good influence on you," he said after a beat. "You seem different from when you came home."

"That's what you want, right?"

"No, Jake, that's not what I want." Jacob dragged a hand through his hair. He wasn't wearing a hat despite the brisk temperature. It was the last race, and the sun was out, so there was no chance of frostbite. "I've always known you had the ability to be more than you were being."

Jake scowled. "I don't want to fight."

"I don't want to fight either. I'm being serious. Kid, you have always been smarter than you gave yourself credit for. Your problem isn't smarts. It might not even be dedication. It's resignation. When things get hard for you, you turn tail and run. Believe it or not, that's the habit I'm trying to break here."

Jake recognized that his father was extending an olive branch. At least that was what it felt like. Instead of exploding or turning petulant, he took the words at face value. "It was hard growing up in your shadow," he admitted. "You were the big man in town. We had money, and people revered you because the resort was the biggest employer in the area."

"And that was hard on you," Jacob surmised.

"I didn't know it was hard when I was younger. I wanted you to be proud of me. I was never the best at anything, though, and you were always the best at everything." Jake was afraid to have a heart-to-heart with his father, especially given their location, but the door had been opened, and he walked through it. He no longer wanted to run. It was time to be a man.

"I'm not the best at anything," Jacob argued.

"Look at this place. You made it into what it is. You're the reason the tourist business in Bellaire is so strong. I can never live up to that."

"Of course you can." Jacob's tone was no nonsense. "You're smart. You're charming. You get both of those traits from your mother, by the way. That charm streak of yours is a mile wide. I have to work for people to like me. They adore you simply because of who you are."

The sigh Jacob let loose was long and drawn out. "I want you to have a good time, and maybe I indulged you a bit when you were younger because I was always so serious as a kid. I wanted you to have more balance. Unfortunately, I feel I encouraged more fun than was potentially warranted."

The laugh that bubbled up caught Jake by surprise. "The easier you made it for me, the less trouble I had doing nothing with my life. Maybe we both needed to learn some balance."

"You were a smart kid who grew into a smart man," Jacob said. "You just needed structure."

"Which is why you saddled me with January."

Jacob hesitated and then nodded. "All I knew of her before she joined the team here was that she was intense. Her recommendations were good, though, and I wanted to take a chance on her."

"Because of her mother." Jake swallowed the sudden lump in his throat. He had no idea where it had come from. "I met her mother."

"Yeah?" Jacob's expression was flat. "What did you think?"

"She's in a hospital, Dad. Did you know that?"

Jacob nodded. "You mentioned it."

"Before I mentioned it though."

"I didn't know."

"That's because she doesn't tell people things. She's afraid that people will judge her." Jake slid his eyes up to the towering resort and blew out a sigh. "She's always had to be the adult. Her mother was terrible to her. Like, well and truly terrible. She said hateful things. She made January feel unloved."

Jacob shifted from one foot to the other, clearly uncomfortable. "I obviously wasn't privy to the inner workings of their relationship, but I'm not surprised. You probably don't remember all the instances where we were called into the office —in elementary, middle, and high school."

Jake's cheeks colored. "We were addicted to torturing each other."

"I'm not sure that's what was going on." Jacob managed a small chuckle. "She needed attention, and you were the only one giving it to her. I saw it. I started watching her.

"The teachers didn't focus on her because she was a good student, and they were overwhelmed by the bad ones," he continued. "Her mother was not a very nice person. I once saw that girl at the age of twelve walking home with groceries. I stopped to give her a ride because it was cold, but she wisely didn't get in the car with an older man she barely knew. She did mention that was all their groceries for the week, though, and it was one bag. One bag of canned soup and SpaghettiOs. I think my heart broke a bit that day."

Jake gripped his hands into fists at his sides. "I want to hate that woman," he admitted. "So much. You have no idea. She doesn't remember anything though. She doesn't even remember January."

"Maybe that's for the best."

"Except January needs to tell her things. She needs to let her mother know how terrible she was so she can move on. She can't though."

"You've obviously given this a lot of thought." Jacob's glance was appraising as he studied his son's profile. "Have you considered taking her there and sitting quietly by her side while she expresses her outrage to her mother? Even if Clara doesn't remember her, it might be cathartic for January."

"I actually made that suggestion. I'm not sure January can go there. She feels responsible for her mother because Clara worked two and three jobs to keep a roof over their heads—something she constantly reminded her of—and January feels as if she has to pay her back."

"January takes things to heart." Sadness washed over Jacob's features. "I realized that after working with her for a few months. She's ridiculously smart. She's driven. She's determined to be a good worker and person. Things hurt her more than she lets on."

"I hurt her," Jake said. "As kids, I did terrible things to her."

"I believe she did them back."

"It's different though. I had confidence. Once, Cassie Bishop was waiting in the parking lot of the grocery store to give January a ride home. It was after dark, and Cassie told me what January was doing. I thought it would be funny to strand January there, so I flirted with Cassie and got her to leave with me, stranding January."

"Well, that wasn't very nice," Jacob chastised on a frown.

"It gets worse. Mickey Jordan followed January home and tried to flirt with her. She couldn't drop her bag and run because that was all her groceries for the entire week. So I put her in the position where the town pervert chased her all the way home while she walked in the darkness and cold, clutching a bag of groceries she needed to survive. I did that."

Jacob made a protesting sound. "Son, you couldn't have known."

"That doesn't make it right."

"No, it doesn't, but you were kids. I don't think January is holding that against you any longer."

Was that true? Jake considered it for several seconds and then exhaled heavily. "She's not. I know I need to let it go if we're going to move forward. I'm just so mad at myself. How could I not see that her problems were so much bigger than mine?"

"Because youth makes for endless blind spots, Jake." Jacob sounded utterly reasonable, which smoothed some of the frayed nerves sparking in Jake's chest. "Listen, I'm not going to pretend you didn't do horrible things to January. She did them to you too though. Also, you're the only one who paid attention to her."

"Negative attention doesn't count."

"Except that was all she ever knew until she got to college, I think. Despite all of that, she's grown into a fine woman. I think she's grown into the sort of woman who would be good for you. If you can get past the baggage that both of you are carrying around, that is."

"That's what I want." Jake saw no point in denying it. "I like her. Actually, it's more than that now."

"Love?"

Jake hesitated. "Isn't it too soon for that?"

"No. I think it's possible you've been falling in love with her since you were a teenager. That night you hooked up out here kicked it into high gear, and you didn't even realize it."

Jake's mouth dropped open. "How do you even know about that?"

Jacob chuckled. "Leo told me you two headed off together. He said it was obvious what was going to happen.

He saw January leaving the next morning, and she looked flustered."

"Well, crap." Jake scratched his cheek. "Does Mom know?"

"Are you under the impression that your mother thinks you're somehow still a virgin?"

"No. I just... I don't know. Mom seems to go back and forth on January."

"Your mother is always going to be your biggest champion," Jacob replied. "She loves you, and she truly believed that January was torturing you when you were younger. She refused to see that you were torturing January back for a long time.

"She was against me hiring January," he continued. "The first time she crossed paths with January upon her hiring, she was cold. January won her over though. So while your mother still wants to protect you, she sees January for what she is."

Jake's mouth was dry. "And what is she?"

"She's a fantastic woman who should've somehow been lost in a sea of uncertainty. Given who her mother is, given how hard she struggled, nobody would've been surprised if she'd somehow fallen through the cracks. She didn't. She remained strong. She made something of herself, and she's going to continue to do that."

"What if I'm not good enough for her?"

"Are you really worried about that?" Surprise registered on Jacob's face. "Is that something you've been thinking about?"

"Yeah." Jake was rueful. "The more time I spend with her, the more I realize she's the superstar. The others make fun of her because she's so organized, but I happen to think that's part of her charm. She actually schedules in time to fall apart if she feels it's going to be necessary. I've never met anyone else like her."

"It sure sounds like love to me."

"I care about her a great deal," Jake acknowledged. "She's fun. Some of the idiots in high school don't see it, but for the first time in my life, I realize it doesn't matter what they think."

"No, it only matters what you think," Jacob agreed. "Is that why you want to buy that chalet? Is it for both of you?"

"I would like it to be," Jake acknowledged. "Part of me thinks it's too soon to live together."

"And yet you've already been living together for a month."

"Yeah." Jake pressed the heel of his hand to his forehead. "She doesn't want to talk about our future right now. She wants to get through the games, get away from the Maxwells, and then figure things out."

"This is her making a list," Jacob acknowledged. "She's always going to be this way. She had to prioritize things to survive as a kid. She can't break that mold as an adult. You're going to have to be the one to compromise when it comes to that stuff. Do you think you can do that?"

"I want to." Sincerity shone in Jake's eyes. "I want to make this work. I want her to teach me to be more responsible."

"And in return, you can teach her to lighten up. You're a good match for each other." Jacob hesitated a beat and then barreled forward. "The forced proximity caused your relationship to grow faster than it might have under different circumstances. You need to take that into consideration."

"I have. I am," Jake corrected quickly. "I feel as if I really know her though. Sometimes, when we're done here at night, we sit in front of the fireplace and just talk. I mean, about mundane crap. I can't ever remember doing that with anybody else."

"That's part of a mature relationship. I talk to your mother all the time, too, even if I couldn't care less about shoes and shopping." He darted a look around the crowd readying to watch the race, as if to see if Enid was eavesdropping. "Don't ever tell her I said that. She thinks I really know the difference between mules and slides."

Jake couldn't contain his laughter. This conversation with his father felt different from all the others. "I want to make January happy," he said when he sobered. "You think I can do that, right?"

"I do."

"She deserves to be happy. I'm just ... afraid."

"I think that's a fair emotion," Jacob acknowledged. "You have to be prepared for her to take a step back after the games. She might want a bit of time to get her head around things. You cannot push her before she's ready. If it's one thing I've learned about January, it's that she'll dig her heels in if she's feeling pressured. Don't be the one who adds pressure to her life."

"She lives in Pendleton Manor," Jake complained. "I don't want her living there. It's not safe."

"Yes, well, I wasn't aware of that until you mentioned it earlier," Jacob replied grimly. "I don't want her there either. She's a stubborn little thing though. Maybe, if she doesn't feel comfortable staying in the lodge with you, I can get her a room up at the resort. Anything has to be better than where she's living."

"You would do that?" Jake was momentarily floored. "Seriously? Because that would be great. We would both be here together, able to see each other, but she would still have her private space if she needed it."

"Of course I would do that. Don't be ridiculous. We can talk to her together if you want, after tomorrow night's party. Let's just get through today and tomorrow and then worry about your future, huh?"

Jake laughed, the weight of the world drifting away. "Thank you," he said in a low voice, his heart in his eyes. "For everything. For all of it."

"Including the tough love?"

"Yes. For that most of all. I needed a kick in the pants."

"Make sure you tell your mother that." Jacob clapped his son on the shoulder and swiveled, jolting when he realized Edward was watching them. "I didn't see you there," he said awkwardly, shooting a worried look toward his son.

How much did he hear? Jake was distinctly uncomfortable. "It's the final race," he said brightly, forcing himself to remain calm. "You must be excited."

"Oh, so excited," Edward drawled. There was a predatory glint in his eyes. "You have no idea how excited I am at the present moment."

Jake knew trouble was coming their way, but he held it together. "Well, I'm glad."

"Yes. Once the race is finished, my father wants to have a meeting with you in your office," Edward said, his eyes landing on Jacob. "I think it's best if your primary team is present. He wants to go over a few things."

A cement brick of horror landed in Jake's stomach. He could read between the lines. Curiously, he watched his father and waited for a response.

"I'm sure that can be arranged," Jacob replied smoothly. "Consider it a done deal."

"Lovely. Make sure January is present too," Edward said. "She's part of this after all."

Jake wanted to punch the other man, but he kept his hands to himself. "She'll be there. She's the reason for this entire event. We're not going to start cutting her out now."

"Lovely. It sounds like a date."

TWENTY-SEVEN

The final race went off without a hitch. January thought they were sailing into the final party without a single big problem popping up. Then she got word of the meeting.

"I don't understand," she muttered in a low voice as she and Jake headed up the spiral staircase toward Jacob's office. "What's happening?"

The look on Jake's face made her blood run cold. "Seriously, what's happening?" she demanded.

There were a lot of people around. January registered them when they landed on the second floor, and she could tell Jake had too. Ultimately, he shook his head. "It could be nothing," he said.

His tone told her that he didn't think it was nothing. "Jake."

"We'll just see what it is," he said as he took her hand. Her hands were clammy, something she was aware of, causing him to frown. "Please don't get worked up."

That was easier said than done. January's heart was a jackhammer as they made their way into the office. Jim and

Edward were already present and seated, and the look of annoyance on Jacob's face as he regarded the two men was enough to have her stomach doing somersaults.

"Close the door," Jacob said darkly when they slid inside.

Jake did as his father ordered, and January moved to the right. There were no open chairs, so she hovered near the window and clutched her hands together.

"Is something wrong?" she asked, hating how shrill her voice sounded.

"I guess that depends on what I hear next," Jim Maxwell said. From all outward appearances, he looked calm. There was an edge to the lines of his forehead, however, and January knew beyond a shadow of a doubt that something very bad was about to happen.

"It's come to our attention that a falsehood has been perpetuated on us," Edward started. He looked smug, which only heightened January's anxiety.

"A falsehood?" Jake asked blankly. "I'm not sure what you're getting at."

"The two of you," Jim replied, gesturing toward January and Jake. "Are you really married?"

January didn't know how to respond, so she merely blinked.

"Why would you ask that?" Jake queried. "I'm not sure why it matters."

"It matters to me," Jim replied smoothly. "I mean, I was told you were married. You're living together, correct? I happen to be a family values man. I made that clear when I agreed to sponsor the games."

"And you somehow think you've been bamboozled?" Jacob challenged.

"We *know* we've been bamboozled," Edward replied. "I heard you and your son talking today. There was chatter about building a future with January. There was no talk of a marriage." He had the audacity to sound hurt. "I mean, you perpetuated a hoax on us to get money for a sponsorship. Do you have any idea how hurtful that is?"

"Oh, grow up," Jake shot back. "You're the ones who feel the need to exert your values on others. I think that's *your* problem, not ours."

Jim's eyes narrowed. "I believe otherwise." He steepled his fingers and rested them on his lap. "Cohabitation without vows is living in sin. I don't promote that sort of lifestyle."

January couldn't find words to respond. That was a rarity for her, but the panic pulsing through her veins was real. She could do nothing but stand there and gape, so that's what she did.

"Jake and January have a long history," Jacob replied. "Their relationship is their own. It has no bearing on your lives."

"And yet you lied to us," Edward persisted. "You told us they were together. Their marriage was brought up numerous times." He shot Jake a pointed look. "In fact, I was made to feel uncomfortable in the shade of this marriage by your son."

"Maybe that's because you were constantly hitting on her and couldn't take no for an answer," Jake shot back.

Shocked horror washed over Edward's face. It was fake—January recognized that—but he was committed to his response. "That is a bald-faced lie." He focused on his father. "They're making that up to cover their misdeeds."

"Of course they are," Jim replied, not a single iota of doubt visible. "I've seen your heart, and it's devoted to your wife. Unfortunately, the three other hearts I'm seeing in this room don't appear to be as true. I cannot be part of a deception like this. I do business with stalwart individuals. I've been lied to since I arrived here."

Jacob tilted his head. January recognized the action. He was reading the room, and he didn't look happy. "What is it you hope to get out of this meeting?" he asked after several seconds. "What is it you want from us?"

"First, I want acknowledgement that you lied to me," Jim responded darkly.

"January and Jake have a complicated relationship," Jacob replied, clearly choosing his words carefully. "They've been in each other's orbits since they were children. As adults, they're in a relationship. Are they married? No. I believe they will end up married though."

January's heart skipped ten beats, and she found herself slumping against the wall. Did he really believe that? If he did, why? Had Jake said something? Her mind was a sandstorm of possibilities.

"But they're not married now," Jim persisted. "You lied."

"We did," Jacob replied evenly. "You seemed upset. We did not understand why you would be upset. Frankly, their relationship is none of your business. It was simply easier to let you believe what you wanted to believe."

"And by doing that, you helped perpetuate a fraud."

January finally stirred. "How?" she squeaked, her voice breaking. "Nobody outside of this resort even knows who I am. They might know who Jake is, but I'm a nobody."

Edward sneered at her word choice. "Your fake husband seems to feel otherwise."

"Knock it off," Jacob warned, extending a threatening finger toward Edward. "I don't even see why you're part of this conversation."

"He's part of it because he wants to punish January for not being interested in him," Jake snapped. "I think that should be fairly obvious."

"You shut up too," Jacob admonished. He appeared utterly reasonable as he regarded Jim. "Nobody is going to be talking about this. Why does it matter?"

"I don't believe in sexual relationships outside of

marriage," Jim replied. "You lied to me to get money. That feels like extortion."

"And how do you want to see this play out?"

"I want her removed from your employment and another sponsorship deal for the next set of races happening in February," Jim replied, not missing a beat. "I know the event isn't as big as the current one, but it's still a good opportunity. I won't be paying for this sponsorship though. I'll just be reaping the visibility rewards."

January thought there was a very real chance she might throw up. Her vision was spotty, and she had to bend over at the waist and rest her hands on her knees to remain upright. Removed from employment? Oh, god, she was going to lose her job.

"That's not happening," Jake snapped as he moved closer to January, his hand landing on her back. "You need to sit down," he said in a low voice.

"I will not work with someone who sees fit to lie to me," Jim argued. "I understand that you can't fire your son, Jacob. That's not how it works. The girl is nothing to you though. I don't want her sexual urges coming back to haunt me. There's only one way this can play out. Otherwise, I'll be forced to take my concerns to the press if you don't give the money I already paid for the sponsorship back."

January blinked several times in rapid succession. If Jacob paid the money back, the resort would be in financial trouble. All the people who worked there would be on the chopping block to cover the costs. If Jacob refused and the news went public, the resort might find itself in trouble for a different reason. If there was a scandal, the skiers—and later golfers, when the season changed—might go elsewhere. It was a no-win scenario for Jacob.

"Do you really see it playing out that way?" Jacob demanded.

"Those are your only options." Jim was firm. "I'll ruin you if I have to. People won't take kindly to the lie you perpetuated on me."

January straightened with a purpose and took a decisive step forward. "That won't be necessary." Her voice was surprisingly strong despite the weakness pulsing through her. "I'll resign. You won't have to fire me, Mr. Jeffries. Nobody has to know."

Jim beamed at her. "That sounds like a reasonable compromise."

"No, it doesn't," Jake snapped. "You're not losing your job over this, January. It wasn't even your idea."

"She can't be here if I'm going to be a regular sponsor," Jim replied. "I don't trust her, and I'll only work with people I trust."

"You don't have to worry about me," January replied. She didn't meet Jake's probing gaze. She couldn't if she wanted to hold back tears. "I'll pack up and be out of here by the end of the day."

"January." Jacob called out to her as she headed toward the door.

She had no idea what he was going to say, but it didn't matter. His back was against the wall, and she wouldn't allow others to suffer when she could fix the problem. "It's okay," she assured him in the strongest voice she could muster. "I'm sure I'll be fine. Don't worry about me."

Jake glared daggers at Jim and Edward before moving to follow. "We'll figure this out," he said in a low voice.

"We certainly will," Jim agreed. "We men will figure it out. I've always been iffy on including women in business dealings. This just affirms I was right. Have a good life, Ms. Jackson."

It took everything January had to keep her chin up. "You, too, Mr. Maxwell."

·   ·   ·

JAKE WAS POSITIVELY FURIOUS. HE WANTED to chase January when she left the office, but one look from his father told him that wasn't what was expected. His heart had fled the office, but his anger remained. Jacob's lone warning glare told him that perhaps he should stay, even though he yearned to go after January and fix things before she fell apart. He couldn't do that without his father, however, which meant he had to wait it out.

"Well, that wasn't nearly as dramatic as I was expecting," Edward drawled.

Jake took two long strides toward the man and jabbed out a finger. "You're going to want to be very careful right now," he growled.

Edward's smug smile was like a knife to the heart. "I knew that woman was trouble the second I saw her. She was leading me on, using her feminine wiles in an attempt to get me to stray. That makes her a demon in sheep's clothing."

Jim nodded in agreement. "It's always that way, unfortunately."

Jake shot an incredulous look at his father. "Are you really going to keep working with these people?" He'd thought he'd found his way to the light, a plan for the future, but if his father allowed this to happen, there was no way he could stay. He would have to venture forth and forge a new path, even though he had no idea what that would look like.

"Jake, take a breath," Jacob ordered. He didn't look nearly as worked up as Jake felt. "As for your offer—all of your offers, really—I'm going to have to respectfully decline."

Jim's eyebrows hopped toward his hairline. "Excuse me? I wasn't bluffing. I will go to the press with your lie. I expect some sort of compensation for what you've done here."

"Oh, stuff it," Jacob replied, causing the tension cramping Jake's insides to ease, if only slightly. "You're not going to the press."

"Oh, but I am."

"You're not." Jacob was firm. "If you do, then I'll be forced to take the footage from the conference rooms and use it in my rebuttal. Your son doesn't look all that stalwart in the footage, so I'm guessing you're not going to want that out."

"What footage?" Edward demanded.

"The footage of you sexually harassing January," Jacob replied evenly. "I have multiple incidents recorded."

"You filmed me without my knowledge?"

"There are cameras throughout this resort for insurance purposes," Jacob explained. "I told you that when you signed the sponsorship contract, Jim. You were well aware. It's in the fine details of the contract."

Jim's expression turned pinched. "You would try to ruin my son?"

"I don't actually want to ruin anybody," Jacob replied. "I was going to keep the footage's existence to myself until this meeting. Since you're trying to ruin January, however, that doesn't seem like an option."

For the first time since entering the office, Jake realized things were going to be okay. His father, while not perfect, would never allow something terrible to happen to January when she didn't deserve it. Sure, he'd allowed her to walk out of the office, but that was so he could verbally brutalize Jim and Edward without upsetting her.

"And what makes you think people will believe you," Jim challenged. "I've done my research. I know that girl is white trash. Her mother has a record. I'll make all of that public."

Jacob leaned across the desk and pinned Jim with a dark glare. "If you do, I'll be forced to make the footage I have of you public."

"Of me?" Jim's confusion was obvious. "What are you talking about?"

"I'm talking about all the female guests you've hit on since they started checking in. I believe I have a good fifteen instances of that on film, including audio." He made a clucking sound with his tongue. "You've been a naughty boy, Jim. That's one of the reasons I decided, long before this meeting, that this arrangement between us would be the first and last instance of us working together."

Part of Jake was angry that his father hadn't owned up to the footage sooner. The other part was smugly delighted. Jim and Edward kept getting smaller in their chairs the longer Jacob talked. They were clearly going to capitulate.

Then something occurred to Jake.

"Wait," he said, holding up his hand. "If you knew that you had them over a barrel days ago—probably even weeks ago —why did you make January and me keep up the marriage ruse?"

Jacob's eyes twinkled. "Why do you think? I've known there was something special between the two of you since you were kids. I had no idea it would get this serious so fast, but I kind of wanted to see how it played out."

"So you manipulated us too," Jake realized.

"I let you figure things out without removing the pressure," Jacob clarified. "You seemed fine with how things were going. I'm not sorry."

Jake didn't want him to be sorry. "I need to find January."

"You do," Jacob agreed. "I'll handle Frick and Frack here." The smile he sent Edward and Jim was predatory. "There might be nondisclosure agreements for both sides to sign before the end of the day, but I think we're pretty much finished here."

"And I can tell January her job is safe, right?"

"No." Jacob shook his head and held up a hand when Jake opened his mouth to protest. "You can tell her that Harold Lincoln is retiring in two months. At that point, she'll be promoted to vice president of the resort, and she'll be in charge of the official rebrand."

Relief washed over Jake, and he had to briefly press his eyes shut as he swayed. "That comes with a raise, right?"

"A big one," Jacob agreed.

"Thank you, Dad." Jake had to choke back tears. "I don't know what to say."

"You don't have to say anything, son." Jacob's eyes were suspiciously glassy. "All you have to do is follow your heart. You know what's right. You know how to make things better. You know what she needs."

"I can't believe we have to sit here and listen to this," Edward complained.

"Oh, you're going to have to listen to a lot more before I'm done," Jacob warned. "You can wait until I'm finished with my son, however." There was no consternation on Jacob's face when he locked gazes with Jake. "It's all right not to know everything. Now is your time to figure it out.

"You and January are going to be okay," he continued, tapping the spot above his heart. "I feel it here. You're going to make each other better."

"That's what I want," Jake said. "More than anything."

"Then go get your girl. We'll have some things to discuss going forward. I want to retire at some point. You're going to need a few years to learn the ropes before that can happen. Together, however, you and January will do great things— together and with the resort—and I can't wait to see how it all turns out."

Jake's heart felt so big he was afraid it would explode from his chest. "Thank you, Dad."

"No thanks are required. You're going to have to do the work. I know you can do it though."

It was the one thing Jake had always wanted to hear from his father. "I'm going to chase January now."

"You do that." Jacob's smile was benign. "I'll handle our friends. I would suggest a family dinner tonight, but something tells me you're going to be doing something else."

Jake's lips twitched. "Probably. How does Sunday sound instead?"

"I'll tell your mother. She'll be thrilled."

Jake was thrilled too. Now he just had to get to January and make sure she was equally thrilled. It was a tall order, but for the first time in his life, he felt up to the challenge.

TWENTY-EIGHT

here would she go?
Jake left his father's office with a clear purpose. He had to find January. She'd fled, likely in panic, so she might not be thinking clearly. The problem was, as far as he was concerned, January was always thinking clearly.

Would she say goodbye to the employees? That seemed like a good bet. With that in mind, he hit up her regular haunts at the resort. He never realized how big the resort was until he had to cover it with an aching heart, however.

She wasn't at the front desk.

She wasn't in the ski rental area.

She wasn't in housekeeping.

She wasn't on the loading dock, where workers gathered when they wanted a break.

He even checked the top of the main ski slope in case she went there to have one last look.

She was nowhere and yet everywhere when it came to crawling through his memories.

With nothing left to do, after at least twenty unanswered

phone calls to her cell, he raced back to the lodge. He figured he'd find her crying or maybe even drinking. If he had to wait for her to sober up, he would. Right now, he just wanted to take care of her.

She wasn't there either. Worse, she'd packed up all her belongings during the time he'd been searching for her in the main building. There wasn't a single sign of her in the lodge, and nothing hurt more than seeing her bedroom—the bedroom they'd been sharing for weeks—empty. The only piece of her he found was a note on the counter.

I'm so sorry.

That was it. That's all it said. There was no indication where she'd gone. She didn't say she'd call him when she calmed down. Just 'I'm sorry.' She didn't even sign her name. If he hadn't become familiar with her fluffy penmanship over the course of the past month, he wouldn't even be certain she was the one who had written it.

Jacob had always considered his son a quitter. It was a major bone of contention between them. Jake wasn't going to quit today. No, he would never quit on January. It hurt too much to even think about.

After crumpling the note—she had nothing to be sorry about—he grabbed his keys and headed out. She lived at Pendleton Manor. That was what she'd said. Someone there would know which unit was hers. If nobody would tell him, he would browbeat Human Resources to give him the address they had on file.

Determination fueled him as he took off. Thankfully, Bellaire wasn't a very big town. He was at the apartment complex in five minutes. To his massive discontent, January's vehicle wasn't in the parking lot. He went through twice before stopping a teenager to ask.

"I haven't seen that chick in a month," the kid replied. He was full of attitude, something that irritated Jake, and his sneer was dismissive as he looked Jake up and down. "Are you her boyfriend or something?"

"Yes," Jake replied, not missing a beat. "I need to find her. There was a miscommunication at work this morning."

"A miscommunication?" The teenager snorted. "Whatever. I don't know where she is. That's her unit." He pointed toward a corner apartment with a view of the dumpster. "She might be up there, but I don't see her car."

Jake nodded in agreement. "Thanks." He headed to the second floor to knock on the door in case she'd hidden her car somewhere that wasn't visible. The odds were slim, but he refused to ignore a single possibility. When she didn't answer, he returned to his Jeep. He could feel multiple sets of eyes focused on him. This place likely had good people living behind its walls. There was danger, too, and he didn't like it.

"Well, she's not coming back here," Jake said to himself as he got behind the wheel. "It's not happening. We'll get her stuff, and she'll move in with me, and that will be that." He felt better after the declaration. He still didn't know where January was though.

Then it hit him.

Jake kept his eyes on the road for the drive to Radcliffe Downs. It was the only thing that made sense. January had unfinished business with her mother, and even though she couldn't finish that business properly at this point, she was shaken. Maybe she figured this was the moment when she should get it all out. If she was going to have to leave—in her busy brain, that's likely what she thought—she might as well tackle everything that was holding her back.

Jake wasn't a relative, so he technically had no right to visit Clara. That didn't stop him from putting his charm on display when the receptionist attempted to shut him down. She put up a valiant fight but ultimately fell victim to his smile and gave him a day-pass badge. Jake affixed it to his shirt for the walk to Clara's room, his heart pounding harder with each step.

What if she's not here? It hadn't even occurred to him that he might not find her until this exact moment. What if January wasn't with her mother? What would he do? His only option would be to hang out in the parking lot of the abysmal apartment building and wait for her to come home. He hated it there, but he would live his life in that lot if it meant finding her. Thankfully for him, that wasn't going to be necessary.

The first thing he saw when he walked through Clara's open door, his hand poised and ready to knock to announce his presence, was an empty chair. Clara was not in the spot she'd been in during his previous visit. Across from the empty chair, January sat and watched. She was still dressed in the same outfit she'd been wearing when she fled from Jacob's office, but she was so pale she was almost transparent.

Had January looked in Jake's direction, she would've seen him stumble. He leaned against the door, his shoulders sagging, his eyes raised, and mouthed a prayer of thanks. He'd found her. That was the most important thing. Sure, he had work to do to make her feel safe, but she was here, and she was okay. That was what he cared about most.

The rest was just details.

"Hey." His voice was soft because he didn't want to scare her.

Her shoulders hopped all the same, and when she whipped her eyes to him, she looked legitimately surprised. "What are you doing here?" she blurted.

It bothered him that she even had to ask, but he ruthlessly shoved his feelings aside and focused on her. Nobody had ever done that for her. *No one.* Not the woman across from her. Not the father who didn't bother. Not grandparents or aunts and uncles. He would be the first to prioritize her feelings, and he was fine with it. He wanted to be her rock.

"We need to talk." He was calm as he moved toward her. Up close and personal, she didn't look as if she'd been crying. He had no idea if that was a good or bad thing. "You scared me. I searched the resort for you, which meant I missed you when you were packing. I don't like being scared."

"I left a note."

"Yeah, and I really appreciate those three words." Jake wanted nothing more than to draw her into his arms and declare everything was going to be okay. Instead, he grabbed the lone remaining chair in the room and drew it to the table. He settled between mother and daughter—the former paying zero attention to them—and grabbed January's hand before she had a chance to pull it away from him.

"You're not fired," he started.

"Um, you were there," January countered. "Edward got his way. Your father has no choice but to kick me to the curb if he wants to save that sponsorship relationship."

"Well, he doesn't." Jake was matter of fact. "You missed the best part of the meeting, January."

"And what part was that?" She refused to meet Jake's steady gaze. He couldn't blame her. She didn't want to fall apart in front of him. If she let herself be vulnerable, that was exactly what would happen. That meant he would have to draw it out of her.

"The part where my father pulled footage from all over the resort," Jake replied evenly. "Apparently, he's been aware of the Edward situation from the start. Jim was also on the footage being a perverted tool. My dad warned Jim that if he tried to make a scene, he would release the footage. It was a good old-fashioned standoff."

January's mouth dropped open, and she finally looked at him. Her eyes were glassy, and the vulnerability he found there was like a kick to the stomach. Rather than fall apart and wait for somebody else to slap him together, however, he remained strong for her.

"W-what?" she stammered.

"Baby, you're not being fired," Jake said. "My father had a plan this whole time. I kind of wish he'd let us in on the plan, but that's neither here nor there. He laid down the law with the Maxwells. They're backing off. We're fine."

"So I'm not fired?" January seemed to be having trouble absorbing the words.

"No, you're not fired. In fact, you're being promoted. How does vice president of the resort grab you?"

Her forehead creased, befuddlement running roughshod over her beautiful features. "I don't understand."

"I know." Jake was tentative when he reached out to stroke his hand over her hair. She felt somehow delicate to him in the moment, which was a foreign feeling when it came to January. She'd always been strong, even when they were torturing each other as kids. Years removed from the situation, he saw so much more than he had then. He needed her to see it too.

"My father values you," he said in a low voice. "He sees what a good worker you are. He wants you on his team forever. I'm sorry you had even a moment of doubt in his office, but he had to lay it out a certain way."

"Okay." January's affect was flat. "That's good. I won't have to move my mother to a county hospital after all. I was just about to break the bad news to her."

Jake hated—*absolutely hated*—how beaten down she sounded. He needed to fix it. Was he up to the challenge? He was about to find out.

"The day we graduated, I had a moment," he volunteered out of nowhere.

January's eyebrows drew toward one another. "What?" She was obviously confused.

Jake squeezed her hand. "Just give me a second," he pleaded. "I need to get this out."

Still uncertain, January nodded and waited.

"You said your high school experience was different from mine, and I get that now. I didn't then, and I wish I had. We can't go back and change that though. I was a real shit."

A startled laugh escaped her lips. "I wasn't any better."

"You were ten times better," he argued. "You fought with me because you needed to be seen. You probably didn't realize that at the time, but I see it now. The thing is, I fought with you because I needed to be seen too.

"I might've been popular, had parents who were involved, and been revered by girls from one end of the school to the other," he continued. "I didn't need any of that. I just needed attention from you."

"Revered by girls from one end of the school to the other?" January challenged in dumbfounded disbelief.

A chuckle escaped, and that was the moment Jake knew it was going to be okay. He just had to finish it out. "I said what I said." He refused to let go of her hand. "I always sought your attention because you made me feel differently, January. Even when we were kids, your disdain was something I craved.

"When we got older, I didn't want that feeling to go away, so I kept chasing the high even if the emotions attached to it were negative," he continued. "They weren't, by the way. Negative, I mean. I convinced myself they were because it was easier than seeing the truth. Looking at you back then, though, it wasn't negativity I saw."

January licked her lips. She looked afraid. "What was it?"

"Desperation?" Jake lifted one shoulder in a shrug. "I'm not entirely certain. I think our feelings for one another are more complicated than they should be. It doesn't matter. That's behind us."

"You're the one who brought up graduation," she reminded him.

"Because that's when I had my first epiphany." His smile was rueful when he fixed it on her. "I saw you across the gym. I was with my parents, and you were alone. Your mother didn't even bother showing up. I remember that now."

A lone tear slid down January's cheek, and she focused on the puzzle. "She had to work."

"She was a terrible mother," Jake countered. "It's okay to say that. She's here." He inclined his head toward Clara. "You can tell her she failed you."

"What does it matter?" January challenged. "She doesn't remember me from day to day. She won't be sorry. Not even in the moment."

"No, but you'll know that you told her and let her go," Jake countered. "You can share my family with me. My father loves you. I love you." The words escaped before he realized what he was going to say, but he didn't want to take them back. He meant them with every fiber of his being.

"You turned yourself into a success, January," he said. "You can have everything you ever wanted, including me."

Her laughter seemingly caught them both by surprise. "You seem pretty certain that I want you."

"That's because we made eye contact that day in the gym," he said in a soft voice. "I remember it. You were alone, and yet you were smiling. You were getting away. In that moment, I wanted nothing more than to be with you. I felt it here." He lifted her hand to his chest and pressed it to the spot above his heart. "I want us to do everything together going forward. I need you to want it too."

January didn't immediately respond.

"I want us to wake up together. I want us to go to work together. I want to learn to be a better worker under you." He leaned close and rubbed his nose against her cheek. "I want to continue to be a better man with you."

January choked back a sob, and he knew he was finally getting through to her.

"I want you to have my father and mother to lean on because they're good parents and they love you," he said. "I want to eat dinner with you. I want to sit with you at night when you make those stupid lists. I want to take you skiing. I want to make you laugh. Most importantly, I want to make you love. Me. That's who I want you to love, in case you're still confused."

January could no longer hold back the tears. They cascaded down her cheeks. "I've always loved you," she admitted on a broken breath. "Even when I hated you, I loved you. I just didn't want to admit it."

"I know, baby." He arranged them so their heads were bent together, their foreheads touching, and they were practically gasping in each other's faces. It wasn't lust fueling them this time. No, this was something bigger.

"It's going to take work from both of us," he said. "It's not going to be easy because we're not easy people. I want you more than I've ever wanted anything in this world. You make me a better man, and I want to keep being a better man with you."

"What if I screw it up?"

"You won't."

"How can you be sure?" She pulled back far enough to stare into his eyes.

"Because I'm even going to love your mistakes," he declared. "Nobody is perfect. You don't realize that true love means there's nothing in this world that can break that bond. I want you to learn that lesson with me."

"And what lesson are you going to learn?"

"That it's okay to be the man my father wants me to be. It

turns out, that man is a pretty good man, no matter what I thought before."

"And what if we don't make it?" January sounded anguished. "What if I give in and let myself love you and we break apart?"

"I don't believe that's going to happen. It doesn't matter though. You're going to regret not giving us a chance if you go that route. This is something we both need. If it doesn't work, we'll deal with it. But if it does work, we have the chance to be happy forever. Don't you want to take that chance?"

"Yes, but I'm afraid."

"Then let's be afraid together." His lips brushed hers, the lightest of touches. "Just give me the go-ahead to try. That's all I ask."

Her breath came out in a shaky gasp. "I don't have a choice, do I?"

"No. Love sometimes grabs you by the throat and doesn't let go. That's what's happening here. We're going to do this together. You're no longer on your own. Have a little faith in me."

She closed her eyes, causing Jake to hold his breath, and then she nodded. "I don't think I can do it alone any longer."

He grinned and leaned close again, ready to kiss her until her lips bled and she passed out from sheer exhaustion. "That's exactly what I want. You're never going to be alone again, and neither am I. Just believe in me. It's all going to work out. I promise."

"It had better. I don't think I can survive losing you."

"Baby, you're never losing me. Watch me prove it."

EPILOGUE

ONE YEAR LATER

"I'm tired." January sank onto the couch—yes, the infamous couch where she and Jake first acknowledged their feelings so many years before, even though their teenage selves hadn't realized what they were getting into—and smiled at the crackling fire.

It was decorating day at the resort. Christmas was coming up. That meant she was exhausted from making sure things looked exactly how she wanted. The feeling of accomplishment she had now that everything was twinkling and pretty was well worth the effort, however. Sure, she was vice president of Sylvan Slopes. Decorating was no longer her job. Some things still felt like her responsibility, though, and the decorations were one of them.

"You look tired." Next to her, Jake's smile was lazy. He'd helped with the decorations. It wasn't his job either. He'd been moved to administration since the previous year, but where January went, he went. "It's done, though, and it's pretty."

"Yeah." January leaned her head against his shoulder and closed her eyes. There was nothing she wanted more than to go home to the chalet she and Jake now shared, but her legs refused to cooperate. "Just fifteen minutes, and then we can go."

"I'm fine with that." Jake plucked her hand from his lap and flipped it over, his fingers light as he traced her lifeline.

It had been a great year, January mused. It hadn't been trouble free—nobody had a perfect existence—but it had been better than she'd anticipated. That day when they left the hospital, Jake had taken her back to the lodge. She'd expected to return to her apartment, but that never happened. Instead, they remained in their cocoon for the next month. Then Jake surprised her with the new chalet.

She'd argued at first because that was her way, but he'd put his foot down. He didn't want her living at Pendleton Manor. It wasn't as if she wanted to live there, but despite his help, she still worried she wouldn't be able to keep up on the bills should something happen.

Should something happen. In hindsight, it made her smile to think about the fears that had plagued her when they'd first embarked on this adventure together. She'd been certain he would change his mind at some point. Jake, however, had remained steadfast in his devotion to her. He'd proven at every turn that he loved her and wasn't going anywhere.

Her first full-on meltdown had come three weeks after she started her new job. She'd been convinced Jacob had made a mistake when promoting her. She was certain Jake already had one foot out the door. He didn't budge when she started yelling though. He stood strong when she started stomping her feet. And, when the tears came, he'd quietly opened his arms. He'd become her rock, which was frightening for a different reason, but now she was used to it.

She didn't know what she would do without him.

"I was thinking we could get pizza delivered," she said as she watched his fingers move over her palm. "Maybe we can eat it in the hot tub."

The corners of Jake's mouth tipped up. "That sounds interesting. There's little I love more than naked time in the hot tub. Pizza is a nice touch. I've already handled dinner though."

January cocked her head, surprised. "You have?"

"Yup. It's being delivered to the chalet even as we speak."

"Who is delivering it?"

"The kitchen staff."

January's smile disappeared. "We've talked about this. They're supposed to be handling the dinner rush in the dining room, not catering to your whims."

"Hey, I've been good." Jake moved her hand back to her lap and fixed her with a pout. "I haven't stolen from the kitchen in months at this point, even though I maintain that you're being unreasonable about that. They like feeding us. They just don't say it out loud."

"Jake." January was exasperated. "That's not their job. You're just entitled."

"Whatever." He leaned in and brushed his lips against her cheek before reclining against the cushions. He seemed fidgety, something January couldn't quite fathom a reason for. "It's a special occasion."

"Because of the decorations?"

"You mean the twelve-hour shift you insisted on working to make sure each and every garland was in the right place? Actually, it has nothing to do with that."

"Those garlands look great," January muttered.

"They do. The lights look great too. I especially like how you color-coordinated each window. It's delightful."

January rolled her eyes. "Whatever. A job well done should be celebration enough. Although what food is waiting for us back at the chalet?"

Jake's smirk told her that he'd expected the question. "I

went all out. There's prime rib, mashed potatoes, turtle cheesecake, and a huge bottle of champagne."

January's frown only deepened. "That's a lot of food."

"I plan on eating the leftovers all weekend. We're not leaving our bed."

"We're not?"

"We're not." He fidgeted with his pocket again, causing January to lift an eyebrow, and then stood out of the blue. He glanced around the lobby, which was empty except for them, and then touched his tongue to his top lip. "We're going to be way too wrapped up in each other to leave the chalet."

"Um, the new sponsors for the Winter Extreme Games come in Monday," January argued. "I have to be ready for them."

"You've been ready for weeks." Jake emphatically shook his head. "You don't need to plan a single second more. You've got this."

"I still don't understand," January insisted. "What's going on that we're going to be locked up at home all weekend?"

"Well, for starters, there's a storm coming in." His smile turned wolfish. "You know how much I love a winter storm."

"You just like being naked and hanging out in front of the fireplace."

"I do. I have very specific plans for you this weekend though."

"I don't understand." January's forehead creased as Jake moved in front of her. He looked nervous. Sweat had even popped up on his forehead. "What's going on? You're starting to freak me out."

"Believe it or not, that wasn't my plan." His smile was sheepish. "I thought I would be much smoother at this. I'm a nervous wreck though."

"What did you think you would be smooth at?"

"This." Jake removed something from his pocket and held

it toward her. She instinctively reached for it, her mouth dropping open when she realized it was a ring box.

"Jake." Her mouth had gone dry.

"Open it," he prodded.

Hands shaking, she did as he instructed. Seeing her fake engagement ring from a year before was a gut punch she wasn't expecting. "What the... I mean, um, what's this? The Maxwells aren't coming back, are they?"

Her reaction was enough to have Jake chuckling. "No, baby. We're free of them forever."

"But why do you have this ring again? I thought your father returned it."

"I talked him out of that." Jake shifted from one foot to the other, clearly worked up. Then he dropped to one knee, and January was convinced her heart was going to rip out of her chest and make a break for the Canadian border.

"W-what?"

"Shh." Jake rested one hand on her knee. "I'm doing this all wrong, but I'm worked up. I guess I'll just ramble and hope you say yes anyway."

She was going to say yes no matter what. How could he not see that? Before she had a chance to tell him that, he launched into his spiel.

"I couldn't let my father return that ring," he started. "I knew it belonged on your finger. That marriage may have been fake, but the feelings were real. I made him keep it until I could pay for it. Surprisingly, he didn't give me grief about it. He seemed to understand."

"Understand what?"

"I want you to have that ring because it has always belonged on your finger. Honestly, I didn't want you to take it off back then. My father convinced me if I told you I wanted to swoop right into a real marriage that I would regret it because you would freak out.

"I knew he was right, but it hurt to watch you take off the ring," he continued. "I wanted us to get married back then. *Really married.* You needed time to adjust, though, and I needed you to believe in me. That meant it had to wait."

Jake swallowed hard before continuing. "Part of me has known you're my forever since we were teenagers. Back then, I would've second guessed that assumption. Now, though, I know."

January blinked back tears. "What do you know?"

"I don't ever want to wake up without you next to me. I don't ever want to go to bed without you wrapped in my arms. I don't want a day to go by without seeing one of your lists on the kitchen table. And, when we're ready, I want you to be the mother of my children. This is simply the next step on the journey we started when you kicked me in the shin and told me I had cooties."

January's laugh ripped from her chest. "I don't believe it was your shin that I kicked."

"Close enough." He winked at her, relieving some of the pressure she was feeling. "You're my forever, and that's not going to change. I want to start moving forward together. So, January Jackson, will you be my wife?"

January knew her answer. She knew what she wanted going forward. Still, she hesitated. "Are you sure? I mean, this seems like a big deal."

"Are you being serious right now?" Jake's eyes narrowed. "My heart is exposed. I'm on one knee. I arranged for freaking prime rib. How can you make me wait for an answer?"

This time when the laughter came, it was chased by warmth and devotion. "Of course I'll marry you." She moved to her knees directly in front of him, noticing out of the corner of her eye that the workers had started to congregate by the front desk. Even though everybody was supposed to be focused on something else, January and Jake were clearly the most exciting thing happening at the resort that evening.

"Yeah?" Jake grinned and reached for the ring box. "When I put this on your finger, it can never come off again."

"I don't ever want to take it off," she assured him. "It's a symbol of your love. That means I'll keep it with me forever because I don't know how I made it before you."

"You made it because you're strong. Now we're going to be strong together."

"Yeah." She held her breath as he slid the ring on her finger, doing her best to ignore the applause echoing throughout the room as the employees—and Jake's parents, she now realized—expressed their enthusiasm at the union.

Emotion choked her, but she managed to say the one thing that needed to be said. "I love you."

"Endlessly," he agreed. "Forever."

"You're my strength."

"No, baby, you're mine."

Made in United States
North Haven, CT
12 May 2024

52410993R00189